SCATTERED LIES 4

"Roman Revenge..."

WRITTEN BY

MADISON

5 Star Publications
PO BOX 471570
Forestville, MD 20753

SCATTERED LIES 4

ISBN -13: 978-0-9854386-4-7
ISBN-10: 0985438649
Library of Congress Control Number: 2012951801
First Printing: December 2012

Printed in the United States

www.5starpublications.net
www.tljestore.com
www.iammadisontaylor.com

Follow Madison for the latest updates: on *www.facebook.com /iammadisontaylor* and *twitter.com/madisonme*

Acknowledgements

As always, I would like to thank **GOD** for His blessings. Without Him, there would be no me. To my family and friends thank you for always being there for me.

To reviewers: **Joey Pinkney, OOAS Book Club (Anna Draper), Myra Panache of Panachereport.com, and** Melody Vernor-Bartel-**Reader's Paradise,** thank you for your reviews.

To the book clubs: **Girls Bay Area (GBC)** and **Sister of Unity (SOU), DMV** and **Columbia S.O.C.I. A.L, Source of Knowledge Book Club** thank you for selecting my book.

To the book stores: **The Literary Joint (Shawn, La Quita), Horizon Book Store (Quita), Source of Knowledge (Patrice, Dexter)**

I also give thanks to my team: **Publicist Makeda Smith, Editor Carla M Dean, Tonya Patterson, Kayon Cox, Maurice Scriber and Tyanna Kiviette.** We did it again!

Special thanks to **Tracey Holder** for convincing me to write Scattered Lies 4... Roman Revenge.

Readers:

I would like to thank you for joining me on the most exhilarating ride of my life . These characters are a part of me and I hope they are now a part of you. They remind me that in one lifetime we can overcome the most devastating circumstances and achieve our dreams. I am also reminded that we are admired for our achievements, but often our greatest accomplishments are how we overcome our failures.

Don't lose yourself in your failures, we all fall down, you are not the sum of your mistakes; falling down shouldn't be your benchmark getting up is.

So once again in the face of adversity our not so perfect, stubborn, powerful and absolutely fabulous characters triumphantly return for the highly anticipated finale of the Scattered Lies Saga, *Scattered Lies 4: Roman Revenge* .

Originally Scattered Lies was conceived as a trilogy but after three installments these characters still have so much to say and so do their off spring; as my mother always says "The Apple doesn't fall far from tree."

Therefore join me once again in following our favorite characters exploits and escapades as they live and love life to the fullest. Let's do this one more time!

As Always
Love and Gratitude,

Madison

SCATTERED LIES 4

"Roman Revenge..."

Prologue

"You have my deepest sympathy." Felix kneeled down and kissed the hands of Denise and Gabrielle's mothers. "I'm so sorry for you loss. If anyone understands, it's me," he added.

With a somber expression on her face, Mrs. Marciano, Felix's mother, flashed a weak smile and thought, *That's what you mullies get for fucking with my granddaughter.*

"Thank you, Felix," both ladies responded.

After the funeral service, Felix met with Mr. and Mrs. Taylor in Denise's old apartment to discuss the custody of his grandchildren.

"I know this might not be the best time, but I wanted to discuss the children."

"Yes, we need to discuss it," Mr. Taylor replied.

"Well, I know you have your hands full with Denise and Jasmine's kids," Mrs. Marciano pointed out.

As Mr. Taylor started to respond, Gabrielle's mother, who was Mrs. Dodson and Denise's sisters were coming through the door.

With a disgusted look on her face, Mrs. Marciano rolled her eyes before continuing. "Like I was saying. We know you're gonna have your hands full with your other grandkids, so Felix and I want full custody of Morgan's babies."

Mr. and Mrs. Taylor looked at each other. While they didn't have the strength or finances to take in any more kids, they knew Mrs. Marciano was pissed that Felix had gotten a black woman pregnant. The only reason she claimed Morgan was because she resembled them. That's why she wanted to raise the grandchildren, because they looked like Italians.

I

"Well, my husband and I are getting older," Mrs. Taylor explained, "but that doesn't mean we don't wanna be in our great-grandchildren's lives either. Morgan was very special to us."

Felix looked at his mother, who had her face twisted up. He knew it was only a matter of seconds before she cursed them out.

"We know, Mrs. Taylor, but as you know, I didn't get a chance to raise Morgan."

"And that's our fault?!" Denise's sister De'shell blurted out. "You chose not to be in her life."

"De'shell!" Mrs. Taylor said.

"No, Ma. I lost both of my sisters. Their children, my nieces and nephews," she stressed as her eyes filled with tears and her voice cracked, "will grow up without their mother. And I know if Jasmine were alive, she would want us to raise Morgan's kids."

"That's not gonna happen," Mrs. Marciano stated in a serious tone.

"Excuse me?" Anita, Denise's other sister, said. "Y'all weren't there for Morgan when she was alive. The only reason why y'all want them is for the money."

Mrs. Marciano had enough with these ignorant mullies. She stood up and straightened out her clothing. "I came to you out of respect, but I refuse to be insulted," she stated.

"Everyone calm down," Mrs. Dodson ordered while standing up, also. "We have to think about the children here. Betty and Roger, you are already raising your daughter's kids. It's only right that Morgan's father and grandmother raise her kids."

"Who asked you?" Anita and De'shell yelled.

"I'm not talking to either one of you, and since we're pointing fingers here, I don't recall you treating Jasmine or Morgan with respect. So, what's your motivate?" Mrs. Dodson shot back.

Both women sucked their teeth, but remained quiet.

"We have to think about it," Roger, Denise's father, responded.

Infuriated, Mrs. Marciano grinded her teeth. "You can think about it, but I'm taking my great-grandkids."

"Over our dead bodies," Anita responded, speaking for herself and De'shell.

Their comment sent flames of rage through Felix's body. "Are you sure about that? Because one thing I promise you is that my grandchildren are coming with me. It's because of your daughter's carelessness that my daughter is gone. She was forced to..." He started to reveal the secret, but caught himself. He didn't want to ruin his daughter's reputation. "...marry and have children at a young age," he continued. "You think I'm gonna allow the same thing to happen to my grandchildren? You think it's about the money? As far as I'm concerned, that coward could've taken his money with him."

Felix's words silenced the room. There was no way in hell he was going to let them raise his grandkids.

Mrs. Marciano lowered her head, praying he didn't reveal what had happened to Morgan.

While the others paid no attention to Felix's ranting, something in his voice caught Roger's attention. "Anita and De'shell, get out of here!" Mr. Taylor told them.

"Daddy..." they whined.

"Out!"

Both ladies stormed out of the apartment.

"Tony raped Morgan," Felix finally revealed.

"Tony raped Morgan?" they repeated, shocked by the revelation.

With one hand, Mrs. Taylor squeezed her husband's hand, and with the other, she covered her mouth. Mrs. Dodson started to feel weak. They had no idea. There was a brief moment of silence in the room as everyone tried to digest the news.

"Impossible!" Betty exclaimed. "There's no way Tony would have crossed Denise like that. They were like brother and sister. Maybe you got it wrong. Maybe Morgan had sex with Tony. I'm not buying that."

"Are you calling my daughter a liar?" Felix said, slowly approaching them.

"Did Denise know?" Mr. Taylor asked.

Felix and his mother looked at each other, both wondering if they should tell the truth.

"She found out years later," Felix mumbled, looking away in shame.

"Years?" Mrs. Dodson said.

Not responding, Felix walked over to window. The wound was still fresh.

Mrs. Marciano looked at her son before saying, "Yes. Morgan was raped by Tony when she was fourteen."

"Oh my God!" Mrs. Taylor cried out. "We had no idea."

Of course you didn't, bitch. You didn't even wanna be around my grandchild. So fuck off with them fake-ass tears, Mrs. Marciano thought. But, instead she replied, "Of course, you didn't. No one did. You see, that's why it's important that we raise her children. We feel like we failed Morgan."

Mr. and Mrs. Taylor nodded.

"Of course...of course. I just wish we had known about this years ago," Mrs. Taylor said.

"Is that why Denise and my daughter are dead?" Mrs. Dodson asked suspiciously.

"No. This had nothing to do with them. I don't know why they were killed," Mrs. Marciano lied.

"I think my wife would agree that the kids are better off with you. However, we still wanna be in their lives," Mr. Taylor stated.

"Of course." Mrs. Marciano reached out and gently touched his hand. "I want them to know their cousins."

"I think we should put our heads together and decide what we're gonna do with our grandchildren," Mrs. Dodson suggested.

"One thing for sure we could never tell the kids what happened to their parents." Mrs. Marciano stated

"I agree, they have been through enough." Mrs. Taylor said.

As they set aside their feelings to come up with a plan for the grandchildren, someone entered the room. "May I help you?" Felix asked.

25 Years Later

"The courtroom is filled to capacity during the trial of the infamous Anthony Omari Flowers, Jr., who is accused of first-degree rape, sexual assault, and kidnapping. His father, rap legend Tony Flowers, was killed by his ex-girlfriend Christina Carrington in a murder-suicide. His siblings, London, Justin and Justine, joined Mr. Flowers in court. Also in the courtroom are his grandfather Felix Marciano and his great-grandmother," the newscaster reported.

"It's hard to believe someone with great looks and with more money than some countries could do this," another reporter stated.

"Well, they say money doesn't fix everything."

"So true," the reporter agreed. "Now we take you inside the courtroom, where the key witness will be taking the stand momentarily."

"All rise!" the bailiff announced.

"You may be seated," the judge instructed as he took his seat and adjusted his robe.

"Clarice Brown, raise your right hand," the bailiff said as he prepared to swear her in. "Do you promise to tell the truth, the whole truth, and nothing but the truth, so help you God?"

"I do," she replied.

"You may be seated," the bailiff told her.

"Ms. Brown, how long have you known the defendant, Mr. Flowers?" the prosecutor questioned.

"For about six years," Clarice responded.

"Intimately?" he asked.

"About five years."

"Can you tell us what happened on…" The prosecutor paused to walk back to the table and pick up a piece of paper. "…October 21st?"

Clarice looked over at the jury. "I bumped into Anthony at a party at Trump Towers."

"And?" the prosecutor asked, prompting her to continue.

"We had a couple of drinks, and he invited me back to his place. I really liked Anthony, so I said okay."

"What happened when you got there?"

Clarice looked over at the jury again. "He started acting strange. He snorted some coke and ordered me to take off my clothes so he could snort some off my stomach."

"Did you do it?" the prosecutor inquired.

"Yes. I mean, I thought it was cool…" she said, her voice trailing off.

"What happened next?"

"He snorted a couple of lines off my stomach. Then he put some on his penis and asked to have sex with me."

"Coke?" he asked, wanting to be clear with her statement.

"Yes, and again, I said okay."

"Then what happened?"

"I started to feel numb down there and asked him to stop."

"Did he?"

"No. He flew into a rage and started choking me."

"Out of the blue, he just started choking you?"

Clarice began to cry. "Yes. I tried to remove his hands, but he overpowered me. He grabbed me by my neck and tossed me across the room."

Gasps echoed throughout the room, and some of the jury members looked over at Tony.

"Then what happened?" the prosecutor asked.

"He raped me," she said, breaking down on the stand.

"No further questions. Your witness," he told the defense attorney.

Bill Fish, Anthony's high-profile attorney, stood up, buttoned his suit jacket, and walked over to the witness. "Ms. Brown, you stated that out of the blue, my client started choking you and then raped you, correct?"

"Yes."

"So why did it take you three weeks to report the rape?"

"I was confused and scared," she responded. "Anthony is very powerful."

"Or is it because my client refused to give you any money?" Bill asked spitefully.

"That's not true! He raped me!" Clarice shouted.

"Your Honor, I would like to enter Exhibit L. This tape will show Ms. Brown plotting to extort my client. At first, she told him that she was pregnant. When that didn't work, she accused him of giving her an STD, and now rape."

As the tape started to play, mumbles filled the room. This time, everyone glared at Clarice. Women twisted their faces up, while men shook their heads.

"He did rape me!" Clarice cried. "Anthony is a monster!"

"Sure, he did," Bill responded sarcastically. "I have no further questions, Your Honor."

Anthony sat with a smug look on his face, staring at Clarice as she stepped down from the stand.

*****

It was the day when a jury consisting of twelve men and women would decide Anthony Omari Flowers' fate. He entered the courtroom accompanied by his family, friends, and legal team. Most people would've been nervous, but not Anthony. At his mother's request, Felix had everything covered. Five members on the jury had been paid off. Even the prosecutor had been paid off to present a weak case. So, either way, Anthony would walk away scot-free

"All rise!" the bailiff said.

"Has the jury reached a verdict?" the judge asked.

"Yes, Your Honor," the foreman replied.

"Will the defendant stand and face the jury," the judge instructed Anthony.

The courtroom was so silent you could hear a pin drop. Like the O.J. Simpson trial, this case had divided a country. Some believed greedy women were setting up Anthony, while others believed he was a serial rapist, with money, power, and political connections, who would get off.

Anthony looked back at his family. His great-grandmother nodded, letting him know everything was going to be fine.

"How do you find the defendant?" the judge asked.

The foreman stared into the defendant's eyes and then at the paper. She knew the world was watching and waiting. As she looked around at the victims in the courtroom, her eyes started to tear up.

"How do you find the defendant?" the judge repeated.

Before she gave the verdict, she said a silent prayer. *God, please forgive us.* Then she replied, "We, the jury, find the defendant not guilty."

The courtroom filled with mixed emotions. Some were crying, while others cheered.

"Order! Order!" the judge yelled, banging his gavel. "Mr. Flowers, the jury has found you not guilty. You are free to go."

Anthony hugged his attorney and then reached over to hug his great-grandmother.

"I told you only in America can you buy this kind of justice," she whispered in Anthony's ear.

Mobbed by the media, with his family and legal team proudly standing behind him, Anthony spoke with reporters.

"Anthony, how do you feel about the verdict?" one female reporter asked.

"I'm happy, of course. I'm happy to be able to put this behind me."

Bill interceded. "There will be a full press conference tomorrow. Thank you."

Family and friends went back to Anthony's penthouse to celebrate. There, Felix pulled Anthony aside.

"Got a second?"

"Sure, Grandpa," he said, walking with him to the other room.

"I think you should lay low for a while. Let things cool down," Felix suggested.

Anthony nodded before smiling.

"I'm serious, Anthony. Next time, you might not be so lucky," he angrily whispered while staring directly into his face.

"As long as I got money, I will always be lucky," Anthony replied arrogantly.

Felix laughed. "Your father would've said the same thing."

"Well, my father was a wise man."

Felix glared at Anthony. The only reason he didn't put a bullet in his grandson's head was because it would've broken his mother's heart. Anthony was everything Felix despised in a man.

"A.J.," he said, using his nickname, "you're my grandson, so I will always be there for you. But, if you rape any more women, I will not help you."

Anthony, being the self-righteous bastard he was, stepped up to Felix. "Help? My father left me a shitload of money. What makes you think I need your help?"

Felix released a devilish chuckle. "You are your father's child...a punk who raped women."

"My father never had to rape women, just like I don't. They just need help saying yes."

It infuriated Felix to hear Anthony praise his father. Maybe if he knew the truth, he might think differently.

"Your father always felt he had to have the best. That's why he's not here today, because the best cost him his life. Now you listen to me, you punk motherfucker. It's only because my blood runs through you that I tolerate your ass. Because if I had it my way, your sorry ass would be spending the rest of your life in prison where you belong with the rest of the niggers."

Anthony smiled. "Now I know how you've really felt about me all of these years. It killed you that my mother married a black man. I knew you were a racist bitch. You never liked my father because he was black."

"No, I never liked your father because of what he did to my daughter," Felix quickly interrupted.

"Bullshit! My father treated my mother like a queen. You didn't like him because he was black. But, that didn't stop you from taking over his estate."

"Is that what you think?" Felix started to tell him the truth, but changed his mind.

"Well, my mother loved my father, and it's because of her that I don't take you out of your misery," Anthony shot back.

"Watch it, boy. Before I forget——"

Anthony jumped in his grandfather's face. "I already did. Now get the fuck out of my house before we do something we both regret."

Felix smirked. Anthony didn't know who he was dealing with.

"There's my favorite great-grandson," Felix's mother cheered, entering the room.

"Hi, Grandma," Anthony said, kissing her on the cheek.

"Be a dear and get your grandma something to drink."

"Sure," he told her, then glared at Felix before exiting.

Once Anthony was out of sight, Felix's mother turned towards him. "What was that all about?"

"That young punk has the nerve to challenge me, when it's because of his fucking father that my daughter is dead."

"Felix, he's your grandson."

"Don't remind me."

Still steaming, Anthony went into the other room to cool off and take a hit.

"Anthony?" London said, knocking on the door before opening it.

With white powder on his nose, he replied, "Yeah."

"You never did stop," London snapped.

X

"What is it, London?" Anthony said, tired of everyone judging him. "What the fuck you want now?"

"You're a son of a bitch, you know that?" London yelled.

By that time, his brother and sister had joined them.

"What the fuck?" Justin said.

"Alright, so I'm caught. Considering the amount of stress I've been under, I deserve a little recreational play."

Everyone looked at him in disgust, while thinking the same thing. *What's the point? Anthony is going to be the cause of his own downfall.*

"Fuck you," Anthony screamed under the stares of the judgmental eyes. "Fuck all of you! This is my father's empire, and he left it to me! I am the king of this empire!"

Chapter One

After the death of his daughter, Felix made sure his grandkids wanted for nothing. Having been awarded fully custody of his grandchildren, he provided them with the best things in life. All the things Felix didn't have the chance to do with Morgan, he did with his grandchildren, from reading them bedtime stories to attending all of their events. They were all he had left. Like Morgan, her children were smart. By the time they turned five years old, they spoke three different languages.

While it was very challenging raising them, Felix received help from his family, mainly his mother who spoiled them. As the children got older, Mrs. Marciano and Felix disagreed on a lot of things pertaining to them. Felix wanted them to have a normal life, which would involve them choosing the direction of their lives, while Mrs. Marciano believed they were royalty and should have the best. Since Anthony was the oldest, she spoiled him the most. As most big brothers did, Anthony protected his siblings. He especially had a strong bond with his younger brother Justin, who looked up to him.

Anthony Omari Flowers stood six feet tall and had olive skin with bluish-grey eyes. He was a younger version of Jesse Williams from *Grey's Anatomy*. But, not only was he handsome, but he was highly educated and very athletic. He was well mannered and dressed like the men in *Ocean Eleven*, wearing a pair of shades as his trademark. Anthony was destined to become successful. However, he had a problem with women. Getting them was never the problem; behind closed doors is when things got ugly.

Anthony and Justin were blessed in the private area just like their father. At the age of ten, Anthony started to experience strong sexual urges. Afraid to tell anyone, he secretly started watching porn. While porn aroused him, S&M porn quenched his thirsty. There were nights when he would watch it for hours until his great-grandmother caught him. While most grandmothers would be repulsed, Mrs. Marciano wanted Anthony to experience the real thing. So, for his eleventh birthday, she hired a nineteen-year-old prostitute to have sex with Anthony. Even the prostitute could not believe the way he was well hung.

Although inexperienced, Anthony was a quick study. After that night, he continued to see the girl, but after a while, he became bored with her. He still had those S&M urges. Therefore, during sex, Anthony smacked the girl across her face while she was performing oral sex on him. When the girl looked up at him and smiled, her reaction sent chills through his body. That night was the beginning of his terror.

By the time Anthony was sixteen years old, he was the most sought after guy in town. Besides being smart, sexy, and handsome, he was known to have a big dick and give good head. He even slept with some of his girlfriends' mothers. In his mind, there wasn't a girl he couldn't have. He'd been through all of his sister's friends with the exception of one, Sofia, who was dating his younger brother Justin. He and London use to fight all the time about his playboy ways. She thought he was arrogant and disgusting, while Justin and Justine laughed at the silly women who ran after Anthony.

All of a sudden, things took a turn for the worse. Suddenly, slapping a girl on the ass or face didn't excite him anymore. One girl had been begging him to come over to her house for months. So, one night, he decided to take her up on the offer. She started off with giving Anthony a blowjob, but when it came time to fuck, she said no. Well, that didn't sit well with Anthony, whose penis was throbbing.

"You gotta be fucking kidding me, right?" Anthony said while standing butt naked.

"I'm sorry, but I can't…" Her voice trailed off as she started to put her clothes on.

"You can't what?" he asked, grabbing her by the wrist.

"I can't…I'll suck it…but…"

"You already did that. You called me over here to fuck and now you're saying no? Well, I want some pussy, and you're fucking me," he ordered, snatching her clothes from her hands and tossing them across the room.

The look on Anthony's face scared the hell out of the girl. His eyes changed from bluish-gray to black devil-like eyes.

"Anthony…" she mumbled, trying to reason with him.

But, Anthony wasn't having it. "Now," he said, pausing to kiss the girl on her neck, "let me show you what a real man feels like, or I can show you what a monster feels like. It's up to you." He moved from her neck to gently kissing the girl on the lips. "Trust me, you're gonna love it," he told her, while guiding the girl back to the bed.

She was the first of his many victims. Whereas she gave it willingly, there were many who didn't. Even though Anthony was popular, he only dated average women from working-class families. That's why he was able to get away with what he had been doing for years. Felix and his mother would pay them off, and the ones who didn't want their money, Mrs. Marciano threatened them with violence. In Italy, the Marciano name rang bells; you didn't want to get on their bad side.

Before things got out of hand, Felix took Anthony to the doctor and had some tests run on him. It turned out he suffered from the same illness that plagued serial rapists and sexual abusers. Felix figured it was hereditary and that Tony had passed it down to Anthony. However, his illness could be controlled if he took the medication.

Once Felix found out the problem, he made sure Anthony took his medication every day. Sadly, the side effects were too much for Anthony. He started to lose weight, slept all day, and became moody. Still, Felix refused to take Anthony off the medication. Mrs. Marciano, however, felt the risks didn't meet the reward; therefore, she secretly switched the pills.

When Felix found out, he hit the roof; however, he agreed to let Anthony stop taking the medication. Anthony was fine for the next couple of months, but then he started having violent episodes. This time it was worse. During one of his sexual outbreaks, Anthony broke a girl's nose. Since it occurred in school, they threatened to expel Anthony and press charges. Of course, Mrs. Marciano could not allow this to happen. Therefore, she paid off the school and the girl's family to sweep it under the rug.

Anthony managed to earn a master's degree in Chemical Biology at Oxford University by the time he was twenty years old. However, because of his great-grandmother always bailing him out of the trouble he managed to get himself into, he grew up to be an arrogant motherfucker, believing he was God's gift to women.

His sister, London Paris Flowers, was different. She was like her mother—involved in sports and didn't rely on her looks to get her things in life. Mrs. Marciano adored London, labeling her Princess. Since she resembled Adriana Lima, the famous Victoria's Secret fashion model, Mrs. Marciano wanted London to pursue modeling and signed her up with an agency when she was just a baby. It was fun at first, but as London got older, it started taking up too much of her time, leaving her little to no time to do the things she loved.

In addition to it being time consuming, Mrs. Marciano made London take diet pills, stating if she wanted to be a runway model, she needed to lose weight. Mrs. Marciano also told London that she could not hang around her friends. She wanted London to only be in the company of young rich men and beautiful women. Wanting to please her great-grandmother, London stopped hanging out with her friends and started dating rich men. As a result, it was only a matter of time before London became a pill-popping, anorexic, self-centered bitch.

One day, London was in the backyard working out, when Felix noticed she had lost a lot of weight.

"Londie, is everything okay?" he asked, taking a seat on a bench.

"Hey, gramps. Yes, why?"

Staring at her, Felix could see her collarbone. "I'm just worried about you. You're not eating, and when you do, it's very little."

London sighed; she didn't want to start no trouble.

"Londie, is someone hurting you?" Felix asked, noticing the sad look in her eyes.

"No, Grandpa, but can we talk?"

Felix's heart started beating fast. *Oh God, don't tell me someone has hurt my baby.*

"Sure," he responded, then braced himself for what she was about to say.

London took another deep breath before speaking. "Grandpa, I don't wanna hurt Grandma, but I don't wanna model anymore," she mumbled, lowering her head.

Having expected news of a more devastating nature, Felix put his arm around his granddaughter and breathed a sigh of relief. "It's okay, honey. If you don't want to model, you don't have to, Londie."

"I don't want Grandma to be upset with me, though. She says women with my looks are princesses who become queens, and that I should marry rich. But, Grandpa, all I wanna do is be me. I wanna hang out with my friends and eat what I wanna eat."

"And you can," Felix said, trying to remain cool. He picked London up and put her on his lap. "Londie, God has blessed with you great looks, but that doesn't mean you have to be a model. You have to do what makes Londie happy. I'm sure Grandma will understand your decision to quit modeling, and if she doesn't..." Felix paused for a moment to choose his words carefully. "Well, it would be her problem, not yours. Understand me?" he said, then kissed her on the cheek.

Relieved, London hugged her grandfather and smiled. "Yes, Grandpa. Thank you so much!"

"Anytime. Now go and have Isabella fix you something to eat," he told her, patting her on the butt.

"Yes!" she giggled, running inside.

Of course, Mrs. Marciano was upset when London told her that she had no interest in becoming a famous model, but eventually she got over it.

*****

London was working towards her master's degree in Asian and Middle Eastern Studies at University of Cambridge, when she met her fiancé Nyennoh Togar, an exchange student from West Africa. Nyennoh worked as a part-time janitor in her dorm. They had several classes together and became close friends. Nyennoh was different from the guys she'd met. He didn't focus on her looks. He was kind, gentle, smart, and appreciated the little things in life. Most of all, she loved his deep blue-black milky skin and pearly white smile. His washboard abs, biceps, and tight ass drove the girls in her dorm crazy. But, he only had eyes for London. He was the only guy that London thought about sexually. In fact, she wanted him to be her first. The first time they made love, Nyennoh made sure to be gentle; he wanted it to be special.

After months of dating, London decided it was time for Nyennoh to meet her family, so she invited him to dinner. Felix and her siblings welcomed him with open arms, but Mrs. Marciano acted cold as ice towards him. Over dinner, she grilled him about his life.

"So Nye…Nye…" She struggled with trying to pronounce his name. "I'm sorry. What's your name again?"

Being the gentle person he was and not wanting her to be embarrassed, he provided her with a short version. "My friends call me Nate."

"Well, I'm not your friend, but Nate is better than that other name," she snidely replied, causing everyone to look at her. "So how long have you been seeing my great-granddaughter? I hope you're not using her to stay in this country."

"Grandma!" London scolded.

"What, dear? It's only right that I ask these questions since you're too naïve to do it. Right, Nate? I'm pretty sure he understands."

Accustomed to this immature behavior, Nyennoh smiled, and responded in a polite tone, "I can understand your concern, but that's not why I'm dating your granddaughter. I love her."

London looked over at Nyennoh with a huge grin on her face. *He's such a gentleman,* she thought.

"Well, I'm happy my granddaughter found someone like you, Nate," Felix cheered.

"Thank you, Grandpa," London said, while cutting her eyes at her great-grandmother.

Mrs. Marciano didn't allow anyone to challenge her, especially in front of others, and Nate would learn that firsthand.

Two days before graduating from college, Nyennoh received notice that he was being deported back to Africa the following day. London was devastated, but then became furious when she found out Mrs. Marciano was behind it. Felix was fuming also when he learned of his mother's involvement. All her life, London had been the quiet one, but this time, she was going to give Mrs. Marciano a piece of her mind. Mrs. Marciano was at The Loft, an exclusive restaurant where old, rich, miserable, stuck-up women hung out. That's also where London decided to confront her.

"Londie." Mrs. Marciano smiled, excited to see her beautiful great-granddaughter.

"Don't Londie me. You caused Nate to get sent back."

Mortified by London's tone and approach, Mrs. Marciano placed her hand over her chest.

"London..." she said, while looking at her friends who were snickering.

"London my ass! You had him sent back so we couldn't be together. How could you?"

"London Paris Marciano, watch your tone of voice with me," she sternly responded, using her full name. "We will talk about it later."

London slammed her hand down on the table. "No, we will talk about it now. I swear if anything happens to Nate, you will regret it."

A couple weeks later, London packed her things and moved to West Africa, where she and Nyennoh got engaged. While Felix was hurt that she had moved away, he was happy London was living her life.

The twins, Justin and Justine, were a different story. From the time they were two years old, they gave Mrs. Marciano hell, especially Justine. Unlike Anthony and London, you could tell Justin and Justine were biracial.

Like his brother, Justin was blessed with great looks. People thought he was related to Michael Ealy because he favored him so much. Justin was a ladies' man, as well. Blessed with a huge package, Justin didn't have a problem getting the girls, and his bad boy image was an added bonus. The only difference between Justin and Anthony was that Justin was built like his father, a lanky figure. That is until he joined the wrestling team and started working out with a personal trainer.

While growing up, Anthony and Justin were very close. Anthony was very protective of his brother and used to take up for Justin when Mrs. Marciano badmouthed him.

Whereas Anthony was the Brad Pitt clean-shaven type, Justin was the sexy bad-boy Tyrese type. Justin was interested in anything hip-hop or urban related. When he wasn't dressed in a school uniform, Justin stayed in a fresh pair of jeans and Timbs. Instead of hanging with a bunch of preppy rich kids, Justin managed to befriend the boys from the hood. Mrs. Marciano called it his ghetto side. For Felix, as long as Justin wasn't robbing and raping women, he didn't see a problem with Justin's desire for urban clothing and hanging out with unfortunate people.

However, Mrs. Marciano wasn't having it. It was one thing to look black, but in her eyes, when you started dressing and acting black, it was time for you to go. But, as Felix stated to her, Justin was just being a kid. So, it didn't bother Felix, especially since Justin maintained good grades.

However, when Justin's girlfriend Sofia committed suicide, all hell broke loose. He went completely wild and started smoking and drinking. Even still, Felix could deal with it, but when Justin was arrested for stealing a car, Mrs. Marciano made Felix send Justin to Horace Mann School in the Bronx.

If they thought Justin was a handful, Justine was ten times worse. Although drop-dead gorgeous, by the way she carried herself, one would've thought she was an ugly duckling. Justine didn't care about her appearance. Favoring actress Denise Vasi, Justine didn't put any effort into her looks. Unlike her sister London, there was nothing girly about Justine. Her hair stayed in a ponytail, and she never wore a skirt. She wasn't outgoing like her other siblings.

Justine had a smart mouth, and from the time she was ten years old, she talked back to Mrs. Marciano. The two didn't get along at all. Mrs. Marciano referred to her as the devil child. Just like her twin brother, Justine was a party animal. Anything illegal Justine was involved in. She even got a tattoo on her lower back, which Mrs. Marciano referred to as a tramp stamp. When she befriended Sofia, things really got wild.

Sofia was a free-spirited person who lived life in the fast lane. She and Justine met at a school function and instantly became best friends. Sofia wasn't like the other girls that Justine went to school with. She wasn't into her looks and didn't care how people dressed. Of course, Mrs. Marciano didn't like her; she felt Sofia was a bad influence on Justine.

Mrs. Marciano was throwing her annual spring party, and Justine invited Sofia. At the request of her grandfather, Justine put some effort into her looks. She wore a strapless summer dress with a pair of sandals. For the first time, she looked like a girl. Like all the other parties, a bunch of snobbish Italians stood around talking about everyone. Justine was getting some punch when she overheard one of the partygoers talking about Sofia, who was at the table talking to Justin and Anthony. They called her trashy and fast and wondered why Mrs. Marciano allowed her around them. Unwilling to bite her tongue, Justine walked over to them and put them in their place. Then she and Sofia left. Once the party was over and Justine arrived back at home, Mrs. Marciano was waiting up for her.

"Do you see what time it is, young lady?"

Tipsy, Justine replied, "I was with Sofia."

Already pissed, Mrs. Marciano walked over and looked her up and down in disgust. "I don't want you hanging out with that trash."

"She's trash because her parents have to work for a living? Unlike some people who muscle people out of their earnings," Justine snidely replied. "Yeah, I know all about the Marcianos,'" she added with a smirk.

"Well, if you know about us, then you know we're nothing to play with. Now, like I said, I don't want that girl in my house."

"What house? This house?" Justine said, stepping closer to her. "This isn't your house. It's my great-grandfather's. Oh yeah, I know your name isn't on the deed. You're a guest just like me."

If Mrs. Marciano knew for sure that Justine wouldn't hit her back, she would have knocked the shit out of her. "We should've left your black ass back with the animals. You will never be a Marciano," she mumbled.

Not the one to back down, Justine instead leaned forward. "Yes, you should have. At least they don't eat their young. And you're right. I would never be a stuck-up Marciano," she shot back before walking away.

Mrs. Marciano was so angry that smoke was coming out of her ears, but she had something for Justine's ass. A couple of weeks went by, and Justine forgot about the whole incident. Since she and her great-grandmother always had words in the past, she brushed it off. Sadly, Mrs. Marciano was tired of Justine's mouth. Also, she knew it was Sofia who revealed that information to Justine about her name not being on the deed. It was time for Mrs. Marciano to teach Sofia a lesson.

One evening, Justine came in the house drunk, and while on her way up to her bedroom, she heard loud noises coming from the guesthouse. At first, she assumed it was Anthony with one of his groupie girlfriends, but then she recognized the voice. The person was begging for the person to stop. Justine went to see what was going on, only to find the unthinkable.

It was Sofia being raped by Anthony. Smashed, Justine thought her eyes were playing tricks on her, and when she saw Mrs. Marciano holding Sofia down, she really thought she was dreaming. Justine and Sofia's eyes met.

"Please," Sophia cried.

With a smirk on her face, Mrs. Marciano got up and walked over to Justine. "Come," she mumbled, leading Justine to the bedroom.

"Is that…"

"That doesn't concern you," Mrs. Marciano said, cutting her off.

Drunk out of her mind, all Justine could do was pass out across the bed. The next morning, she woke up with a massive headache and unable to remember anything from last night. She figured no one had seen her come in last night. It wasn't until she saw Anthony standing shirtless in the kitchen that it started coming back to her.

"Hey," she said.

"Hey, Justine," Anthony replied, while fixing a sandwich.

Noticing scratches on Anthony's back, she asked, "How did you get those scratches on your back?"

In a nonchalant tone, Anthony responded, "I don't know," before walking out.

It was then that Justine realized what happened. Quickly, she got dressed and ran over to Sofia's house to find her in the yard drunk out of her mind.

"I thought you were different. I thought we were close," Sofia sobbed. "How could you stand there and allow Anthony to do that to me?" she rambled, snot and tears covering her face. "I trusted you!"

Speechless, Justine lowered her head. Just as she feared, it hadn't been a dream. Anthony had raped her friend.

"Sofia, I was drunk. I didn't know," Justine cried while slowly strolling over to her.

Sofia held her hand up. "Don't come near me. Don't you fucking come near me!" she screamed, then fell to her knees on the ground.

"I swear, Sofia. I didn't know. Listen, let's go to the police. I'll tell them what he did to you."

While the idea was great, Sofia knew crossing the Marcianos was something you didn't do.

Sofia stumbled to her feet. "Police?" she giggled. "Yeah, like your grandma would allow that to happen. Wake up, Justine. You know how many women your brother Anthony raped!" she exclaimed, causing Justine's eyes to widen. "Yeah, everyone knows Anthony is a rapist, and the Marcianos pay them off."

"I didn't—"

"Of course, you didn't," Sofia spat, cutting her off.

"Sofia, I swear I will fight this with you. I will make sure my brother and Grandma pay for what they did to you." She reached out for her arm. "We can tell Justin."

"Oh God, Justin," Sofia sobbed. "He's not gonna speak to me after he hears this." Sofia smacked Justine's hand away and glared at her. "Leave me alone! I'll handle this myself!"

Two days later, Sofia jumped in front of a car and killed herself. Justine was devastated. She couldn't believe she had witnessed her brother raping her best friend, and it changed her relationship with Anthony forever. As far as she was concerned, he was dead to her.

A week after Sofia's funeral, Felix and Mrs. Marciano invited Sofia's parents to the house. Justine later found out that Felix had paid for Sofia's funeral and gave her family some money. Once Justine learned this, she started acting out. She became withdrawn from the world. Her grades dropped. She started dressing gothic. Every other night Justine would come home drunk out of her mind, rambling about how she hated this side of her family. Everyone just assumed she was going through something because she had lost her best friend.

Things got so bad with Justine that Felix eventually had no choice but to send her to Trinity Boarding School in Manhattan. Before she was scheduled to leave, Justine decided to confront her great-grandmother. Mrs. Marciano was in her bedroom.

Knock!Knock!

"Come in," Mrs. Marciano called out.

"You finally got your wish," Justine said as she entered.

"You have a lot to learn, little girl," Mrs. Marciano sneered. "I tried to warn you."

Glowering at her, Justine responded, "I know Anthony raped Sofia, just like I know you paid her family off. I'm gonna make you..."

"Make me what? Who's gonna believe a drunken slut? Look at you! You could never be like your sister." Mrs. Marciano walked over and whispered in her ear, "If you even breathe one word to anyone, I will make sure you join Sofia."

For a brief second, Justine was scared. She couldn't believe her own great-grandmother was capable of killing. However, Justine's pride wouldn't let her back down.

"You're gonna die screaming, and I'm gonna watch, bitch!" she retorted before exiting. After that night, Justin and Justine never returned. In fact, they got their acts together once they left Italy. Sadly, it was the last time Felix saw his grandchildren.

Chapter TWO

For years, Roger blamed himself for the death of Denise. Maybe if he had been a better father, her life would've been different. In the beginning, it was very difficult for them raising four children. Although Jasmine and Denise had life insurance policies, Roger and Betty were pushing sixty years old with health issues and on a fixed income. However, Roger refused to allow his grandchildren to go in the system. If his other two daughters weren't such fuckups, he would have let them take in two of the kids, but judging by how his other grandchildren were being raised, he declined. Besides, Anita and De'shell were selfish; they would only do something if money were involved.

Roger wasn't surprised to find out Denise had left everything to the kids in her will. She also left a trust for them. A couple weeks after Denise's death, Mr. Rubin, her lawyer, flew down to visit them. Denise had arranged it so whoever took in her children would receive a monthly stipend until her children were of legal age. She also had a lot of stipulations. For instance, the person raising the children was required to provide Mr. Rubin with receipts of school tuition, clothing expenses, etc. The children must also be taken to the dentist twice a year and have a yearly checkup. Roger and Betty couldn't help but to laugh at some of the things Denise listed.

With the help of Mr. Rubin, Roger and Betty moved into a five-bedroom, three-bath Victorian House right outside of Atlanta, Georgia. While Roger hadn't planned on raising any more kids, he couldn't have asked for better grandkids.

Like their mother, Derrick and Halle were focused; both got good grades in school. As Denise's will stipulate, Roger enrolled Derrick and Halle into early childhood school, which paid off. By the time they were five years old, both kids knew how to read and write on a first grade level. Although Roger had to admit raising four kids took up a lot of time, he was happy that he and Betty were alive and able to do so.

Sadly, his other two daughters reverted back to their old ways after Denise died. For the life of him, Roger didn't understand why they were so negative. Denise had left them ten thousand dollars apiece, and once they ran through it, they were begging for more. When Roger said no, they became resentful. Every time they visited, De'shell and Anita would torment Derrick, and Halle by saying mean things about Denise. That was one of the reasons Roger and Betty didn't invite them over.

De'shell and Anita had children. Shameka was Anita's child. By the time Shameka turned eighteen, she'd had several abortions. However, she decided to keep her last child, Kasheem, who stayed in trouble. One day, Shameka said, "Fuck it," packed up her shit, and moved to Kentucky, leaving her fourteen-year-old son to fin for himself.

De'shell was the mother of Ronisha, who had a daughter named Diamond. Diamond went to live with her grandmother De'shell at the age of ten when her mother got busted for insurance fraud. But, she was off the hook—drinking, smoking, and partying recklessly. So, De'shell sent Diamond to live with Roger and Betty. By then, Michael and Monique had gone away to college.

Roger didn't want them around Derrick and Halle, who were the children of Denise and Derrick Sr., but somehow Betty convinced him, claiming they could be saved. However, Roger would forever regret his decision.

Derrick and Halle had bright futures ahead of them. Before their lives took a turn for the worse, they were attending The Westminster School in Atlanta. Derrick Johnson was tall, dark, and handsome like his father, but hot tempered like his mother. He was straight A student and the star of his basketball team. He had the potential to be the next Kobe Bryant. Halle Johnson was average looking, but had sex appeal like her mother. She too was also hotheaded. When she wasn't running track, she practiced playing the piano. Roger knew Denise and Derrick Sr. were looking down smiling at their children.

Happy to be around family, Derrick and Halle welcomed their cousins Kasheem and Diamond with open arms, but Kasheem and Diamond had much animosity towards everyone. As most people today, they blamed the world for their mistakes.

Kasheem, the older of the two, was nice looking. However, because of his front rotten teeth and dark marks left behind from busting his pimples, he was standoffish and insecure about his appearance. Having dropped out of school, his vocabulary was limited.

Even though Derrick knew Kasheem was jealous of him, he still included him in things. Since Roger had explained to him and Halle about the abuse Kasheem and Diamond endured while growing up, they went out of their way to make them feel loved. Sadly, Kasheem had different plans. Once he knew his way around Atlanta, Kasheem started hanging out with the wrong crowd. Every other night, he would get into fights with guys in the street.

One night, Derrick took Kasheem to a party, where Kasheem spotted a pretty girl dancing across the room. He walked up to her, and they started dancing. When the night was over, Kasheem asked the girl for her number. She laughed in his face and stated that the only way he would get her number was if it were for Derrick.

Humiliated, Kasheem wanted to stomp the shit out of her. While looking over at Derrick, who had a flock of girls smiling at him, he decided to destroy him.

Diamond was what they called "damaged goods". Ever since her mother was busted, Diamond had a *fuck the world, don't ask me shit'* attitude. Before she knew how to shave her pussy,

Diamond was fucking. At a young age, Ronisha showed Diamond how to fuck for money, and Diamond was about to introduce that lifestyle to Halle.

Halle wasn't popular like her brother. In fact, girls only hung out with her to get closer to her brother. That's why Diamond had no problem manipulating Halle. Within two months, Diamond introduced Halle to sex, money, and drugs. As a result, Halle's grades started dropping. Everyone tried talking to her, but it was like Diamond had cast a spell on Halle. She was so out of control that she started doing pornography movies with girls.

What Halle didn't know was that Kasheem and Diamond had secretly planned to ruin her and Derrick's lives?

*****

It was supposed to a celebration for Derrick, who was leaving for Duke University the following week. The party was going great until Diamond gave Halle LSD, a hallucinating drug. Diamond then led Halle to a dark room where some guy was passed out on the bed. She lied telling Halle it was a guy named Rob who Halle had a crush on.

"Hey, Rob is in the room passed out. Why don't you wake him up with a blowjob?" Diamond suggested while opening the door.

High off the drug, Halle thought it was cool. "I'm gonna give him the blowjob of his life," she said, giggling and high-fiving Diamond

"That's what I'm talking about. Show that nigga what he's been missing. I'm gonna wait until the right time before I turn the lights on. Okay?"

Giggling like a schoolgirl, Halle replied, "Okay."

Being that the guy had on sweat pants, it was easy for Halle to pull out his penis. Also, the guy had a towel thrown over his head. Since Diamond had showed her how to suck dick like a pro, the guy became aroused in no time.

While massaging Halle's head, the drunken guy moaned, "Oh shit. What the—"

"Shhh," she whispered. "I'm gonna make you feel good."

Once he was fully erect, Halle removed her clothes and started riding him. By then, Diamond had entered the room.

"You alright, cuz," she asked Halle.

"Yeah. This nigga's dick is big," she said, while bouncing up and down.

"Halle," Diamond called out, "look at the camera. Let's show this nigga how we handle big dicks in the ATL," Diamond boasted, while recording Halle.

Completely out of it, but motivated and horny, Halle smiled at the camera. She even licked her lips and blew a kiss.

"Ride that nigga, Halle. Use them pussy muscles like I showed you."

Excited by Diamond coaching her on, Halle gently pulled up the towel a little so she could lean over to kiss the guy, who was semi-awake and holding Halle by her waist as she continued to ride him. Kasheem quietly entered the room and started cheering them on.

Diamond moved closer to get better footage. "Jump off and suck it, girl. You know how we do. Let it hit the back of your throat."

Doing as instructed, Halle jumped off his dick and started sucking it, making slurping sounds. "You like that?" she asked him.

"Look at the camera. Put it in your mouth and look at the camera like they do in the porn flicks."

Doing as she was told, Halle looked directly in the camera. She even smiled and hit herself in the head with the tip of the penis. "He has a big dick. I like sucking big dicks."

Not only was the guy drunk, but he was high on LSD, too. Horny as hell, the guy flipped Halle over on all fours and entered her. This time, Kasheem cheered the guy on.

"Fuck that pussy. Fuck that bitch," he said, disguising his voice.

Sadly, their chemistry was off the chain. Fucking and sucking each other, Halle and the guy gave each other numerous orgasms.

*****

The next day, Halle was in the bed sleeping, when her grandfather busted into the room screaming, "What did you do?"

"What?" she answered in a groggy voice. "What are you talking about now?"

"I know your mother and father are turning over in their graves!" he shouted.

By now, Derrick had already seen the video. "What the fuck did you do to me? OH MY FUCKING GOD!" he screamed, storming into Halle's room with the video.

Fully awake now, Halle jumped up to see what all the commotion was about. She wanted to die when she saw the video. Apparently, someone had posted a video online of Halle and Derrick having sex.

Disgusted, Roger yelled, "What has gotten into you? It's not bad enough that you allow someone to videotape you having sex, but you go and do it with your brother? I don't know you anymore!"

Feeling as though her eyes were deceiving her, Halle snatched the iPad out of Derrick's hand to get a better look. *Oh my God*, she thought, starting to feel sick.

"This can't be happening," she mumbled, dropping the device on the floor. "I had sex with my brother?"

Too sickened to look at her, Derrick ran back to his room and slammed the door, damn near taking the hinges off. Halle put her hands over her mouth and ran to the bathroom to throw up.

"How did this happen?" Roger and Betty asked as Halle walked back into the bedroom.

Unable to remember, she remained silent.

"Answer me goddamnit!" he screamed, while Betty stood next to him waiting for a response.

"I don't know."

Roger was so upset that he wanted to beat the shit out of them. "Ever since Diamond moved in, you've been acting like a whore, drinking, partying, messing with every Tom, Dick, and

Harry, and now this. I don't know what has gotten into you, Halle, but you better get your shit together or else," he scolded.

"Roger!" Betty said.

"Roger, my ass! Denise did a lot of things, but one thing's for certain. She was never a follower. Now look, just because you live your life recklessly, don't mess up your brother's life."

"I'm sorry," was all Halle could say.

Roger was right. For the past couple of months, she'd been out of control.

Feeling sorry for Halle, Betty took a seat next to her. "Sweetie, did we do something wrong?" she asked, trying to find out why Halle was behaving like this.

Ashamed, Halle stared at the floor as tears rolled down her face. "No."

"Then what's wrong? What's gotten into you lately?"

Halle jumped up, went over, and grabbed her family photo.

Betty went up behind her. "I know you miss your parents. I miss them, too."

However, Roger wasn't buying that bullshit. Halle was on the right track until Diamond's ass moved in. Before he said or did something he would regret, he left to check on Derrick, who was so upset that he tore his room apart.

"Derrick," Roger said, entering with caution.

Breathing heavily, Derrick punched his fist against the wall. "I don't wanna hear it, Grandpa."

"Okay then, I won't say it. But, I'm here when you're ready to talk," Roger stated before closing the door back.

Roger and Betty went down to the kitchen to discuss what had happened. When Kasheem and Diamond arrived home after having left earlier that morning, they could tell something was wrong.

"What's going on?" Diamond asked, both of them pretending not to know what happened.

Betty was too upset to talk, but somehow, Roger had a gut feeling that they were behind it.

"What happened last night at the party?" he asked in a nasty tone. "What did you give Derrick and Halle?"

Offended, Diamond answered in a standoffish tone. "What you mean, what did we give them?"

"Word? What are you talking about?" Kasheem said, fighting hard to keep a straight face.

Roger only twisted his face; he knew their asses were behind it. Since Roger didn't reply, Diamond and Kasheem brushed him off and went upstairs.

On the way upstairs, Kasheem and Diamond gave each other high-fives.

"Good for those motherfuckers," Diamond said, boasting.

Within an hour, every social media site had the video posted online. Over two million viewers watched the clips. Derrick and Halle's lives were ruined. After this, no NBA team would touch Derrick. The only way Derrick could come back from this was to find out who was behind it.

*****

A couple of weeks went by, and of course, Kasheem and Diamond found it hard to keep it a secret any longer. Both confided in people, and one of them told Derrick's teammates.

Since the incident, Derrick and Halle had been keeping a low profile and avoiding each other like the plague. If it weren't for school, they wouldn't leave the house.

It was Saturday night when one of Derrick's teammates came over to the house. At first, Derrick told his grandfather to send him away, but Wez insisted on seeing him.

Knock! Knock!

"Yo, Dee," Wez said, entering the room.

"Yo, didn't I tell my grandpa—" he said, jumping up off the bed.

Wez held up his hand for Derrick to sit back down. "Chill. I told him I had something to tell you. Yo, I know who was behind that sex tape shit," he informed Derrick, gaining his full attention.

"What? Who?" he asked.

Wez paused. He wasn't sure if Derrick could handle it.

"Who?" Derrick asked, jumping up from the bed again. "Who the fuck was behind it?"

"Your cousins Kasheem and Diamond," Wez replied, then looked away ashamed.

"What?" He was unsure if he had heard Wez clearly.

"Word! Kasheem told his girl that he and Diamond drugged y'all and then taped y'all."

In a state of shock, Derrick asked, "Why?"

"I told you that nigga's been hating on you. And you should see the shit Halle got Diamond doing."

As Derrick looked Wez in the face, his body started getting hot. All he saw was blood. "You know where he's at now?"

"Yeah, he's at Pocket's party."

Derrick threw on a sweat suit and grabbed his keys to head over there. "Yo, let's go."

On their way out, they bumped into Halle. Judging by Derrick's body language, she knew something was wrong.

"What's going on?" she asked him.

Derrick didn't respond, but Wez did. "Your cousins were behind that sex tape shit."

"What?! Are you serious?"

"Yeah. Dee and I are about to go holla at Kasheem now," Wez responded.

"I'm coming," Halle told them.

"No, you're not!" Derrick said, stopping her. "I got this."

However, Halle was just as hot tempered as him. She waited until they pulled off and then jumped in her car to follow them.

Upon entering the party, Derrick spotted Kasheem whining with some girl. Without saying a word, he walked up to Kasheem and knocked the shit out of him. Delivering blow after blow, Derrick knocked Kasheem's teeth out.

Diamond, who was in the other room with some guy, came out to see what all the commotion was about. That's exactly what Halle was waiting for.

"What the..." was all Diamond could say before Halle started pounding her non-stop.

To show them what it felt like to be humiliated, Derrick and Halle dragged Kasheem and Diamond's battered bodies outside. As everyone watched in shock, Derrick and Halle almost beat their cousins to death. Someone called their grandparents, but by the time Roger and Betty got to the scene, Halle and Derrick was getting it on with the police.

The car hadn't come to a complete stop before Roger jumped out. "What are you doing? Get off of them?" he cried, trying to stop them from placing the cuffs on Halle and Derrick.

When the smoke cleared, Kasheem and Diamond were being transported to the hospital, while Derrick, Halle, and Roger were on their way to jail.

Once the ADA reviewed the video footage taken from camera phones and witnesses came forward, most of the charges were dropped against Derrick and Halle. The most serious charge, aggravated assault in the first degree, stuck and carried up to a twenty-year prison term.

Feeling guilty, there was no way Roger would let his grandchildren be convicted. So, he called Kasheem and Diamond over to his house and tried to reason with them. At first, Kasheem and Diamond declined the invite, but Roger promised to make it worth their while. Once they arrived, Roger didn't waste any time.

"How can we make this go away?" he asked them.

"You see my fucking head?" Kasheem replied, pointing at his injury. "I have staples in it and a fucking rod in my knee. Fuck that nigga."

With her jaw wired shut, Diamond just screwed up her face and nodded.

Roger glared at them; at that moment, he wished they weren't related to him.

"Would you drop the charges for twenty thousand dollars?" His words got Kasheem and Diamond's full attention. "Come on, you can use the money. I'll give y'all twenty thousand."

Kasheem looked at Diamond before saying, "Nah, fuck that. We want a hundred thousand dollars each, or your grandson is gonna become someone's bitch."

As bad as Roger wanted to snatch the life out of him, he replied, "Okay. I'll have the money in a couple of days."

Gloating, Kasheem and Diamond gave each other high-five.

"That's what I'm talking about," Kasheem said, satisfied.

Although they agreed to drop the charges, the state of Atlanta decided to pick up the case. Derrick was seventeen, and Halle was fifteen when they were sentenced to two years in a juvenile center. As a part of the agreement, if they stayed out of trouble, when they turned twenty-five years old, their record would be sealed. While Derrick found God, Halle started using drugs.

Though they were released eighteen months later, Derrick and Halle's lives would never be the same. However, it was Monique and Michael who made them get counseling to talk about the incident. It took a couple of sessions, but Derrick and Halle finally started working toward building their relationship.

Chapter THREE

Fulfilling a promise she made to her daughter, Sadie made sure Greg Jr. and Gracie had a well-balanced upbringing. Like Felix, Sadie changed Greg and Gracie's last name to Dodson. Until they found out who killed Gabrielle and Greg, Sadie wasn't taking any chances.

Sadie managed to raise four girls, and none of them compared to Gracie, who was outspoken, stubborn, and hot in the ass. She ran Sadie's blood pressure up so bad that she thought she would have a stroke.

Gracie was nothing like her mother. Gabrielle had class and morals. Sadie couldn't believe Greg and Gracie had been birthed from the same woman. Gracie was pretty and smart like her mother and had the spirit of a hustler like her father. Just like her mother, Gracie didn't believe in men taking care of her. From the time she turned thirteen years old, Gracie knew she wanted to run the world. As for men, her motto was "fuck'em and leave'em." The only thing they were good for in her eyes was a good lay.

At the age of sixteen, Gracie was hanging out with some of the prettiest socialites in Miami. However, one night, she was at an exclusive party on Fire Island, when one of her girls caught her boyfriend with her friend. When confronted, the guy dismissed both of the girls, saying since he made the money, he made the rules. That's when Gracie realized these women didn't have much of anything and were just arm candy, which was something she refused to be. After that night, Gracie vowed not to be one of them. Therefore, she did everything in her power to learn everything about the nightlife business, from bartending to bookkeeping. She even lied about her age, stating she was twenty years old.

It took some time, but Gracie's ambition caught the eye of one of her friend's father. Stuart was an old Cuban who had just purchased a nightclub. He was looking for someone fresh, young, and sexy to run his nightclub, and Gracie was just the person.

Instead of asking her friend to ask her father if she could work for him, Gracie decided to approach him herself. Stuart was at one of his nightclubs when Gracie found him. Since she was his daughter's friend, Stuart agreed to see her.

"Ahh, Gracie, what can I do for you?" he asked as he stood and greeted her with a kiss on the cheek.

With a smile, she replied, "Hello. I was wondering if you found someone to run your nightclub."

"No. Why?" Stuart sat back down at his desk.

As Gracie strutted over closer to him, she said, "Because I wanna run it."

Stuart released a loud laugh. "You? You're not even legal."

"So? No one has to know. Mr. Stuart, trust me, I'm the person."

Stuart stared into Gracie's eyes. Something about her tone and the look in her eyes told him she was serious.

"Have you ever worked in a nightclub before?"

"Yes, I bartend at one after school and on the weekends. I'm good at bookkeeping, and I get the customers to spend their money."

For a second, Stuart considered it, and then he laughed at the idea. Hiring her would be like hiring his daughter.

"Gracie, while I'm flattered, the club scene isn't a place for a young, pretty girl like yourself. You should be——" he tried to say but was cut off

"Be what, someone's arm candy? Or a waitress?" she said, cutting him off.

Annoyed, Stuart responded, "Neither. You should be studying to become a nurse, a doctor, or a lawyer. I wouldn't want my niña working in a nightclub."

Gracie sucked her teeth at his sexist remark. She was about to say something slick, but had an idea. "Can I talk to you in private?" she asked.

Stuart nodded at his bodyguards, which was a cue for them to leave. Gracie then seductively walked around the desk while licking her lips.

"What do I have to do?" she softly whispered before dropping to her knees.

Stuart tried to get her to stand up, but she pushed his hand away and proceeded to unbuckle his pants. Quickly becoming turned on, Stuart pulled out his penis. He had totally forgotten Gracie's age and that she was his daughter's friend.

She gave Stuart one of the best blowjobs he'd ever had, making him explode in less than ten minutes.

Breathing heavily, Stuart pulled out his handkerchief to wipe away the mess. "Damn, where did you learn how to suck dick like that?"

Gracie giggled. "So are you gonna give me a try?"

Stuart stared into her eyes, wondering if it was a setup. "Okay," he finally replied. "I'll try you out for two months, but if I don't see anything, you're gone."

Gracie flashed a sexy smile and then dropped back down to her knees.

*****

Within six months, Gracie turned Stuart club into the hottest spot in Miami. It was so hot that there was a waiting list for parties. Overnight, she became the "it girl" of the party scene. Every club owner wanted her to manage their club, and they would wine and dine her in an attempt to win her over.

By the time Gracie turned eighteen, she wore only designer clothing, drove expensive cars, and only ate at five-star restaurants. She did whatever it took to make it to the top. She mingled with drug lords, sport athletes, moguls, and even terrorists. Not only did Gracie have the gift of gab, but she could also fuck her ass off, which she didn't mind doing if it meant closing a deal. Nothing was going to get in her way of having what she wanted, not even Sadie.

It was Greg and Gracie's eighteenth birthday, and Gracie was getting ready for work when Sadie knocked on her door. For the past couple of years, Sadie had watched Gracie turn into Lindsay Lohan. Gracie had disrespected her on so many levels that Sadie refused to tolerate any more. She was tired of fighting with her. She prayed many nights, asking for some guidance. That's why tonight she decided there could only be one woman in the house. Therefore, Gracie had to go

"Gracie, are you in there?" Sadie asked from the other side of the door after knocking.

"Yeah," she answered dryly.

Sadie opened the door, but didn't enter the room. "I wanna talk to you and Greg. Are you going to be home tomorrow?"

Gracie looked Sadie up and down, wondering what she was up to. "Depends on if I get lucky," she told her.

Sadie looked away in disgust. Gracie always tried to get under her skin, but Sadie refused to let her tonight.

"If he's sleeping with you, I wouldn't call that luck," she shot back. "Have your ass in here by the time I wake up in the morning," she stated, then slammed the door. "Slut," she grumbled.

Greg was the total opposite of his sister. From day one, he knew what he wanted out of life. He was the perfect child; he got good grades in school and helped his grandmother out. You really had to piss him off for him to act up, which Gracie did. While growing up, Gracie referred to Greg as a wimp because he avoided fights. Greg was far from a wimp, though. He just didn't see the point of proving his manhood to anyone. Like his father, Greg was very quiet and laidback. He didn't have a lot of friends; he kept his circle small for a reason. He was also very giving and inspired people to better themselves. One example of his unselfishness would be when one of his friends was forced to drop out of school to get a job because his family fell behind in their bills. When Greg found out, he took the money he had saved up for a car and gave it to his friend. When his other friend started hanging out with the wrong crowd, it was Greg who convinced him to stop.

Tall, dark, and handsome, Greg was a ladies' man. Like most typical boys, Greg messed with a lot of girls, until one of them gave him a STD. That's when Greg learned that just because a girl is beautiful doesn't mean she's clean. After that scary experience, Greg only slipped up a few more times. One of those times led to him getting a girl pregnant at the age of seventeen. Of course, Sadie found out, but instead of scolding him, her silence said it all. The last thing Greg wanted to do was disappoint his grandmother, who was like a mother to him. When the girl decided to get an abortion, Greg vowed never to slip up again.

Greg and Sadie were very close. Sadly, that wasn't the case with Gracie and Greg. When they were kids, Greg and Gracie were inseparable. Then, as time went on, Gracie and Greg fought like cats and dogs. Greg didn't like the way Gracie treated people, especially Sadie.

Gracie believed Sadie was strict. Unlike her friends, Gracie wasn't allowed to wear revealing clothing or make-up until she was sixteen, and her boyfriends had to pick her up from the house. Most of all, you couldn't stay in Sadie's house if you did drugs and didn't go to school.

At times, Greg also felt Sadie was too strict, but he knew she was only doing it out of love. Things had gotten so bad between Sadie and Gracie that Gracie barely stayed home. Greg could tell his sister's absence was taking a toll on his grandmother. So, Greg

decided to take both ladies out to lunch, hoping it would smooth things over. Sadly, it would be something he later regretted.

Gracie was now staying in Blue & Green Diamond Condominiums after being put out by Sadie.

"If you're coming here to convince to move back, I'm not," Gracie snapped when she opened the door to greet Greg.

"Well, hello to you, too, sis," Greg snidely replied while entering. "Nice pad. One of your rich boyfriend's?"

Gracie sighed and then closed the door. "Does it matter? You should take a page out of my book."

"No, thanks. Besides, dating rich old men isn't my thing," he jokingly said, causing Gracie to chuckle.

"What, she sent you over here to force me to come back?" she asked.

Taking in the beautiful view, Greg replied, "Nope. I think she's happy you're gone."

His comment caught Gracie off guard, and for a second, she felt sad. "Figures. Oh well, that makes two of us."

Greg faced his twin. "Chill. You know grandma's upset you're gone. What's gotten into you, Gracie?"

"You want something to drink?" she asked him, totally disregarding his comment as she walked into her luxury kitchen.

Greg followed her. "No, thanks. Don't ignore me. Look at you. You're like one of those stuck-up rich bitches we use to make fun of."

Gracie slammed a bottle of *Naked* juice on the counter. "Fuck you! Who died and left you my father? Grandma had too many rules. Hell, you said it yourself. We're almost nineteen years old and have curfews. I'm in college for Christ's sake, but does she see that? No! All she wants to do is control our lives. I'll be by later to get the rest of my things."

Greg sighed. Gracie was so stubborn; it was pointless talking to her. Meanwhile, Sadie knew Greg was wasting his time going over there. Like a lot of people, Gracie was going to have to learn the hard way.

★ ★ ★ ★ 32

*****

Sadie had just finished preparing dinner, when Gracie entered the house.

"Are you hungry?" Sadie asked, trying to be cordial.

"No, thanks. I'm just here to get the rest of my things."

Just as Gracie was about to leave, Greg entered. This was the perfect time.

"Gracie...Greg, have a seat," Sadie said.

Gracie pouted. "I can't."

"It won't take long," Sadie stated.

Gracie exhaled. "How—"

"Gracie, can you give Grandma a minute," Greg said, cutting her off. "I'm pretty sure your rich friends won't mind."

"Screw you," Gracie spat.

"Alight!" Sadie yelled. "Give me a second," she then said in a lower voice and exited the room.

Moments later, Sadie returned with a folder. "Have a seat," she said, gesturing for them to sit down. "I was trying to wait until you guys turned twenty-one or at least until you graduated from college, but judging by the way things are going, that might never happen," she snidely commented while looking at Gracie.

Gracie smirked at her grandmother's slick comment. "Can we get on with this? I have some place I need to be."

Greg shook his head and thought, *Ungrateful bitch.*

"Of course," Sadie said. "Your grandfather left both of you a trust fund," she lied.

"Our grandfather?" Greg asked.

"Actually, he left it to your mother, but since she's gone, it belongs to you," Sadie told them while trying to hold back the tears

Gracie and Greg looked at each other.

"Grandma, are you alright?" Greg asked.

Unable to hold her tears back, Sadie smiled and replied, "Yes. It's been a while since I said it out loud."

"Said what?" Gracie questioned.

"About your mother being gone. You never got over losing your child," Sadie said, causing the twins to lower their heads. "That's why I stay in your asses a lot. Because even though your mother is not here, she would've wanted the best for you."

Feeling ashamed, Gracie's eyes filled with tears.

Sadie giggled. "Your mother was a lot of things, but most importantly, she was her own person. She knew what she wanted out of life and was determined to get it."

"Mommy was outspoken, huh?" Gracie said, wiping her tears away.

"Yes, just like you," Sadie told her, causing Gracie to giggle. "I know you guys are older and are gonna make your own decisions. And though I may not agree with them, all I ask is for you to use this money wisely. Don't be like others and blow it. Make your parents and me proud. You understand me?"

Greg reached out for his sister's head and rested it on his shoulder. "We will," he told her.

Gracie looked at her grandmother. It was the first time she realized Sadie only wanted the best for her. Sadie could've taken their money and blew it, but instead, she held it for them.

"Grandma," Gracie said, "I know these past few years have been rough. I know I haven't been exactly the best granddaughter, but I just wanna say I'm sorry for all the things I've done."

"I know I'm strict and stubborn," Sadie responded. "I guess that's where you and your mother get it from." Her comment caused them to giggle. "But, I'm like that for a reason. I've watched so many people who I loved be taken away from me. This world doesn't care about no one; it never has. I just want you and Greg to become something in life. I owe that to my daughter. Now, you can take this money and live happily for the rest of your life, or you can live miserable. That's your choice."

"Grandma, I'm so sorry." Gracie cried as she stepped forward to hug her.

"I know, sweetie," Sadie said, embracing her granddaughter.

Greg joined them. He was happy they were able to put their differences aside.

"Alright," Sadie said, handing them each an envelope. "Here."

Greg looked over at Gracie. Both thought it was few thousand dollars, but when they opened it, their eyes almost came out of their head.

"Twenty million dollars?" Greg said in shock.

Again, Greg looked at Gracie, whose face displayed the same look.

"Grandma, is this for real?" she asked.

Sadie laughed at their expressions. "Yes. It accumulated over the years."

Both dropped into nearby seats.

"I didn't know our grandpa had money like that. I mean, we lived so modest," Greg stated.

Sadie laughed. "Just because you have money doesn't mean you have to wear it on your sleeve."

"So all of these years we were millionaires." Gracie smiled.

Sadie got up to check her food "Yes. I wanted you to know the true meaning of life. If I would've given it to you or exposed you to it at a young age, you wouldn't know what hard work felt like," Sadie told them as she went to check on her food on the stove. "That's the one thing your parents knew...*hard work*," she emphasized.

"Wow! What did our grandpa do to become a millionaire?" Gracie asked.

For a brief second, Sadie looked at her grandkids. She thought about telling them the truth. Sadie wanted to see their faces when she told them that the money had actually came from their parents, but she was afraid of the questions that would follow, ones she wasn't ready to answer.

"Grandma, are you okay?" Gracie asked, noticing Sadie deep in thought.

"Yes...yes. Oh, your grandfather was a professor."

"Professor? I didn't know they made money like that. Maybe I should become a teacher," Greg jokingly stated. "No, that money came from his insurance policy." After Sadie checked her food, she faced the twins. "Now, are you gonna question me about the money or enjoy it? Because I know a lot of people who would love to be in your shoes," she stated with her hand on her hip. "Yes, ma'am," both replied, and then promised to invest their money wisely. Greg went to college to become an architect. After graduating, he relocated to New York and started his architect and design company. At twenty-five years old, Greg was engaged to his college sweetheart, and they were expecting their first child. Instead of going to college, Gracie attended a two-year business school. Although Sadie wasn't thrilled about it, she was happy Gracie hadn't blown her money foolishly. Gracie invested her money in hotels and restaurants, owning several in South Beach and New York. While Sadie was proud of their accomplishments, she prayed money, power, and respect wouldn't lead them to the same fate as their parents.

Chapter FOUR

Like many great artists, Tony's estate tripled after his death. While alive, Tony was worth one hundred and fifty million dollars. With the help of Felix, Tony's estate tripled courtesy of Christina Carrington's estate. Although Tony had agreed to give her back her publishing rights, they never signed the final papers, which Felix eventually had voided.

The children had proven themselves to be responsible adults. So, that's why Felix asked them to meet him at a house in Lake Minnetonka. He felt it was time for them to learn the truth about their parents' inheritance.

After the death of Morgan and Tony, Mrs. Marciano wanted Felix to sell all of Tony's properties, but he didn't. He thought it was important for his grandchildren to know they had lived in a home filled with love. Felix left the house exactly the way it was upon the death of Tony and Morgan, with the exception of cleaning and locking the room where Morgan had been murdered.

Before the kids arrived, Felix took a stroll through the house. It's been over Twenty years since he'd been there, and it was still painful. Smiling at the pictures and paintings on the wall, he took notice of how Morgan was just like her mother, classy.

Ironically, the kids pulled up to the house at the same time, but in different cars.

"Justy!" London screamed as she exited the car.

"Londie!" Justine shouted, running into London's arms.

"Just!" The ladies smiled while walking over to him.

"In the flesh," Justin joked, greeting them each with a kiss.

Anthony hopped out of his car like he was a star. "La familia," he jokingly greeted them in Italian. He hugged his brother and kissed his sisters before asking, "Do y'all know what this is all about?"

"No. We were just about to ask you," London replied.

"Well, I guess there's only one way to find out," Anthony said as he brushed something from off his jacket while leading them inside.

With everyone living in different states, the kids rarely saw each other. Anthony traveled back and forth between London and New York, managing the research department of Pfizer Pharmaceutical Company. London, who was now married to Nyennoh, lived in West Africa and became a teacher. She was also working on her first documentary. Justin lived in Yonkers, New York and was studying journalism at NYU grad school. He worked at *The New York Times* as a part-time writer. Justine, finally getting her act together, also lived in New York. Unlike her siblings, Justine partied hard. In fact, today she was celebrating one year of being clean. She was finishing up her Psychology degree at Columbia University.

Before they could knock on the door, Felix opened it.

"Come inside. It's so good to see you," he said hugging and kissing each of them as they walked inside.

After entering the house, they looked around at their surroundings and then at each other before turning to their grandfather. Strangely, they felt a sense of comfort, as if they had been there before.

"Grandpa, where are we?" Justine asked.

Felix took a deep breath and shut the door. "This was your home."

"Our home?" Anthony repeated, confused.

Felix sighed. "It was your parents' home."

Stunned, their eyes filled with tears.

This time, it was Justin who repeated what he'd heard. "Our parents?"

"Yes. All of you lived here," he answered, then led them into the living room to show them a huge family portrait.

"Oh my God! That's Mommy," London cried, running over to get a better look. "She's beautiful," she commented as the others joined her.

"Is that our father?" Anthony asked.

"Yes, that's Tony," Felix flatly replied.

"His face looks familiar," Anthony added.

"Come on. Let me show you the rest of the house," Felix said, ignoring Anthony's comment.

They were amazed at how beautiful and warm the house felt. That is until they came upon a room that was locked.

"What's in here?" Anthony asked, trying to open the door.

Felix lowered his head as his eyes filled with tears. "It's the room where your mother was murdered," he informed them.

There was a moment of silence while they tried to comprehend what Felix had said.

"Murdered? You said our mother was murdered?" Justine repeated and then pointed to the door. "In this room?"

Unable to respond, Felix nodded as tears rolled down his face.

"I thought you said our parents were killed in a plane crash." Anthony's tone was one of disappointment.

When the kids were younger, Felix told them their parents had been killed in a plane crash, which was something he now regretted doing.

"But you said our parents died in a plane crash," Anthony repeated, this time in a louder, stern tone.

Felix reached in his pocket and pulled out a key. "I told you that because I didn't think y'all could handle it," he said, then unlocked the door and walked inside.

Stunned by this revelation, they just looked at each other. Unlike the other parts of the house, this room had a dark, cold,

gloomy feeling. However, nothing was more disturbing than the huge bloodstain on the carpet.

"Oh my God!" Justine gasped when she noticed the huge stain.

Since he hadn't been to the house in over twenty years, Felix had forgotten about the reminder permanently left behind.

"How was she killed?" Anthony asked.

"She was shot," Felix answered.

"Why? By whom?" Justin questioned with tears in his eyes.

Although Felix didn't know who pulled the trigger, he believed Denise and Tony were responsible for her death.

"We don't know, Justin. The police believe she interrupted a burglar who was trying to rob the house," Felix lied, his voice cracking.

"Where was our father?" London asked.

"He was in the other room sleeping. He ran in after he heard the shot, but it was too late. She died in his arms."

Overwhelmed with grief, Justine ran out of the room with London following her, while Anthony and Justin remained with Felix.

"What about our father?" Justin asked. Tears were now rolling down his face.

"What about him?" Felix retorted.

"How did he die?" Anthony inquired.

"He was killed a couple of weeks later."

"So they never caught their killers? Where were we, and why weren't we killed?" Anthony asked.

Felix took a deep breath as the kids bombarded him with questions. By then, London and Justine had rejoined them.

"Your mother had just given birth to Justin and Justine before she was killed. Afraid for your safety, your father sent you to live with us."

Before they could ask any more questions, Felix took them back downstairs. "I'll answer all your questions, but first, I want to show you some things," he said, leading the way.

★ ★ ★ ★ ★ 40

He took them into the movie room, where he recovered some home videos of Tony and Morgan with the kids. Just as he was about to press play, Felix paused and turned around to look at his grandchildren. He couldn't wait for them to finally see their mother.

As the video started, the children watched the recording of Morgan feeding London while telling Anthony to leave something alone. It also showed Tony pick up Anthony, kiss him, and tell him how much he loved him. With his son in his arms, Tony bent over to kiss his daughter and Morgan, telling them how much he loved them, also.

So they wouldn't feel left out, Felix showed them another video of when the twins were brought home from the hospital. Tony and Lil' Anthony were dancing. Lil' Anthony was asking his mother could he hold his brother. The video ended with Tony and Morgan expressing their love for their children and thanking God for their wonderful blessing. Sadly, it was the last video they made before their untimely death.

Overwhelmed with the pain and joy of seeing their parents, there wasn't a dry eye in the house. After the video ended, Felix took them into the formal dining room.

"Have a seat," he told them, then continued. "Your father..." His voice trailed off as he searched for the right words.

"What about our father?" an eager Anthony asked.

"He..." Felix paused, wondering if he should tell them the truth.

"He what?" they all asked in anticipation.

"He left you guys some money," Felix said.

"He left us some money?" Justine repeated, confused and wondering why her grandfather was talking in riddles.

"Grandpa, what exactly are trying to say?" London asked, growing frustrated.

Felix sighed and then blurted out, "Your father was Anthony Omari Flowers, better known to the world as Tony Flowers."

"Tony Flowers?" the room echoed.

Felix went to great lengths to keep his grandchildren out of the limelight. That's why he never allowed them to visit their other grandparents or any other family members. He had even changed their last name. Especially since Tony and Morgan's killers were never caught.

"Grandpa, who is Tony Flowers?" Anthony asked.

Felix lowered his head. "Tony Flowers was a rapper."

"You're not talking about *thee* Tony Flowers that was killed by his girlfriend, are you?" Anthony questioned.

Felix's eyes widened. "You know about that?"

"Yes. He's a legend. Everyone knows about that," Justin answered.

"Grandpa, Tony Flowers was our father?" London seemed to be in shock

"Yes. Your last name is Flowers," he said, handing them some documents.

Glaring at Felix after having reviewed the documents, in a raised voice, Anthony said, "How could you? So, all these years you—"

"I did it to protect you," Felix retorted, cutting him off.

"To protect us? All these years we thought our name was Marciano!" Anthony shouted in a nasty tone. "Now you tell us it's Flowers. What else are you hiding?"

"Anthony, calm down! Let Grandpa finish. I'm pretty sure he has a good explanation," London exclaimed.

"She's right. Let him finish," Justin agreed.

Felix glared back at Anthony and took a deep breath before continuing. "As I was saying, I did it to protect you. In a year, your father's entire family was killed. His business partner, former assistant, and driver were all killed."

"Why?" Justine asked.

"It was rumored that Tony owed some money to drug dealers," Felix lied. "The police believe Tony was killed by Christina Carrington, but I never believed the rumors about the dealers or Christina. I think whoever killed Tony's family and

friends also killed my daughter and him." Felix's statement silenced the room. "You see, that's why it was important for me to protect y'all. I owed it to my daughter."

They looked at each other and nodded.

London stood and went over to him. "We understand, Grandpa," she mumbled, hugging him.

"I lost my daughter, but I refuse to lose my grandkids, too," he cried. "I'm sorry," he said, taking out his handkerchief to wipe his face after London released him. Felix took a seat. "I need y'all to understand that I owed it to my daughter. You guys were her life," he stressed while looking each of them in the face.

"We know, Grandpa," London said in an attempt to comfort him.

"So Tony Flowers is our father?" Anthony asked, disregarding Felix's feelings.

"Yes, he's the father to all of you. He was married to your mother. Tony had set up a will, leaving everything to Morgan and his children. Since she's gone, you guys inherit everything."

"What did we inherit?" Justine asked.

Felix picked up some documents and looked at it them. "At the time of your father's death, his estate was worth about one hundred and fifty million dollars. It now has tripled. His estate is currently worth seven hundred and fifty million dollars."

"That's a quarter of a billion," Justine said as they looked at each other.

"How?" London questioned.

"How what?" Felix replied.

"How did he reach that amount? Who was running my father's business?" London inquired.

"Me and other board members," Felix stated.

"You? What happened to my mother's family? Why didn't you tell us about this years ago? You made us go to school and get job, when all along we were millionaires!" Anthony exclaimed nastily.

Felix glared at Anthony. He was getting tired of his little tantrums. "That's what my daughter would've wanted."

"Oh please! My mother was rich and beautiful. I doubt education was on her mind," Anthony shot back.

"You little bastard! Don't you dare tell me that my daughter wasn't educated. Your mother went to Dalton, one of the best schools in the country. All the top schools wanted her. By the time she turned twenty-one, she had a Bachelor's in Economics. She was valedictorian of her class. Before her death, my daughter...your mother," Felix highlighted as spit flew from his mouth, "...was accepted into Woodrow Wilson School of Public and International Affairs at Princeton University. This program allowed students to obtain a Master's in Public Administration and a Juris Doctorate. So, don't tell me that my daughter wasn't about education," he grumbled, shutting Anthony up.

"Well, it's not like she had to work," Anthony grumbled, sitting back in the chair.

"Why don't you keep your damn mouth closed and listen sometimes? That's why you stay in trouble, because you think you know everything!" Justine yelled. "You weren't there. You don't know anything about our parents."

"Exactly! Has it ever occurred to you that Mommy wanted this?" London added.

"What are you talking about? We're rich, London," Anthony said, dragging her name out.

"That's all you ever think about, women and money," Justin pointed out, shaking his head.

"That's what life is all about, lil' bro," Anthony snidely responded.

Felix looked back and forth at his grandchildren. Sadly, he could see Anthony was going to be a problem.

"Enough!" Felix yelled, taking control of the conversation. "Before you go out there spending money you don't have, there are a few things you need to know. One, your father's estate will be divided equally. You will each receive a monthly allowance."

"Monthly allowance! Are you kidding me?" Anthony said.

Felix ignored Anthony. "Like I said, you will receive a monthly allowance until you turn thirty years old. After that, you will get a large lump sum of money." Felix shuffled through some more documents. "In addition to the money, you also inherit several homes throughout the country, a mansion in Alpine, New Jersey, one in Aspen Colorado, two luxury penthouses in Manhattan, a small island, and a private jet among other things," Felix said, reading off the list.

"Grandpa, who's running our father's company now?" Justin inquired.

"A board of trustees."

"Do you oversee this board?" Anthony asked in an insinuating tone.

Felix laughed. "As a matter of fact, I do. Let me tell you something. If it wasn't for me, your father's estate would've died right along with him. It was my idea to incorporate a board, so no one has the final decision but me. I made sure I owned the majority."

"How much did you get?" Anthony questioned.

"Anthony!" London shouted in disbelief.

Felix smirked. "No, London, let your brother talk. I have nothing to hide."

Everyone grew quiet and turned to look at Anthony, who had a cocky smirk on his face.

"I'm not saying that. Grandpa, you know I love you, and I appreciate everything you have done for my siblings and me. But, I found it a little strange that you took us in for free."

London shook her head while thinking to herself, *Anthony's just talking because he has a hole in his face.* Felix, on the other hand, was immune to Anthony's bullshit. This wasn't the first time Anthony had challenged him. In fact, he'd been doing it ever since he was a child. Felix blamed his mother for that. In her eyes, Anthony could do no wrong.

Felix got up from the table, put his hands in his pockets, and slowly strolled over to Anthony while the other grandkids watched in anticipation. Anthony, cocky and arrogant, wasn't going to allow his grandfather to punk him. Therefore, he stood up.

As the men stood face to face, Felix mumbled, "Are you accusing me of stealing, boy?"

Before Anthony could respond, Justin jumped up and got between them. "Come on," he mumbled, pushing his brother away. "Anthony, you know Grandpa would never take anything from us, so cut it out."

Having had enough of Anthony's shit, and before he did something stupid, Felix handed London the documents. "Here. I'm done," he said before exiting.

Meanwhile, Anthony's siblings glared at him as they shook their heads.

"What?" Anthony shouted in a defensive tone, then snatched the documents from London.

Pissed off, London snatched them back. "He didn't give them to you."

"But I'm the oldest". Anthony snapped, trying to grab them from her.

London pushed him away. "Not tonight you're not," she snidely replied before walking away.

Disgusted, Justin and Justine followed behind her.

"After all Grandpa did for us, you act like this," Justin grumbled, bumping Anthony as he walked out.

Anthony fiercely stared at them as they walked past him. Then he slammed his hand on the table and followed them. "London!" he shouted. "Wait! Wait, guys!"

London stopped and walked over to him. "What, Anthony? What do you have to say to us?" she asked while the twins looked him up and down.

"Alright…I'm sorry," he told her.

London shook her head. "No, you're not. You always think someone is out to get you. After all Grandpa did for us…especially you…and you're going to accuse him of lying and stealing."

"London—"

London put her hand up to silence him. "London, my ass. You may be the oldest, but I will not let you ruin what our parents have built. Do you understand me?" she warned.

As for Felix, he refused to stay under the same roof as Anthony. Another wrong thing said, and he would forget that Anthony was his grandson. Sadly, Anthony felt the same way.

Anthony went into the den to pour himself a drink. Then he took a seat on the couch and stared at the huge portrait of his father. Smiling, Anthony sipped from his drink and mumbled, "I am king."

Chapter FIVE

Two years had passed since Derrick last seen his sister Halle. Although they talked over the phone once a week, the last time they were together was at their grandmother's funeral. Today, they were attending their grandfather's funeral.

It had been years since the incident between Derrick and Halle, and Atlanta had left a bad taste their mouths. That's why as soon as both were released from jail, Derrick moved to South Carolina, where he was finishing up his degree in Theology.

Halle moved to New York. She was a part-time substance abuse counselor at Daytop Village. She had just celebrated twenty-seven months clean and was also working to become a Credentialed Substance Abuse Counselor.

Avoiding the stares, Halle entered the church searching for her brother. *God, I can't wait to get back home.* From afar, Derrick waved while walking over to her.

"Hi, sis. So glad you could make it," he said, embracing her.

"I almost didn't," Halle told him.

"Well, well, look who's here?" Kasheem said, walking up on them. "Derrick and Halle. You know I still watch that tape."

A man of God, Derrick answered, "Hello to you, too, Kasheem."

As for Halle, she didn't say anything. Seeing Kasheem was like throwing salt on a fresh wound. A part of her wanted to run and hide, but when she noticed Diamond walking over to them, Halle instantly saw rage.

"Diamond, look who's here," Kasheem said.

Diamond giggled. "I was just watching you guys on tape the other day."

"Which tape? The one of us busting your ass?" Halle shot back. "Now that's something to watch."

Kasheem was about to charge her, but remembered what happened the last time. In fact, he was blind in one eye because of that ass whipping. Now washed up, overweight, and with slow reflexes, Diamond decided not to challenge her.

As the four of them stood staring each other down, Michael and Monique came over to defuse the situation.

"Derrick! Halle!" Monique cheered, ignoring Kasheem and Diamond. "Oh my God, it's so good to see you."

Kasheem and Diamond looked at them, then waved their hand and walked off.

"Why are you letting them get under your skin?" Monique said, noticing Halle's nostrils flaring up.

Halle rolled her eyes and exhaled. "They're just—"

"Miserable," Michael said, finishing her sentence. "We all know that. You can't keep letting them get to you, though."

"Mike and Moe is right," Derrick said. "Come on. Let's go get our seats. It's about to start.

After the service, everyone came up to give their condolences to the family. Derrick and Halle may have not known this, but a lot of people were happy to see them. Everyone was aware of the tape, but they also knew they had been drugged.

In truth, that incident is what really killed Roger and Betty. They blamed themselves for ruining their grandchildren's lives. Everything was perfect until they allowed Kasheem and Diamond to move in. Sadly, before their deaths, Roger and Betty were in debt, but they refused to use Derrick and Halle's money. In fact, Derrick and Halle weren't aware of Roger and Betty's deteriorating health until they had passed away. It was Roger's way of protecting them from any more pain. Unfortunately, Derrick and Halle were upset at the fact that they didn't get to say goodbye. They didn't even get a chance to thank them for raising them.

Monique convinced Derrick and Halle to stay a couple of days to help with the house. Halle said no, but Derrick talked her into it. She agreed only if she could stay in a hotel.

They were on their way out, when a white old man approached them. "Sorry to hear about your grandma," he said, extending his hand.

"Thank you," they replied and turned to walk off.

The man cleared his throat. "Derrick and Halle," he said, causing them to stop in their tracks. "Is there someplace we can talk?"

Confused, Derrick responded, "I'm sorry. Do we know you?" Puzzled by how the man knew their names, he instinctively guarded Halle.

The man looked around to make sure no one was listening. "No. My name is Roger Rubin. I knew your mother, Denise Jackson I was your mother's attorney."

Mr. Rubin's words silenced them. It was the first time they had met someone who knew their mother other than family.

"You were my mother's attorney?" Derrick asked.

"Yes. Listen, I would really like you to come to New York so we can talk."

"About what? Is something wrong?" Halle asked, concern lacing her tone.

Mr. Rubin reached in his pocket and handed them a business card along with two plane tickets. "Why don't you come to my house sometime next week so we can talk?" he suggested and then walked off, leaving them puzzled.

*****

Back at the house, Halle was helping Monique clean up.

"Moe, have you heard of a man named Roger Rubin," Halle asked her.

"Roger Rubin? Yes. Grandpa spoke to him all the time. He was at the funeral," Monique said, cleaning off the table.

"Yes, but I didn't see him at grandma's funeral."

"I think he was sick or something. Why?"

Halle walked over to Monique. "He said he needed to talk to me and Derrick. He said he knew our mother."

"Well, Aunt Dee did know some powerful people."

"Yeah, but why does he want to see us?"

Monique laughed at Halle being such a worrywart. "I don't know. It's probably nothing."

Halle remained quiet.

"What's wrong?" Monique asked.

Halle sighed and took a seat. "I don't know. I just wish we knew more about my mother."

Monique took a seat next to her. "I know the feeling."

"It's like we're cursed. Everyone in our family is gone," Halle said. "Well, at least the good ones," she added when she heard Diamond and Kasheem in the background.

Both ladies laughed.

Monique put her arm around her little cousin; she knew all too well about losing someone you love. She had lost her mother and sister. "Yeah, the good die young. I know. Sometimes I still can't believe my mother is gone. I always wondered how I would've turned out if she were alive."

"Exactly! I know my life would've been different. I just wonder if it would be for the best."

"Why you say that?" Monique asked.

Halle took another deep breath. "Because all you hear about is how my mother was a killer, drug dealer, and got herself killed. How she abandoned us."

"Who told you that?" Monique asked, stunned.

Halle looked over her shoulder in De'Shell and Anita's direction.

Monique shook her head. "Hold on," she said while placing the dirty plates on the table. Then she went and got Michael and Derrick to join them. "Michael, Halle told me that De'Shell and Anita said Aunt Denise was a drug dealer and killer. Can you believe it?"

"Yeah, they called me slow, stupid, and talked about how my mother got pregnant by a retard" Michael responded. "So, nothing surprises me. They even talked about my dead sister. They're miserable. Look at them," he said, causing everyone to look in their direction. "Look at their kids. Yes, our parents might be gone, but look at us. We still turned out better."

"So true," Derrick concurred. "We all made mistake, but at least we learned from ours."

"Halle told me that Mr. Rubin wanted to see you," Monique said, talking to Derrick.

"Yes. He invited us to his house next week."

"Mr. Rubin, the lawyer?" Michael asked.

"Yes. You know him?" Halle said.

"Yes. He was the one who gave Grandpa the money to pay off Kasheem and Diamond."

"What?!" Derrick and Halle said in unison.

Oh shit, Michael thought, *I thought they knew. Well, no need of hiding it anymore.*

Michael and Monique led them to a private room so they could talk.

"Grandpa felt bad about what happened to you guys," Michael continued.

"He thought it was his fault. So, he paid Kasheem and Diamond to drop the charges," Monique explained.

"But we still went to jail," Derrick stated.

"We know. The state picked up the charges. You guys were facing twenty-five years each." Monique told them. "There was no way Grandpa was going to let y'all go to prison."

"How much?" Derrick calmly asked. "How much did Grandpa pay them?"

"A hundred thousand each. It was his life savings."

Hearing this sent flames through Derrick and Halle's bodies. While Derrick said a silent pray, Halle wanted to send them to hell. She was about to go confront them, but Monique grabbed her.

"Halle, don't."

"They ruined our lives, Moe," she cried. "It's not fair." She broke down sobbing into Monique's arms.

Derrick started reciting scriptures in his head while tears dropped from his eyes. It pained him to see Halle hurt like this.

"I know, but don't worry. Their day will come," Michael said, consoling Derrick.

*****

After learning what their grandfather did for them, Derrick and Halle were very curious to talk to Mr. Rubin. During the ride to Mr. Rubin's Long Island home, Derrick and Halle were silent, both lost in their thoughts and wondering what he could possibly want to talk to them about.

Anxious, Mr. Rubin was standing in the driveway waiting for them.

"Derrick, Halle, I'm so glad you could make it." He embraced them in a hug.

"Thanks for inviting us," Halle replied.

"You know, there's not a day that goes by that I don't think about your mother," he said, while leading them inside to his office where he had several pictures of Denise.

Immediately, Derrick and Halle noticed them, especially their parents' wedding photo.

"Oh my God, is that my mother and father?" Halle asked.

Mr. Rubin smiled and replied, "Yes." Then he paused for a moment to reflect back. "Everyone couldn't believe someone was brave enough to marry your mother. She was a firecracker."

"Yeah, from what we heard, she was something else," Halle mumbled in disappointment.

 54

Noticing her expression, Mr. Rubin responded, "What do you mean? What exactly did they tell you?"

"Mr. Rubin, we know about the money you gave my grandpa," Derrick informed him.

The look on Mr. Rubin's face confirmed everything. "Please," he said, gesturing for them to sit down while he took a seat. "Your grandfather called me up crying. He had lost his daughter and was afraid of losing you guys, too."

"So you know about the tape?" Halle mumbled, embarrassed.

"Yes, I do. It didn't surprise me that your cousin would do something like that to you. Denise has always outshined everyone in the family. That's why I had to send the money."

"Yeah, but it left my grandparents broke. They gave up their life savings for us," Derrick stated.

Now Mr. Rubin was confused. "Their life savings?" he repeated. He stared at Derrick and Halle for a moment before asking, "What exactly do you know about your parents?"

Derrick and Halle took a deep breath and told Mr. Rubin everything. Certainly, Mr. Rubin was distressed at what they told him. For years, they were lied to about their mother.

"Your mother..." his voice trailed off. "Your mother was nothing like that. Yes, she had her ways, but your mother was one of the strongest women I know."

"How did you meet our mother?" Derrick asked. "You said you were her attorney, right?"

"Yes. I represented her on several criminal cases," he replied.

"Criminal?" Halle's voice became high pitched. "So it's true our mother was a criminal?"

"No, she wasn't." Mr. Rubin stood and walked over to his desk. "Now, that doesn't mean she didn't have her issues, but criminal is such a strong word," he stated.

"I don't understand," Derrick said.

"Why don't I let her tell you? Before your mother died, she made a tape. She called it her testament. She made me promise if something happened to her, I would show it to you."

Anxious, Derrick and Halle followed Mr. Rubin into the movie room and took a seat while he started the tape.

"I'll leave you alone," he said before exiting.

On the screen, the legendary Denise Taylor sat in a chair with a black background, dressed in a tailored white blouse, black slack, and red pumps. Her hair was cut in a bob, and she was draped in pearls and diamonds like a boss.

"I prayed that you would never have to watch this, but if you do, I want you to hear it from me as to why I'm not there. This is very important," Denise emphasized, lowering her eyes.

"My name is Denise Taylor, but legally, it's Denise Jackson." She smirked. "I think people will agree I don't deserve to be called Mrs. Derrick Jackson once they learn that I killed my husband, the father of my children," she confessed "Yes, I killed the only man who's ever loved me. He gave me two beautiful children, Derrick and Halle. Isn't it ironic that I killed my first love, Grant Tiger, and my last love, Derrick Jackson." She giggled. "At the time of my killing spree, I didn't understand my action. I was in a devil state of mind. I would've killed my family if they had gotten in my way, starting with my sorry-ass sisters Anita and De shell. It's only because of my parents that I didn't put a bullet in their heads. Bitches." Denise grinded her teeth and added, "Including their kids. I bet they didn't amount to shit." She laughed. "That's why it killed me when I found out what Tony did to Morgan. She was so innocent, so pure, and Tony took all of that away when he raped her in my apartment. Morgan was like a daughter to me, and hurting her was like hurting my Derrick or Halle," she said, squinting her face from the painful thought.

"How could I allow him to live? My sister Jasmine trusted me with the most precious thing in life, her daughter Morgan, and look what happened. Like Morgan, Derrick didn't understand Tony had to be dealt with accordingly." Denise paused, looking away from the camera. "Death was the only option. Unfortunately, innocent people get killed in wars," she snapped before continuing. "Why didn't they understand that? How could I not do something about it? Morgan…" Her voice trailed on in sorrow. "Why? How can you love a man who brutally raped you? How can you bear his children? She didn't understand that I needed to make it right. Tony was one of my best friends, and he not only violated her, he violated me, too. And where I'm from that's punishable by death." Denise lowered her head. "She chose him over me. What was I supposed to do? I had my two kids to think about, and not even Morgan came before them." Denise smiled. "She made her choice, and I made mine. Tony didn't deserve that kind of loyalty. I just hope someone is taking care of her children. Would you believe before she took her last breath, Morgan asked me to take care of Tony and the kids? Oh yeah, I took care of Tony alright. I sent him and his family a first-class ticket to hell." Denise grilled the camera with an icy stare, then leaned back and put her arm over the back of the chair.

"I know you're watching this tape and wondering why. No matter what I say, you will never understand. But, I want you to know I gave my life for you to have a life. I loved you so much that I would lie down for my children. I remember someone saying I was a demon—that I was a cold heartless bitch—and I always wondered if what they said was true. If so, I prayed I didn't pass it down to my children?" She looked away from the camera again, then flashed a devilish grin. "But, when you have people like Tony and Grant who exist in the world, I prayed that I did pass it down to them," Denise said, leaning closer to the camera. "Because in order to catch a monster, you have to become a monster." She laughed, got up from the chair, and faded into the back, leaving Derrick and Halle speechless.

Mr. Rubin entered the room and smirked at the looks on their faces. He, too, had the same look after seeing the video.

"Come in here. I wanna give you something," he said, taking them back into his office.

Still flabbergasted, Derrick and Halle looked like zombies.

"Before your mother was murder, she sold most of her businesses and left three trust funds: one for each of you, and the

other for whomever cared for her children after her death. That's where we got the money from to pay off your cousins."

"I don't understand," Halle said.

"Your parents were multi-millionaires. Your father owned his own consultant firm. Some of his biggest clients were Paramount, Apple, and DreamWorks. Your mother owned over fifty buildings from South Bronx to Delaware." Mr. Rubin stood up from behind his desk. "You see, your mother started out on the wrong foot, but everything she did was for you guys. Before her death, she made me promise to make sure you both were okay and never let anyone spend your money."

"Money?" Derrick repeated. "How much did she leave us?"

Mr. Rubin reached across the desk, picked up some papers, and then put his glasses on to start reading. "To my children Derrick Jordan Jackson and Halle Jasmine Jackson, I leave my entire estate, which is fifteen million dollars."

Chapter SIX

Sadie couldn't have been more proud of the way her grandchildren invested their inheritance. Greg managed to double his inheritance in two years, whereas Gracie tripled hers. With Greg living in New York and Gracie living between South Beach and New York, they rarely saw each other. Mostly, they communicated through FaceTime and Skype. Today, they were meeting in New York at the site where Gracie was opening a hotel in lower Manhattan. Greg had designed it for her.

"Greg!" Gracie cheered, greeting him with a hug and a kiss on the cheek.

"Grace!" He smiled and kissed her back.

"The place is looking great," she said, looking around.

"Of course, look who's designing it." He winked. "Come on, let me show you around."

After he gave her a tour of the place, they went to get something to eat.

"So, bro, when is the big day? Are you ready to be a dad?" Gracie asked, playfully hitting his arm.

Greg laughed. "We haven't decided on the big day yet. She doesn't want to be pregnant walking down the aisle. What about you? When are you gonna settle down?"

Gracie smiled. *When I find a man with a huge dick and a bank account to match,* she thought.

"Settle down, Greg. I'm not even thirty yet. I'm still finding myself." She winked. "Besides, when I find the right person, I will, but I don't have time for a relationship right now."

"Gracie..." he said, raising his eyebrow.

"What, Greg? I'm too young to settle down."

"Yes, but I still want you to be happy. Running around with every Tom, Dick, and Harry isn't good either," he commented, knowing his sister's history.

Gracie frowned up her face. "Wow, bro, that's low even for you."

"Come on, this is me you're talking to, or did you forget I'm in the same circle as you? Don't you think I get tired of men whispering about my sister?" he proclaimed.

"So it's your reputation you're worried about. Were you worried when I was directing clients your way? Did you think about that?" Gracie viciously retorted.

Greg laughed. "I'm not one of your little boys, I was well established before you. And I didn't know we were playing tit for tat."

Gracie exhaled. She didn't like fighting with her brother. "You think I'm out there sleeping with everyone? Out of all people, I figured you would've given me the benefit of the doubt. Gee, thanks," she said, tossing her napkin on the table.

Greg reached out for her hand. "And when do you care what anyone thinks?"

"Greg, I'm not working in a nightclub as a waitress or some struggling actress who's stripping to make ends meet," Gracie snapped, leaning forward. "I owned them. There's a difference." She pointed a finger at him. "And you know I care what you think"

Greg shook his head while thinking about what his grandmother would say about Gracie being just like their mother. "Boy I feel sorry for your man," he said with a chuckle.

"Me, too."

"So are we ready for the grand opening?" Greg asked, changing the subject.

She smiled and responded, "Of course. I was born ready."

*****

It was the night of the hotel's grand opening, and the place was packed. Gracie looked stunning in her one-shoulder canary yellow dress. Despite the fact that she had slept with every powerful man in the room, Gracie still held her head up high.

As for Greg, he held the same presence as his father; he owned the room. Women threw themselves at him. While flattered at the attention, Greg had no intentions on ruining what he had with Tracey. Besides, he learned early on that a pretty face doesn't always mean a clean, disease-free body.

Characteristically, Gracie and Greg worked opposite sides of the room stroking the egos of the rich and powerful.

"Gracie, this is Anthony Marciano," her accountant introduced.

Quickly, Anthony corrected him. "No, it's Anthony Flowers."

"Hello! Welcome to Gracie's!" She smiled and extended her hand.

Gawking at her, Anthony kissed her hand. "Thank you for having me. And may I say you look stunning in that dress."

Impressed, Gracie looked over at her accountant, her eyes asking, *Who is this tall, handsome man?* With more guests to meet, Gracie said, "Well, Mr. Flowers, please help yourself to anything at the party. Excuse me, but I have some people I need to say hello to."

When Gracie tried to walk away, Anthony reached out for her hand and pulled her close to his body. "Does that include you?" he whispered.

Flirting back, Gracie said, "That depends," before walking away.

Confident, Anthony just smiled as he watched her disappear into the crowd.

Gracie finally met up with Greg, who was networking with potential clients.

"Isn't my brother a genius?" She smiled and kissed him on the cheek.

"Yes…yes." Mr. Strong reciprocated her smile. "I was just telling Greg that my wife loves his work. I wanted to schedule a meeting with him to discuss designing her new accountant office."

Gracie beamed. She loved when people spoke highly of her brother. "Greg is the man for the job."

Humble, Greg smiled and said, "Well, just let me know when, and I'll make myself available."

"How about tomorrow?" Mr. Strong asked. "We can meet at Ayres' Place on West 4th Street at noon."

"Sounds like a plan to me," Greg told him.

"Okay. See you then," Mr. Strong said before walking off.

Throughout the evening, Anthony and Gracie flirted with each other. She couldn't take her eyes off of him. His five-thousand-dollar tailor-made suit accentuated his athletic built. His deep olive skin and big blue-grey bedroom eyes undressed Gracie. But, it was his confidence that Gracie admired.

The party was coming to an end, when Anthony caught up with Gracie at the bar.

"You still here?" she asked with a seductive look.

"Is that a problem? I thought you said help myself to whatever I wanted," he flirted back while moving closer to her.

"As I said earlier, it depends," Gracie said, licking her lips.

Anthony laughed. "Has anyone ever told you, you are truly beautiful," he told her while staring deeply into her eyes.

Feisty, Gracie replied, "Yes, about five minutes ago."

Her response caused both of them to laugh.

"Okay…okay, you got me," he said, raising his hand. "Anyway, I would love to take you to dinner."

Gracie looked him over. While he might be a great lay, she didn't have time for a relationship. And judging by the way he had been sweating her, he was looking for one.

"I don't know. I'm really busy. Besides, I have to look over my books."

A little irritated at her response, he placed his hand over the papers. "Don't you have an accountant to do that?"

★ ★ ★ ★ ★ 62

Gracie gently moved his hand. "As the great Oprah Winfrey said, no one can count your money better than you. Now, as for you offer..."

With a smug look on his face, Anthony chuckled. "I'm not asking for your hand in marriage. I just wanna take you to dinner, and then who knows after that. But, I can tell you haven't been fucked real good in a while," he said while staring directly into her eyes.

Gracie's vagina tingled. No man had ever spoken to her like that. Normally, she was the aggressor, but his statement left her speechless.

Anthony pulled out his card and placed it in her hand. "Call me when you're ready."

*****

The next afternoon, Gracie and Greg celebrated by meeting for lunch before Greg's meeting with Mr. Strong and his wife. In addition, they wanted to go over a few things about the hotel. Although exhausted, Gracie arrived first.

As usual, Greg greeted her with a kiss on the cheek. "The event was a success," he said. "Thank you. It wouldn't have been without you. Everyone loved the architect."

Greg blew on his index fingers like they were the barrel of guns and then rubbed them on his shirt. "Well, I do my best," he joked.

As they continued to laugh and talk over lunch, they lost track of time.

"Uh-um." Mr. Strong, who was standing over them, cleared his throat to get their attention.

"Oh shit, it's noon," Gracie said, looking at her watch.

Greg jumped from the chair and extended his hand. "I'm sorry."

"It's fine. This is my wife, Stacey Strong. Honey, this is Greg and Gracie Dodson."

Stunned, Stacey stood silent for a second. She couldn't believe her eyes. Sitting there were her godchildren.

"Dodson," she blurted out before catching herself. "I'm sorry! Nice to meet you," she said, extending her hand to shake theirs.

Just as Gracie was about to excuse herself, they asked her to stay.

"So my wife wants to redesign her Atlanta office," Mr. Strong stated.

"Okay. Mrs. Strong, do you have any ideas how you would like your office designed?"

Still in shock, Stacey didn't respond.

"Mrs. Strong?" Greg repeated.

"Oh, sorry. What did you say?" she asked.

"Do you have any ideas for your office?" he repeated.

Just then, Mr. Strong's phone rang and he excused himself to take the call.

Stacey looked over her shoulder to make sure her husband was out of sight. She then cleared her throat and mumbled, "I can't believe it."

"Believe what?" Gracie asked, noticing how distant Stacey was acting.

"How much y'all look like your parents," Stacey told them.

"Our parents?" they replied in unison.

Trying to hold back her tears, Stacy replied, "Yes. Gabrielle was my best friend. She called me by my nickname Stevie. I'm your godmother."

Greg and Gracie looked at each other before looking back at Stevie.

"Is this some kind of joke?" Greg said.

Stevie lowered her head and then looked up at them. "I wish it was. Your mother and father are Gabrielle and Greg Brightman."

"Yes, but..."

"And your grandmother is Sadie," Stevie stated, interrupting Greg.

"So that's why you called Greg and used the excuse about your office needing to be redesigned, because you know our parents?" Gracie snapped.

When Stevie was about to respond, she suddenly remembered some pictures she carried in her wallet. She reached into her bag for the photos.

"Look," she said, handing them two photos: one with just the two of them and another taken with them and their parents. "Look on the back."

Speechless, Greg and Gracie's eyes got watery as they looked at the photos together.

"After your parents were killed, your grandmother took you away. She promised to keep in touch, but she wouldn't return my calls. I never got the chance to say goodbye. I wanted so badly to be in your life." Unable to hold it any longer, she started to cry.

Greg reached out and touched her hand. "It's okay. We were just stunned that you knew our parents," he said and then looked at Gracie, who had a suspicious look on her face.

"You said our parents were murdered, but they weren't," Gracie informed her.

Stevie giggled, amazed at how Gracie was just like her mother. She questioned everything.

"No, your parents were murdered. Your mother was shot in y'all's home in Rye, New York. Your father, Greg Brightman, was shot to death along with his best friend, your cousin Denise Taylor, in lower Manhattan."

This revelation silenced them once again.

By then, Mr. Strong had rejoined them. "Sorry, did I miss anything?" he asked, taking his seat.

"Ask your wife?" Gracie snapped, then jumped up, tossed her napkin on the table, and stormed off with Greg following.

Emotional, Gracie started to cry as she exited the restaurant. Her mind was running a mile a minute. "So do you believe her?" Gracie asked while pacing back and forth. "Our parents were murdered!" she shouted through her tears.

★ ★ ★ ★ 65

Greg embraced his sister. "I don't know, Gracie," he mumbled.

There was only one way to find out. So, Greg and Gracie took a deep breath and decided to go back into the restaurant to talk with Stevie. Stevie and her husband were about to get up to leave, when Greg and Gracie caught them.

"Okay, say we believe you," Greg said. "Tell us about our parents."

"What do you wanna know?" she asked.

"Since you knew them, why don't you tell us?" Gracie spitefully replied.

Stevie glowered and then giggled. "It would take all day. But, I will tell you that your mother was a powerful attorney, who had her own practice. Your father, after being released from prison, opened up a few nightclubs and bought a couple of buildings."

"My father was in prison?" Greg asked.

"Yes," she responded in a confused tone. "What exactly were you told about your parents?"

"Evidently, not the truth," Gracie sarcastically stated.

Stevie took a deep breath and told them everything from sunrise to sunset about their parents. However, she didn't mention Tony Flowers. They were flabbergasted at what they heard. Like the others, they had been fed lies while growing up.

They thanked Stevie and agreed to stay in touch. Infuriated, Greg and Gracie hopped on the next flight back to Florida. Sadie had some serious explaining to do.

*****

Sadie was in the kitchen when they confronted her. Gracie wanted to go off, but Greg told her to be cool, thinking maybe there was a good reason why Sadie didn't tell them the truth.

"My babies!" a surprised Sadie cheered as they entered the kitchen.

Greg played it cool. "Hi, ma," he said, kissing her on the cheek.

However, Gracie blurted out in a nasty tone, "Why didn't you tell us that our parents were murdered? Why didn't you tell us that our parents were married and that our father was in prison?"

"Excuse me. Do you ever come in my house questioning me? Hello to you, too."

Gracie looked at Greg, who shot her a "chill the fuck out" look.

Gracie sighed. "Hello. So why didn't you tell us about our parents?" she repeated.

Sadie took a deep breath before sitting down at the table. She didn't bother asking where they got the information. "Yes, your parents were murdered. I didn't tell you because the killers were never caught."

"So is that why you didn't use our father's last name?" Greg asked, sitting next to her while Gracie leaned against the kitchen island.

Remorseful, Sadie nodded as she cried. "Yes. Within a year, I lost my husband, daughter, and son-in-law. I couldn't stand to lose you, too."

"We understand, Ma," Greg said, trying to comfort her.

"No, we don't, Greg!" Gracie shouted as she stood with her arms folded. "You lied to us. You said our inheritance came from our grandfather, when in fact, it came from our parents."

"Gracie, I did it to—"

"You did it because you and Grandpa were upset that my mother married an ex-con," Gracie blurted out, cutting her off.

Pissed at Gracie's tone, Sadie got up from the table and walked over to her. "Is that what think? I lied to you because I was ashamed of who my daughter married? No, I wasn't proud of who my daughter married, but after getting to know Greg, I realized he was a good person and was proud Gabrielle had chose him."

"Is that before or after the money?" Gracie spitefully asked.

Sadie slapped her hard across the face. "Don't you ever talk to me like that. You may not like the decisions I made, but damnit you will respect me, you hear me? I lost my daughter. She was shot in the head while looking through the peephole. The bullet blew half of her skull off, and we had to have a closed casket. As for your father he died in the street like a dog. The police cheered when they heard he murdered" Sadie was in her face and pointing her finger. "Until you've been through...Until you give birth to your own, don't you ever...ever question my decision."

The smack caused Gracie's face to turn cherry red and her ear burned. She had to compose herself and remember Sadie was her grandmother. Honestly, she wanted to beat the fuck out of her.

"I lost my parents, and whether you like it or not, I'm going find out who killed them. And God help you if you're behind it," she warned, then walked out.

Speechless, Sadie looked back at Greg.

Like always, Greg shook his head and ran after Gracie. "Gracie, wait!" he called out.

"Greg, I don't wanna hear it," she yelled back, getting in her car.

But, Greg wasn't going to let her drive off upset like that. "Gracie, chill the fuck out." He snatched the keys out of her hand before she had a chance to put them in the ignition. "Why don't you see it from Ma's point of view?"

Gracie glared at Greg and thought, *Has he lost his mind, too?*

"Are you fucking kidding me? Did you come out of the same pussy I did? She lied to us, Greg! We are Brightmans, not Dodsons, and you wanna give her a pat on the back? Well, I'm not! As far as I'm concerned, she's dead to me!" Grace said, then snatched the keys back and drove off.

Greg watched as Gracie sped off steaming. She was about to write a check her ass can't cash.

 68

Chapter Seven

If the world thought Anthony was cocky before he had money, he was about to take it to another level. When you looked up the word "arrogant", Anthony's picture would be there. Felix immediately gave them five million each to start. Whereas the others continued to work and attend school, Anthony quit his job the following day. He was Tony Flower's son, and the only business he would be working for was his father's company.

Unlike the others, Anthony splurged, dropping five to ten thousand dollars on tailor-made suits, thousand-dollar shoes, and five-hundred-dollar ties. Secondly, Anthony changed his last name to Flowers and hired an attorney, an accountant, and a personal stylist.

In a couple of weeks, Anthony was the most sought after man in the world. He was fucking a different woman every night, and he was just getting started. Whether Felix liked it or not, Anthony was determined to live like a king, and he would start by taking his father's belongings out of storage. From what he read, Tony had expensive taste, so Anthony felt he could use everything that had been stored. Lastly, Anthony moved into his father's penthouse and old office in New York.

His siblings were a little different with the way they handled their money. London didn't quit her job; however, she took a leave from it. With so much going on, she wanted to handle her business before flying back to Africa. Although she treated herself to a new wardrobe, London didn't need anything to make herself look good. She could wear a paper bag and still be the baddest bitch in the room.

Justin looked at some luxury apartments and vehicles. He also took a leave from work to sort out things. Still, he continued to attend school since he was close to finishing.

On the other hand, Justine was the total opposite. She didn't spend a dime of the money. She didn't need anything to enhance her looks, either. In fact, Justine pretended as if her grandfather hadn't even given her the money. She was more concerned with learning about her parents. She had a gut feeling Felix wasn't telling them the truth.

One day, though, London finally convinced Justine to at least purchase some clothing. They were in Bergdorf Goodman, and it was amazing how men tripped over their feet staring at them. Certainly, London and Justine were use to it. That's why they didn't pay them any mind.

"London, can I ask you a question?" Justine said while trying on some Celine pumps. "Do you feel like Grandpa told us everything about Mommy and Daddy?"

"What do you mean?" she asked, then turned to the salesperson and said, "May I have this in a size seven."

"I don't know. I just got this feeling he was holding back something. Like there's more to the story than he's telling."

London pondered on Justine's statement. "Yeah, kinda...sorta, but I thought it was for our own protection. You know how Grandpa is when it comes to us."

"Yeah, that's why he shipped me and Justin off to boarding school," Justine snidely remarked, raising an eyebrow.

"Come on, Justine. You know that's not the case. You and Justin were out of control," London said, defending her grandfather. "Y'all were drinking and carrying on. What else could Grandpa do?"

"Has it ever occurred to you that maybe we were doing that for a reason? You and Anthony were always treated differently."

Concerned, London grabbed Justine by the arm and pulled her over to the corner of the store.

"What do you mean treated differently? Did something happen to you?"

Justine lowered her head. She wanted to tell her sister about Sofia, but didn't know if she would believe her. Mrs. Marciano had blackballed Justine from the family years ago.

"No, but everyone knows Grandma treated you better."

"No, she treated *Anthony* better. Only if you knew she was the real reason why I moved away."

Justine was surprised by her sister's admission. "I thought it was because you got a job out there."

"No." London twisted her face up. "She didn't accept Nyennoh and made all kinds of racist remarks about him. I guess she thought that was supposed to make me leave him. Justine," she said while staring into her eyes, "I refuse to live to make someone else happy, and you don't have to either. I'm always here for you. Understand? No matter what, you are my little sis, and I love you." London started getting emotional.

Justine smiled. It had been years since she and London spent time together, and it felt good.

"I love you, too, Londie."

"Good. Now let's finish shopping."

The ladies spent the entire day shopping, going to the spa, and getting their hair done before heading over to Anthony's place for dinner. The last time things got a little heated between Anthony and Felix. Therefore, Mrs. Marciano decided to attend, hoping to settle things. Felix and Mrs. Marciano arrived first.

"Grandma," Anthony said, greeting her with a kiss on the cheek.

"How's my favorite great-grandson doing?" She smiled and hugged him tightly.

"I'm great now that my favorite lady is here."

"Wow, you didn't waste any time," Felix snidely commented.

"Well, hello to you, too, Grandpa. And why should I? My father would've wanted me to have it, don't ya think? Beside I'm tired of living like a peasant, I'm a king now." he replied as he led them into the other room.

"Of course, A.J. you've always been a king," Mrs. Marciano confirmed, glaring at Felix.

Repulsed, Felix shook his head. Anthony was like that because of Mrs. Marciano. Although she spoiled all of her great-grandchildren, Anthony was her favorite. In her eyes, Anthony could do no wrong. Every time he got into trouble, he would run to her and she would make Felix take care of it.

Looking around, Mrs. Marciano said, "I love what you did with the place. You gave it a touch of class, just like a Marciano."

Anthony laughed. "Thank you, Grandma, but this was my father's stuff. I took it out of storage."

Felix looked over at his mother, who had a disdained look on her face. "Oh, I see," she simply said while cutting her eyes.

Moments later, the others arrived and were surprised to see their grandfather and great-grandmother there.

"Hello," London and Justin said in unison, while Justine flashed a phony smile, waved, and damn near ran over to hug Felix tightly.

"Grandpa!" Justine greeted, happy to see him.

Obviously, Mrs. Marciano noticed that and said, "Justine, aren't you gonna come and give your great-grandma a hug and kiss?"

"You sure you want me to?" Justine sarcastically asked.

"Of course. I don't bite. Only when I have to," she retorted.

Given the history between these two, everyone knew shit was about to hit the fan. Therefore, Anthony decided to lead everyone into the formal dining room. Before they could get settled in their seats good, the doorbell rang.

Not expecting anyone, Anthony mumbled, "Who can that be?"

"Oh, I asked Mr. Bostick and Mr. Kempt to join us at the meeting," Felix said smirking. He thought, *You're not the only one who can play the game.*

Felix knew Anthony and Mrs. Marciano had something up their sleeves. Therefore, he invited the board's attorney and accountant to this meeting.

"You invited Mr. Bostick and Mr. Kempt?" his mother asked in a disgusted tone.

"Why not? They've been with the company for years," he said, then walked out the room to go open the door.

London and her siblings wondered what the hell was going on. When Felix and his invited guests returned to the room, Mrs. Marciano, who was sitting at the head of the table with a deadpan expression, began speaking.

"Thank you all for coming. The last time your grandpa met with y'all things didn't go so well. So, I thought it was best that we meet again and talk about your futures."

"Things went great for us," London said, sitting across from Anthony. "It was Anthony who had the problem."

Anthony shot London a nasty look. "No, I'm just the only one who spoke up, as I always do."

Before London could respond, Mrs. Marciano raised her hand. "Now let's be respectful to each other. London, it's alright if Anthony doesn't agree with your grandfather's decision."

"Of course you would say that. He's always been your favorite. Great-grandma to the rescue," Justine chimed in.

Pissed, Felix glared at his mother and Anthony. "Why don't we let Mr. Bostick and Mr. Kempt talk?"

Annoyed that Felix cut her off, Mrs. Marciano mumbled, "Very well. Speak, Mr. Bostick"

"Okay," he said, then pulled out some documents. "After your father passed, he left everything to his wife and children. With his wife being gone, everything was left to you. Your grandfather went to court, and they appointed him executor over your father's estate. But, over the years, your father's empire grew. So, to protect you and your father's empire, Felix implemented a board. A board is…" Mr. Bostick tried to say, but was rudely cut off by Anthony.

"Mr. Bostick, we are all educated here. We know what a board is."

Mr. Bostick glared at him for a moment before continuing. "Very well. Your grandfather owns eighty percent and has the majority of the say."

"We know all of this, but why can't we take ownership of our father's estate?" Anthony questioned.

"Why should we, Anthony?" Justin asked in a pissed tone. "It's not like we're not getting an allowance. "

"Typical for you to say that, lil' bro. We're grown-ass men. What do we look like getting an allowance from our father's estate? Maybe you like living like a peasant, but I was born a king."

"And even kings are overthrown" Justin shot back

"Exactly!!! How about we learn the business first before we start claiming offices. How about that?" Justine said, directing her comment towards Anthony.

"I don't see any reason why they can't take over their father's business," Mrs. Marciano suggested.

Felix glared at his mother, annoyed by how she always undermined him.

"Taking over the business isn't an option, Mother. I'm not gonna allow anyone to destroy what I've built. It was me who took their father's empire to the next level, and I didn't ask for a dime."

"It's not your empire for you to decide, Felix," Mrs. Marciano stated.

"Yours either," he shot back.

If looks could kill, Felix would've been dead because of the way Mrs. Marciano was staring at him. She looked as though she wanted to blow his head off. Not only had he raised his voice, he challenged her in front of people, which was something she didn't tolerate.

Composing herself, Mrs. Marciano took a deep breath, ignoring the smirks on everyone's faces. "Very well. Let's ask the children," she said, giving them the cue to speak.

"Well, I agree with Grandpa. If it's not broke, don't fix it," Justine said.

Anthony sneered. "Of course you would agree with him. You don't know how to run a business. All you know how to do is put a bottle up to your mouth, career student."

Years ago, his comment would've hurt Justine, but she had learned in the NA meetings not to let anyone put you down.

"And you do?" she simply responded.

"Of course, I do. I work for a prestigious company. While you were out drinking and partying, I was running a Fortune 500 company," Anthony boasted.

"Yeah because Grandma put in a good word for you, or did she threaten the CEO? Please!" Justine said, glowering. "We all know you can't land a two-dollar whore without Grandma's help. But, I tell you something, brother. This is our father's empire, too, and just like they have kings they also have queens and I will not let you ruin what he or Grandpa built just to satisfy your ego. So, as far as I'm concerned," she said, standing up, "this meeting is over."

"Justine!" Mrs. Marciano called out as Justine walked toward the door to exit. "Justine, you are..."

Justine stopped and faced her. "I'm what, huh? You're still fighting his battles, I see," she said, then continued to walk out.

London and Justin looked at their great-grandmother and shook their heads before following after Justine. It was no secret Anthony was her favorite. For a second, Felix stared angrily at his mother and grandson before going after his grandchildren.

Mrs. Marciano got up and closed the door so she and Anthony were alone with Mr. Bostick and Mr. Kempt. "Sorry for my son and great-granddaughter's rude behavior."

The men acknowledged her with a nod but remained quiet.

"Gentlemen, I'm pretty sure there's something we can do to accommodate my grandson."

Mr. Bostick and Mr. Kempt looked at each other. Felix had already warned them that his mother was conniving.

"Yes, but only if all children agree. If not, Anthony would have to prove Felix was incompetent and negligent with their money," Mr. Bostick stated.

"And the board will support that he isn't. No disrespect to your grandson, but why don't you learn the business first and then look to take it over?" Mr. Kempt suggested.

Pouting like a child, Anthony glanced over at his grandmother.

"Learning the business is something I'm sure he can do. So you mean there's no other way?" she asked.

"Yes, if he dies, then the children would be awarded his share."

Anthony looked over at his grandma again. Both were thinking the same thing.

"Well, that's not gonna happen," Anthony stated in a spiteful tone.

Meanwhile, Felix was in the kitchen with the other kids.

"Sorry for acting like that, Grandpa, but Anthony gets on my damn nerves, calling himself *King*" Justine explained.

"No need for an apology. If he doesn't want me to have control, it's fine. You know I would give my life up before I steal from y'all."

"We know, Grandpa." Justin patted him on the back.

"Anthony is gonna have to go through this *Queen,* because I'm not overruling you!" Justine yelled.

Felix smiled. "Thank you, but your brother might feel differently if he knew the truth about his father," he said before exiting.

Unfortunately, Mrs. Marciano and Anthony were planning their next move.

"So now what?" Anthony asked, disappointed.

Mrs. Marciano walked up to him. "You were born a king, and no matter what, you will claim your throne."

*****

Mrs. Marciano was unaware, but she had just created a monster. Anthony knew with his great-grandmother on his side there was no stopping him. For the past couple of weeks, Anthony had been making all kinds of business connections due to his father's name. Tonight, he was getting ready to meet with some investors, when Gracie popped into his head. Anthony was surprised she hadn't called him yet. Knowing her, she probably thought he was some smuck looking to come up on her. Little did she know he had his own paper. *Maybe I should give her call,* he thought. *After all, I'm a millionaire now.*

It rang twice before she answered.

"Gracie, speaking."

"Gracie, it's Anthony."

"Anthony who?" she asked in a snobbish tone.

"Anthony Flowers. We met at your grand hotel party a couple of weeks ago."

"Oh, that's right. Sorry I've met so many people that I can't remember everyone. How are you?"

"Wonderful now that I heard your voice."

Gracie chuckled. Now she definitely remembered him. He was so full of himself. "I have a million and one things to do. Being charmed by you isn't one of them."

Caught off guard, Anthony replied, "Okay. How about I take you to dinner tonight?"

"I can't. I'm meeting with someone tonight."

"What about a nightcap?"

Gracie looked at the phone. *Is this guy serious?* Gracie started to say no, but then replied, "A nightcap is fine. You remember how to get to my hotel, right?"

"Yep."

"Well, meet me there about ten. Is that okay?"

"See ya then."

"Can't wait."

For the attitude she has, that pussy better be good, Anthony thought.

Anthony didn't tolerate shit from women. If they acted up, he quickly dismissed them. But, for some reason, he liked Gracie. She reminded him of his grandmother: a boss. She was young, ambitious, and beautiful. Everything he wanted in a woman.

While Anthony was working on Gracie, his siblings went to see the other properties. They were visiting the house in New Jersey to decide what they should do with it. Not to their surprise, Anthony didn't join them. He was too busy spending his money.

Since the gruesome killing, Felix had the house remodeled and bought some new furniture. Arriving together, London and her siblings toured the house. Strangely, it felt damp and cold.

"Is it me or does this house has an eerie feeling to it?" London asked, looking around.

"No, I thought it was just me," Justine said, feeling creeped out, too.

As they were finishing up their tour, someone pulled into the driveway.

"Are we expecting someone?" Justine asked her siblings.

"No," Justin said while walking to the door to find out who was there. "Hello. May I help you?" he asked the man.

"Hi, my name is Phil, and I take care of all the empty houses on this block," he said in a strong Spanish accent

Judging by the looks they were giving him, Phil knew they were confused. He laughed before adding, "People in this neighborhood paid a lot of money for their homes, and they expect every house to be well kept. So, I come by once a week to check on everything, I make sure the lawn is taken care of..."

"Oh, you're the maintenance man." Justine smiled.

Phil chuckled. "Something like that. Are y'all realtors or buyers?"

London looked at her siblings and then back at Phil. "Buyers," she lied.

Phil's eyes widened. "Oh, that's great. This house has been on the market for years. It has become a tourist attraction, a pilgrimage place for the fans. It's like National Historic Landmark now"

They looked at each other.

"Landmark and tourist attraction?" Justin repeated.

Phil shot them a puzzled look. "You don't know about this place?"

"No," London said, curious.

"The rapper Tony Flowers and his wife Christina Carrington were killed here."

"What?" Justine looked at her brother and sister, who had a shocked look on their faces.

"Wait...you said Tony and his wife were killed in this house?"

"Yes. Didn't you know? They were found chopped up."

Justine and London held their mouths as if they were going to throw up.

"Chopped up?" Justin asked.

"Yes. They said some of his body parts were hanging from the balcony, and the girl was found on the floor in the foyer."

Justin looked at his two sisters, then back at Phil. Not knowing if he was telling the truth, Justin thanked him before going back into the house.

"Did you hear that?" London said, looking up at the balcony.

"Daddy was killed in this house," Justine mumbled.

For years, they didn't know their parents were married. All they were told by Felix was that their parents had died in a plane crash. Then he said they were murdered, with their mother killed in one mansion and their father killed somewhere else weeks later. However, Felix never mentioned their father being killed with another woman, let alone that woman being his wife. As far as they knew, their mother Morgan had been his wife. Something wasn't right, and they were determined to get to the bottom of it.

Conversely, they agreed to leave Anthony out of it for now.

*****

While Anthony was living the life of luxury, London and her siblings hired a private investigator to find out what really happened to their parents.

It didn't take long for Addy, the private investigator, to dig up stuff on their parents. Strangely, he asked them to meet him at the mansion in Alpine. After exchanging greetings, Justin led them inside. Addy could tell by the look on their faces that they were anxious to know what happened. Therefore, he didn't waste any time.

"Your father was murdered here, but you already know that."

"What about our mother? Is it true she was murdered at the house in Lake Minnetonka?" London asked.

"Yes. She was killed with a single gunshot wound. The police are still baffled by your mother's death."

"Why?" Justin asked.

"The house your mother was killed in had one of the best security systems in the country," Addy explained. "It would've been impossible for the killer to slip in and kill your mother without any alarms going off."

"So what are you saying? My father had my mother killed?"

Addy reached inside his briefcase and handed them the police notes. "At one time, they suspected it was either an inside job or your father."

Shaking their heads, the kids passed the documents back and forth between each other.

"But, before they could investigate the case, your father was killed."

"What about this Christina Carrington? Was she really married to my father?" London inquired.

"No. I did some research and found no marriage license. Not even an application of them applying for one. However, I did find your parents'," he said, handing them a copy.

After carefully reviewing it, London noticed their mother had married their father a day after her eighteenth birthday.

"Wait. This says our parents were married a day after Mommy turned eighteen. That's impossible because Grandpa said Mommy went to college, even law school." London looked up at Addy for answers.

"Yes, she did. According to her social security number, she even worked."

Now the children were even more confused. Addy figured they would be, so he had created a timeline.

"It's confusing, so I put something together for you."

Like Stevie and Mr. Rubin, Addy gave them a history on their parents. While he provided them with more details than their grandfather, they were still confused about their parents' relationship.

"So, for years my father was dating, engaged to, and supposedly married Christina Carrington. Then, all of a sudden, he married my mother a day after her eighteenth birthday," Justin reiterated.

"Yes," Addy replied.

"What about our mother's family? Did Grandpa know any of this?" Justine asked.

Addy sighed. "It's interesting that you asked about your grandfather. I ran a background check on him. Your grandfather was deported to Italy. Until the untimely death of your mother, he wasn't allowed into the United States."

"Huh? Why was he deported" Justin asked, confused.

Addy handed over some confidential documents. "This is from Immigrations. He was deported for drug trafficking."

With their mouths hung open, London and her siblings sat there in complete shock.

"He was deported for drugs?" Justine repeated.

"Yes. Your mother lived with her mother Jasmine and her aunt Denise. She went to Dalton."

"So how did my mother meet my father? According to my father's death certificate, he was thirty-eight when he was killed. And Mommy wasn't even twenty-five when she passed," Justin said, thinking out loud. "So how did they meet?"

Addy pulled out a picture of Tony, Denise, Jasmine, and Greg. "This might help," he said, handing it to London. "Your father knew your grandmother and aunt. They grew up together."

"What!" London blurted out.

"Yes, they grew up in Melrose Project."

Justin stood up and started pacing back and forth. "It doesn't make sense. Why would our grandma allow our mother to marry someone twice her age?"

"Maybe we should ask them. Do you know where we can find them?" Justine asked.

Again, Addy sighed. "Your grandma died of cancer twenty-seven years ago, and your aunt Denise was killed two years after your parents."

"So you're telling us there's no one on our mother's side who can explain this to us?"

"Well, your grandmother had two other children, Monique and Michael. I tracked them down. They live in Virginia. I also found Denise's children."

"That's a start," London said.

Before departing, Addy provided some additional information about Tony's parents, and then gave the last known addresses of Denise's children and their aunts and uncle.

Overwhelmed and confused, the siblings went back into the family room.

"So what do you think about this?" Justin asked.

"Just, I don't know what to believe. I mean it's crazy. Our father marries Mommy a day after her eighteenth birthday. Our father is a friend of our grandma and aunt. Grandpa was deported for drug trafficking. I mean, none of this makes sense," London said, recapping what they were told.

"No, it doesn't, which means someone is lying," Justine said. "And I have a feeling it costs our parents their lives."

Chapter Eight

It's not every day you find out your mother was a contract killer or that you inherited forty millions dollars. While most kids would've been thrilled about inheriting millions, Derrick didn't want any part of it. Watching that tape confirmed what everyone had been saying about his mother. As a man who served God, how could Derrick be associated with that? It was unfortunate, but Derrick didn't want anything to do with his mother. That's why he decided to donate his half of the money to various churches and charities, praying some good would come out of it.

Halle was a different story. She couldn't give a shit what her mother did. After what she'd been through, Halle understood why her mother sent people back to their essence. When you have people like Kasheem and Diamond in the world, they don't give you a choice. Learning this made Halle want to know more about their parents. She was pleased to learn their mother left them a house right outside of New York. According to Mr. Rubin, their mother wanted them to have it. After weeks of arguing, Halle finally convinced Derrick to drive up there with her.

"What's wrong?" Halle asked, noticing Derrick's quiet demeanor as he drove.

"What do you mean?"

"Derrick, I know when something is wrong."

He sighed before replying, "It doesn't bother you that our mother killed our father, or that she's responsible for a lot of deaths?"

"Yes, it does, but she is still our mother. Or have you forgotten that?"

"No wonder we're so freaking screwed up. Look at who gave birth to us," he grumbled.

Halle glared at her brother for a second. "Are you fucking serious? You think what happened to us is Mommy's fault."

Derrick shot her a nasty look. "I can't believe you don't. For Christ's sake, we had sex with each other."

"And you think that's our parents' fault. You're right. You really are screwed up. Our parents didn't drug us. Our parents didn't make us have sex with each other, Derrick. Our cousins did."

Derrick was steaming inside. "Do you know what I would've been if I didn't go to jail? I lost everything," his voice cracked.

Halle lowered her head. Derrick was right. She had also lost everything, but it wasn't their mother's fault.

"I lost a lot, too, but we can't dwell on the past. Didn't you say that?"

Derrick cut her off. "We're here," he said while getting out of the car.

"Derrick!" Halle called out as she exited the car, too.

"Halle, I don't wanna talk about it."

"And you call yourself a man of God?" she snidely remarked as they walked to the house.

Derrick didn't respond. Instead, he shot Halle another nasty look and followed her.

What in the name of Jesus, he thought, looking around. The house was in a rural wooded area.

"Are you sure this is the place?" he asked.

"Come on with your scared ass," she told him and then entered the house.

However, the sight that greeted them upon entering made them look at each other and then take a step outside to make sure they had the right house. There were so many guns scattered everywhere that it looked as if someone was getting ready for World War One.

Nervous, Derrick got in front of his sister and walked around. "This looks like an assassin's house," he commented.

"Is this where she came to plan her attack?" Halle asked.

Shaking his head, he replied, "I don't know," while still looking around the room.

Derrick wanted to leave. Seeing this house had solidified his decision.

"I'm ready to go?" Derrick stated.

"Derrick, can we look around, go through some boxes? I'm pretty sure Mommy left this house to us for a reason."

Derrick frowned up his face. "Of course, she did. She prayed we'd be just like her. Are you ready?"

Halle glared at him. "Yes, let's leave," she said before it turned into a heated argument.

*****

Halle wasn't aware of it, but before flying back to South Carolina, Derrick made a stop at Mr. Rubin to get the tape of his mother. When your world has been turned upside down, you try to make some sense of it. Derrick prayed that maybe if he watched the tape alone, he could see things through his mother's eyes. However, after watching it several times, Derrick felt nothing. In fact, it made him angrier.

One Sunday afternoon, the deacon at his church preached a special service about forgiveness. His words weighed heavily on Derrick's heart, and he returned home thinking about scriptures that would help him with his feeling. He came across Matthew 6:14-15.

"For if you forgive other people when they sin against you, your heavenly Father will also forgive you. But if you do not forgive others their sins, your Father will not forgive your sins," he muttered, then closed the bible to ponder on this passage.

He started to think Halle was right about their mother not having a choice. Just look at what happened to him and Halle; their own family had ruined their lives. While playing every detail

back in his mind, Derrick decided in order to forgive his mother he must learn more about her. So, he packed his things and caught the next flight back to New York, straight to the house.

The sun had just set when Derrick arrived. Still hesitant, he stayed in the car for a couple of seconds, saying a quick prayer before getting out. As he slowly walked to the door, Derrick looked behind and around him. *Mother must've been one bad person to come up in these woods by herself,* he thought.

Derrick took a deep breath and then went inside. *Here goes nothing.* Looking around, Derrick didn't know where to start. Then he spotted what appeared to be a diary on the table. He picked it up and started reading it.

April 11, 2002

It's been two months, and I'm still living in this nightmare. I know I'm not supposed to question God's actions, but why did he allow this to happen to me? What did I do to deserve this? I wanna tell my aunt, but Tony said he would kill her. However, I don't know how much more my body can take. If he's not sexually hurting me, he's beating on me. Oh please, GOD, help me. Please end this nightmare

Sincerely,

Morgan

This was the first of many diaries that Derrick read. It was seven o'clock in the morning when he looked up at the clock. After reading and watching tapes of Morgan being sexually assaulted, he understood his mother's actions.

Is this the reason Mama was killed? he wondered. One thing for certain, Derrick was determined to find out. He felt in order to find out who killed his mother, he needed to go through everything. That's why he secretly moved in the house. For the next few weeks after moving in, Derrick studied tapes and documents among other things. Not only did Denise leave them money, she left them a shitload of evidence. Everything was detailed and organized; it appeared as if she wanted her kids to pick up where she left off.

The information was overwhelming for Derrick at times. Although he didn't know Morgan personally, he felt her pain.

The past couple of weeks, Derrick had shut off the world to absorb this horror. Laying there in the dark and staring up at the ceiling, Derrick tried to get the images and words of everything he had watched and read out of his mind. Sadly, he couldn't. Like his mother, Derrick felt the need to do something. Also like his mother, Derrick had a demon in him. He realized it when he almost beat Kasheem and Diamond to death.

It was raining outside, and oddly, it felt like the drops were pounding on the house. As the thunder crackled, Derrick placed his hands over his ears, hoping to silence his thoughts, but it seemed like they were only getting louder. Not knowing what to do, Derrick starting praying out loud.

"Father, please help me. What am I supposed to do? Ma, if you're up there, help me," he cried.

The voices and thunder grew louder, and he started hearing chanting sounds. He closed his eyes and fell back on the bed. Moments later, the voices ceased. All of a sudden, Derrick sat straight up like the girl in *The Exorcist*. He looked to his left and his right. Then he walked over to the window, where a black panther with deep golden eyes greeted him with a growl. Derrick nodded, closed his eyes tightly, and recited his mother's words. *In order to kill a monster, you must become one.*

The devil was back!

*****

Meanwhile, Halle was enjoying her newfound wealth, but she didn't splurge. She moved out of her one-bedroom apartment and into a house in Teaneck, New Jersey. She brought a new Lexus and wardrobe.

Her biggest purchase was two buildings that she would use to open Taylor's Youth Center. After learning about her parents and how hard they worked to build their empire, she thought it was best to follow in their footsteps. That's why she was meeting with an architect at Greg Dodson Architect and Building Design Company to design the layout. According to *Daily Architect Magazine,* he was the best in the business.

While getting ready for her meeting, Halle paused for a second to soak it all in. Just a couple of months ago, she was living in a one-bedroom apartment, struggling to pay her rent. Now she was millionaire, but was it worth it?

Although saddened to learn her mother was not only a murderer, but had killed their father, too, deep down inside Halle believed she had no choice. She prayed Derrick would one day see it, too. Since that night at the house, there had been a strain on their relationship. If anyone knew how Derrick felt about the rug being pulled out from under him, it was Halle. Before that tragic night, she had a bright future ahead of her, too. But, Halle remembered an old Alicia Keys' song titled "Lesson Learned".

"If you don't know what the struggle's for…falling down ain't falling down. If you don't cry when you hit the floor…it's called the past 'cause I'm getting past…and I ain't nothing like I was before. You ought to see me now," she sang, smiling.

Hopefully, one day, Derrick will move past this, but Mr. Rubin said Derrick had been by to pick up the tapes and other things, so who knows, she thought

As for his share of the inheritance, Derrick told Mr. Rubin to hold onto it for now. Mr. Rubin told Halle not worry. He felt Derrick just needed some time and then he would come eventually come around.

On her way out the door, Halle glanced up at the huge family photo on the wall that Mr. Rubin had given them and smiled. "No one is perfect," she mumbled before leaving.

*****

Halle was both nervous and excited about her meeting with the architect.

"Ms. Taylor, Mr. Klein will see you now," the receptionist announced, then led her down the hall to a conference room.

"Thank you," Halle said, following the receptionist.

"Ms. Taylor," Mr. Klein greeted, extending his hand.

"Hello," Halle responded, smiling as she took a seat.

Getting right down to business, Halle shared her vision of what she would like her building to look like. Mr. Klein was impressed by the fact that Halle had done her homework. Just as the meeting was coming to an end, Greg walked in.

"Klein, I need... Oh, I'm sorry. I didn't know you were with a client. I wanna see you when you're done," he said and was about to close the door.

"Greg, this is Ms. Taylor. We're designing her youth center."

Greg stepped back in the room. "Wow, that's great," he said, shaking her hand. "What made you decide to open a youth center?" he asked.

"Well, I was just informed that my mother, who is deceased, owned a couple daycare centers. It's kind of my way of keeping her dream alive."

Greg smiled at her statement. "That's good. It's always good to give back. Well, let me know if we can do anything for you. But, I assure you that you're in good hands with Mr. Klein." He patted Mr. Klein on the shoulders. "It was nice meeting you, Ms. Taylor," he said before exiting.

Leaving that meeting made Halle feel like a million bucks. Just a few years ago, she was on drugs. Now she was on her way to opening up her first of many youth centers around the world.

Afterward, Halle headed into the office to catch up on her caseload. Most people would have quit once they found out they had inherited millions of dollars, but strangely, this job gave her a balance. Besides, she cared about her clients.

It was going on eight o'clock when Halle decided to call it a night. Still excited from her meeting earlier that day, Halle felt like

going out to celebrate, but she didn't have anyone to celebrate with. Since that incident, Halle had shut out a lot of people in her life. The only friends she did have were drug users who had been in rehab with her, and most of them had relapsed. She thought about calling Derrick, but he'd been so cold and distance lately.

Fuck it. I don't need anyone to celebrate with. I'll celebrate by myself, she thought.

Halle went to Gotham Bar and Grill. Since it was packed, she went to the bar to wait for a table to become available.

"What can I get for you?" the bartender asked.

"Ginger ale with a twist of lime," she said.

Halle noticed a huge picture on the wall behind the bar. Recognizing the faces, Halle asked the bartender, "Who's that on the picture?"

"Who's who?" he asked since there were a lot of pictures on the wall.

"In that picture," she said, pointing.

"Oh, that's Tony Flowers, his wife Christina Carrington, and their friends."

Curious, Halle asked the bartender to pull down the picture. At first, he was reluctant, but a fifty-dollar bill quickly changed his mind. *Oh my God*, Halle thought when he handed her the picture. It was her mother, Denise.

"Excuse me," she called to the bartender. "Who did you say this was?"

"Tony Flowers, the rapper that was killed with his ex-wife Christina Carrington."

"What about the other people in the pictures?"

"Oh, I don't know. I guess they were fans or friends," he responded nonchalantly.

Oh shit! Please don't tell me that my mother killed thee Tony Flowers, Halle thought.

*****

The following morning, Halle got up, went straight to her computer, and pulled up everything on Tony Flowers. There was

nothing linking Denise or Morgan to Tony, so maybe it wasn't him. From what Halle read, Tony had been married to Christina Carrington and they were murdered together. To make sure, she called Mr. Rubin.

"Hey, Mr. Rubin, it's Halle."

"Hi, Halle."

"Mr. Rubin, did my parents know Tony Flowers."

"Your mother did. In fact, he was one of her best friends. Why?"

Uncertain if it was the same Tony that her mother was talking about on the tape, Halle replied, "Nothing. I just saw a picture of them, that's all."

"Oh yes. Tony, Greg, and Denise were best friends."

"Okay. Well, I won't keep you. Thank you," she said before hung up.

Halle was about to give up, but then she remembered the house upstate. Maybe her mother left behind some additional information. Halle hopped in her car and headed up there. This time, she could take her time and look around since she didn't have Derrick's angry ass with her.

After arriving at the house, she reached in her bag, pulled out her keys, and went inside. *Someone's been staying here*, she thought while squinting as she looked around. She noticed dishes in the sink and found food in the refrigerator. Then again, she hadn't got a good look at the place the first time, so those things could have already been there. However, as Halle did a quick walk through, she noticed some clothing on the chair. She walked over and picked up the shirt. *This looks like one of Derrick's shirts.* Then she went into the bathroom and saw his toiletries. *Derrick is living here. Mr. Rubin did say he came by to pick up the tapes. Maybe he wanted to view them in private,* she thought while walking back into the living room.

Halle was about to leave, when she noticed some open boxes and videotapes scattered on the table and floor.

"Hmmm, what is this?" she mumbled, picking up a diary from the table.

Although horrified at what she read, she took the book and placed it in her bag. Then she saw an old photo of Monique and Michael with Jasmine and Morgan. Monique had the same picture.

Oh my God! Morgan is Michael and Monique's oldest sister.

Slam!

"What are doing here?" It was Derrick.

"You've been staying here?" Halle asked, startled by the sound of the slamming door.

Derrick stormed past her. "None of your business," he said, snatching the picture out of her hand.

Halle glared at him. This wasn't her brother. He looked possessed. His eyes were bloodshot red; he was sweaty looking and stunk.

"What's wrong with you?"

Derrick started straightening up, avoiding her stares. "There's nothing wrong with me," he snapped. "I wish you would stop asking. Anyway, what are you doing here?"

"The question is, what are you doing here?" Halle shot back, raising an eyebrow.

Now both of them were glaring at each other, not willing to back down.

"Are we back to our old habits?" he snidely asked.

"Fuck you! How dare you accuse me of getting high?" Halle was about to charge him, but stopped herself. Instead, she released a loud laugh. "You know what, Derrick? I'm not gonna let you or anyone else 'cause me to relapse." Halle gathered her things and proceeded to walk out, but before leaving, she turned around and faced a somber-face Derrick. "Don't do anything you might regret!" she exclaimed, looking him up and down before exiting out the door.

Damn! Derrick thought, hurling a glass against the wall.

★ ★ ★ ★ 94

Chapter Nine

Gracie immediately changed her name to Brightman. While Greg forgave Sadie, Gracie could care less if the bitch lived or die. As far as she was concerned, Sadie was a non-motherfucking factor. After learning that information about her parents, Gracie decided to hire a private investigator to find out more. Although Stevie gave them a lot of information, Gracie knew there was some stuff Stevie either left out or didn't know. Either way, Gracie was going to get to the bottom of it.

However, tonight, she was having dinner with Anthony. They were supposed to meet for a nightcap a couple of weeks ago, but one of her meetings ran over and she had to cancel. They were meeting at his penthouse for an intimate dinner. Gracie was hesitant at first, thinking he was up to something, but he assured her that she would be in good hands.

Anthony knew Gracie was a powerful woman with money. Therefore, he pulled out all stops to impress her.

"Wow, you look stunning," Anthony said, greeting her with a kiss on the cheek.

Gracie blushed. "You clean up nice, too."

Anthony gave her a tour around his penthouse, showing off his expensive art collection, but that wasn't the only thing she noticed.

"Oh, that's my father, Tony Flowers," he told her while she stood in front of the picture.

"Thee Tony Flowers was your father?" she asked.

"Yes, and that's my mother and other siblings."

"Beautiful. Your mother was young. I didn't know he was married."

"Yes," he responded. "You didn't know about my father?"

"Only that he was a good rapper who became a great businessman," she replied.

Anthony smiled like a proud son. "Yes, he was a great man, but enough about him. Tell me, Ms. Gracie, why a woman so beautiful, powerful, and classy is single."

"The same reason why you're single. Now I know you didn't invite me to dinner to ask if I'm single," she said, gazing into his eyes.

Anthony bit his bottom lip while flashing a sexy grin. "Actually, I didn't," he said, leading her to the eating area.

Over dinner, they talked about everything from new technology to business ideas. Gracie was a breath of fresh air for Anthony. Surprisingly, she thought the same thing about him. Not only was he fine as hell and rich, Anthony was smart. He even spoke several languages.

One thing for sure, Anthony knew how to romance a woman. Once they moved to the living room, Anthony turned on a little music.

He extended his hand to her. "Would you like to dance?"

Playing along, Gracie put her drink down. "Sure."

While dancing to the sounds of Trey Songz, they gazed into each other's eyes. Anthony then leaned over to kiss her. Horny and tipsy, Gracie didn't turn away. It started with a simple kiss and would lead to an enchanted night of passionate sex. With both being aggressors in the bedroom, it made the sex even hotter.

Gracie ripped open Anthony's shirt, causing his to moan.

"Slow down, baby. I'm not going anywhere," he whispered.

Gracie giggled. "You're right about that," she told him, then licked his neck.

But, Gracie didn't know who she was fucking with. Anthony loved being in control in the bedroom. He knew women like Gracie who had everything liked to be fucked.

He slipped his hand between her legs, massaging her clit. "Hot and wet," he moaned, tonguing her down.

"Why don't you taste it?" she shot back.

Caught off guard by her request, Anthony looked at her. This was the first time a woman had boldly made such a request of him.

Anthony bit her bottom lip and replied, "With pleasure."

He lifted Gracie up and placed her on the arm of the chair. Anthony then kneeled down, putting himself face to face with her wet pussy. He wrapped her legs around his neck. Burning with anticipation, Gracie massaged his head while gently pushing it in between her legs. She was so hot that she squirted in his face. Seeing this made Anthony's dick jump. He started playing with her clitoris, gently massaging the little man in the boat, before sticking his fingers inside.

Anthony looked up at Gracie, who was playing with her titties. Oh yes, she was ready. He started eating Gracie's pussy as if his life depended on it. He ate it to the point where she couldn't stand it anymore.

Drooling from her mouth, Gracie begged in ecstasy, "Please stop. I can't take it anymore."

But, Anthony wasn't ready to stop. He wanted Gracie to remember this fuck. In fact, that's how Anthony got most of the women that he didn't sexually assault, by putting it down.

"Oh God, Anthony. Please," she said as her body trembled.

Gracie finally found the strength to push his head away, close her legs, and jump to her feet. Anthony stood smirking with her juices all over his face. Gracie pulled him closer to her and kissed it off.

Okay, two can play that game, she thought.

She pushed him against wall, dropped to her knees, and unbuckled his pants, only to be greeted by the biggest dick she'd ever seen. Gracie had seen some huge cocks, but Anthony's looked like a toddler's arm. She wasn't sure if it would fit in her mouth. Nevertheless, she was up for the challenge. After a few tries, she managed to get most of it in. Even though she had to breathe through her nose, Gracie sucked Anthony off until he burst in her mouth.

Fortunately, they were just getting started. Anthony pulled Gracie to her feet by her head, turned her around, and walked her back to the armrest. He then bent her over, arched her ass up in the air, and smacked it. Excited, Anthony pulled out an extra large condom, ripped it open, put it on, and then thrust himself inside of her.

Gracie's body went into shock at the size of his penis. She tensed up and tried to move away, but Anthony held her by the waist, giving her all of him.

"Don't run now," he panted. "Take all of this, baby. This is want you came over here for. You wanted some of this big dick."

After a few strokes, it started to feel good to Gracie. She relaxed her body and threw it back like a quarterback.

"Unfucking believable," he huffed.

"Fuck me harder," Gracie commanded, arching her ass up more.

Obliging, Anthony pounded in and out of her. They were fucking so hard that they moved the sofa to the other side of the room. They went at it like two wildebeest mating until they collapsed on the floor.

*****

Meanwhile, Greg was searching for his father's side of the family. Sadly, his father's family was small. His grandmother passed five years after his father's death, and his father's only sister died last year of lung cancer.

While he sat in his office reading about his father, Greg's fiancée Tracey entered. "Hey, you're still up? You usually fall asleep in here," Tracey half-joked.

Greg reached out and pulled her onto his lap. "Yeah," he said, leaning over to rest his head on her stomach.

"What's wrong?" she asked, rubbing his head.

Greg took a deep breath. "Besides finding out my parents were murdered, my father was in prison for murder, or my sister disowned our grandma?" He sighed and released a slight giggle.

"Gracie will come around. She's just hurt."

He laughed. "You don't know, Gracie. She can hold a grudge."

Tracey laughed, also, while lifting Greg's face up by his chin. "You can't blame her. I would be hurt if I found out someone lied to me about my parents." ¬

"Yes, but I'm pretty sure my grandma didn't do it intentionally. I just wish Gracie could see that. She's even questioning our godmother's intentions."

"Why?"

"Because she's Gracie. Always thinking someone is hiding something."

"Greg, she's just being careful. We live in a world where people do have hidden agendas."
He sighed again and hugged her tightly. "I guess."

Tracey looked into his eyes. "You know what? If your parents were alive, they would've proud of you. You're gonna make a good father."

Greg smiled. "Thank you. I just wish..." He paused for a moment before continuing. "I just wish they were here to see their grandson. I'm grateful for the money, but I would rather have them."

"I know, baby. I know, and they know. Do you know who killed them or why?"

Shaking his head in disappointment, Greg answered, "No."

"Damn. Well, maybe you should ask your godmother. She might know something."

"Yes, and she invited Gracie and I out to Atlanta for dinner this weekend. Perfect."

*****

Ever since Gracie had been seeing Anthony, she'd been avoiding Greg. Although she knew he would be happy that she

finally settled down, she wanted to make sure Anthony was the right one. Initially, she and Greg were supposed to meet with some business investors and then fly out to see Stevie for the weekend. However, Gracie cancelled at the last minute, claiming an emergency came up.

Yeah, right. The emergency was nothing other some cock, Greg thought to himself during the ride to Stevie's house.

Greg wanted to bring Tracey along, but with her due date so close, they thought it would be best if she stayed home. Therefore, he arrived at Stevie's alone.

"Greg!" She smiled and greeted him with a kiss.

"Hello, Mrs. Strong," he said, hugging her.

"Please…call me Stevie."

"Okay, Stevie," he obliged with a chuckle.

Stevie led her godson into the house. She was so delighted to have her godchildren in her life. They were all she had left of Gabrielle. Stevie cooked up a feast for them, and just as they were about to sit down to eat, Gracie arrived.

"Sorry I'm late."

Stevie giggled at how Gracie was just like her mother.

"So what did I miss?" Gracie asked.

"Nothing. Stevie was just telling me about the day Mommy told everyone she was pregnant."

"Yes, it was your father's birthday. I swear those two were meant for each other." Stevie smiled while thinking about them.

"Stevie, did you know any of my father's family?" Greg asked.

"No."

"How did you meet our parents?" Gracie inquired.

"It's funny you should ask that. I actually met your father first. I use to mess with one of his friends named Tony. Your father was dating your mother at the time. From day one, Gabrielle and I hit it off. She wasn't fake like other girls."

Greg and Gracie smiled at Stevie's comment.

After dinner, Stevie led them to the family room to show them pictures. Upon entering, they were greeted by a huge photo of some people. Gracie immediately noticed one of them in the photo. At first, she thought she was seeing things. So, she walked over to get a closer look.

"Yeah, I dated Tony Flowers," Stevie said when she noticed Gracie staring at the picture. "He was one of your father's best friends."

Gracie placed her hand over her mouth. "Oh my God," she gasped, turning pale.

"Are you okay?" Greg said, noticing his sister's expression.

"Tony Flowers knew my father?" Gracie asked.

Stevie shot Gracie an apprehensive look. "Yes. That's your father Greg, Tony, Denise, Gabrielle, and me."

"Wow, I didn't know my father knew Tony Flowers," Greg stated.

Stevie took a seat on the sofa, with Greg sitting next to her. "Yes. In fact, if it weren't for your father, there would have never been a *Tony Flowers*. It was your father who convinced Tony to become a rapper. He started a record company and signed Tony. But, when he went to prison, he gave it to Tony. That's the kind of man your father was; he was honorable."

Stunned, Gracie took a seat, but remained quiet. Greg looked at her and then back at Stevie.

"That's good to know, considering all I've read has been bad things about him," Greg commented.

"Oh, the newspapers? Well, they didn't know the real Greg. Yes, he did bad things, but he helped a lot of people. You see that, young lady." Stevie pointed at another photo. "That's your cousin Denise Taylor. Greg took her and molded her into a real estate tycoon."

"That's my mother's cousin?" Gracie asked, looking at the picture.

"Yes. You never met her kids. Denise had two kids." Stevie stood and went to retrieve photos of them. "Here, that's her husband Derrick and their kids, Halle and Derrick Jr."

"Our wonderful grandma didn't tell us," Gracie snidely told her.

Stevie twisted her face. "Now that's strange, considering Gabrielle and Denise were close. I know they would've wanted y'all to keep in touch."

"What happened to Denise?" Greg asked.

"She was killed with your father. I think her parents got custody of her kids."

"Damn, they're all dead," Greg mumbled, shaking his head. "Why?"

Stevie lowered her head. She had an idea why, but didn't know if it was her place to tell them. Taking a deep breath, she decided to tell them what she knew.

She put her hand on Greg's knee and said, "Something happened before your parents were killed. They found out your grandfather was behind Greg being sent to prison. He had a daughter by the ADA, and ironically, Greg messed with her and your mother at the same time. Greg didn't know, but your grandfather did. So, he and the ADA set him up for murder."

Angry, Gracie asked, "Did my grandma know about this?"

"She found out later."

Gracie released a fake laugh. "Figures!"

Greg looked over at Gracie and then at Stevie, who was confused. "Gracie thinks my grandma deliberately didn't tell us about our parents," he explained to Stevie.

"And hearing this, you don't?" Gracie snapped.

Stevie looked at Gracie and nodded. "Gracie is right, Greg. For years, she and your grandfather didn't approve of your parents' marriage. In fact, they didn't start getting along until y'all were born."

Greg looked away, avoiding Gracie's "I told you so" stare. "Why?" he asked.

"Your father was a drug dealer. They only wanted the best for their daughter. When you have children, you will see."

"So Denise is from what side of the family?" Gracie inquired.

"Denise is from your grandfather's side."

"I still can't believe our parents knew Tony Flowers. He's like a legend. And you dated him?" Gracie got up to study the picture.

"I dated him before he became the infamous Tony Flowers."

"Why didn't you marry him?" Greg asked her.

Now it was Stevie who lowered her head. She got up and started pacing. "Tony...good ole Tony. Only if people knew the real Tony Flowers."

Gracie turned around. "What do you mean the *real* Tony Flowers?"

Although it had been over twenty years, Stevie could still remember that night as if it was yesterday. "Tony Flowers was an abuser. He used to beat me."

"What!" Greg said.

"But that's just a small part of it. Tony raped Denise's niece, Morgan. He was raping and beating her since she was fourteen years old."

"What!" Gracie walked up to Stevie. "Tony Flowers was a rapist? Why didn't he go to jail?"

Greg got up and walked over to join them. "Because he's Tony Flowers."

"No," Stevie responded."Morgan didn't tell anyone until she and Tony were married."

"She married him?" Gracie blurted out while looking at Greg.

"Yes, they were married with kids."

Gracie slowly walked away. "Did they have a son?"

"I believe so. I think his name was Anthony."

Gracie damn near shitted on herself. *Oh my God!*

*****

Since that evening, Gracie couldn't get what Stevie revealed to them out of her head. *Was she telling the truth or is she just a jilted ex-girlfriend?* Doubtful, Gracie wanted to talk to her brother about her feelings. She finally located Greg, who was working late in the office, and went to see him.

So, he wouldn't get alarmed, Gracie took dinner to him.

He smiled, greeted her with a kiss on the cheek, and asked, "What's wrong?"

Gracie playfully patted him on his arm. "Nothing. I can't bring my big brother dinner?"

Greg twisted his face up. She had brought pizza and wine, his favorite.

"What did you do?" he asked, causing them both to laugh.

"Greg," she whined, "that's not fair."

"Alright," he jokily stated, then laughed and hugged her.

Although they were different, Greg could sense when something was bothering her. Growing up, Greg was the only person Gracie listened to. He stood by her no matter what. For him, Gracie was the only real family he had. So, it was only natural that he wanted to protect her from the world. Still, it didn't mean Greg didn't want to kill her ass at times.

"So what are your thoughts on our fairy godmother," Gracie asked, biting a slice of pizza.

"What do you mean? She seems nice."

"Yes, but are you buying her story?"

"I don't understand what you're saying."

"You know the information about Tony?"

Greg shrugged his shoulders. "Oh, I really never gave it any thought. But, it doesn't surprise me. Most famous people have hidden secrets."

Gracie took a sip of her wine. "True, but, Greg, she knew all of this information and never wrote a tell-all book? Come on."

Greg got up to get another slice of pizza. "Maybe she isn't like that. Not everyone is out to make money like that, Gracie. Besides, she seems like the type to get her own. Or maybe she didn't want to smear his name."

"Yeah, but this is Tony Flowers. And why haven't we read anything about her? I Googled her, and her name doesn't appear in nothing that has to deal with Tony."

"So you think she's lying? I mean, she has pictures and..." Greg pointed, "...she did say it was before Tony was famous."

"Okay, but why tell us? She doesn't know us like that. Shit, we can sell this story to the tabloids."

"I don't know. Maybe she wants to start her own reality show." He burst into laughter.

Gracie giggled. "I'm serious. I think she's up to something."

Greg plopped down in a chair. "Okay, what do you think she's up to and why do you care? Stevie has shared with us more than Grandma ever did...things we should've known. Why would she lie about anything now?"

"I don't know, but I have a feeling she's up to something."

Greg dropped his head. He knew Gracie wasn't going to let up.

Chapter Ten

While London and the others continued to search for answers about their parents' death, Anthony was living like a king, partying every night, and taking different women back to his penthouse. Once word got out that Anthony was Tony Flowers' son, everyone wanted a piece of him, from rappers to Wall Street. Anthony Omari Flowers became an overnight celebrity.

Sadly, even money couldn't change the anger Anthony had inside him. He experienced a sick thrill when he humiliated women. He thrived on their vulnerability. Anthony didn't believe in women telling him no. That's why he helped them say yes.

Tonight, he was attending an exclusive party. From the door, women were throwing themselves at him.

Awaiting him in the private section was the best champagne and cigars. In addition, there were about five women who were on him like flies on shit, and Anthony loved it. These parties were the new way for closing business deals. Anthony was meeting with some movie producers, Pioneer and Star, who wanted to bring his father's story to the big screen. Of course, Anthony thought it was a great idea.

"So did you look over the proposal?" Pioneer asked.

Sipping on a glass of champagne and puffing on a cigar, Anthony replied, "Yes. I just wanna meet the writers for this movie. I know there's a lot of unauthorized books and shows about my father. So, this movie must be done right."

Pioneer and Star looked at each other before Star told him, "Of course. That's why we came to you. You're his son. Hopefully, you can work with the writers so the story is told correctly."

"Sure," Anthony absently replied while flirting with one of the girls.

Pioneer and Star could tell Anthony's mind was preoccupied with the readily-available ass. Therefore, they toasted to their new business deal and left. Not long after they departed, Anthony took one of the girls back to his place.

Wasting no time, the girl gave Anthony a blowjob in the backseat during the ride to his place. As she sucked on his cock, Anthony sniffed a few lines of coke. He even put some on his penis and made her lick it off. His cocaine use started in college, the drug helping him to stay up for those big exams, but now he was using it every other day.

By the time they reached his place, Anthony had busted in the girl's mouth. However, with his huge appetite for sex, Anthony wanted more. He was the perfect gentleman until they got into his apartment. That's when Anthony revealed his true colors. After going to freshen up, the young girl found Anthony in his spare bedroom.

While standing there butt naked, in a seductive tone, the girl said, "Ready to finish what we started?"

Anthony snorted a couple lines and glanced up at her with a disgusted look. "Clothes do hide a lot of things," he snidely remarked, making the girl feel uncomfortable.

"Excuse me?" she said with her hand on her hip. "You didn't have a problem with my body when I was sucking your dick."

Anthony wiped his nose and glared at her. She was fucking up his high. He got up and slowly glided over to her. "Why don't you give me another one of your blowjobs?" he asked while unbuttoning his pants.

For the girl, the mood to please him had dissipated. She felt disrespected and wanted to leave. "Why don't you suck your own dick?" she shot back and turned to walk away.

Anthony grabbed her by the back of her neck. "You crazy bitch, don't you know who I am?" he grunted. "You should be happy I allowed a hoe like you to even touch my dick," he added, then smashed her into the wall.

"Get off of me!"

She wildly swung, trying to pry his hands off of her. But, Anthony overpowered her, tossing her across the room like a rag doll. He snatched off his jacket and tossed it across the room, as well.

"I'm gonna teach you some manners, bitch."

Hurting and scared, the girl pleaded with him. "Please don't," she said, putting her hands up to block her face.

Anthony smiled inside, feeding off her fear. Effortlessly, he picked up the girl and put her on the table. "Shhh," he told her.

Shaking and crying, the girl mumbled, "Please...I'm sorry."

Her begging only turned Anthony on more; he was now hard as a rock. He unbuttoned his pants, pulled out a condom from his pocket, put it on, and rammed it inside of the girl. Within seconds, it was over.

Anthony pulled out and walked into the bathroom. As for the girl, she laid motionless. A few moments later, he returned, picked up his jacket, went inside of it, and pulled out a wad of money. He tossed it at the girl.

"This is for your trouble," he said to her, but that was just the beginning.

*****

What little leads Addy left them, they decided to follow up on. Unfortunately, all the leads turned up empty. Tony's entire family was gone. They went around his old neighborhood hoping to find someone, but no one knew Tony Flowers personally. They had only heard about him.

As for Morgan's side, the information Addy gave them turned out to be correct. Monique lived in West Virginia, and Michael had just moved to California. Scared of being disappointed, Justin and Justine waited in the car while London rang the bell. When no one came to the door, London turned to walk away. Just then, the door opened.

"May I help you?"

When London turned around, Monique immediately recognized her.

"Oh my God! London, is that you?" she asked with her hand over her mouth.

Both of their eyes filled with tears as London nodded.

London tried to speak, but was cut off by a hug from Monique.

By then, Justin and Justine got out of the car.

"Oh my God! Justin and Justine!" Monique hysterically praised, hugging them tightly.

Crying with joy, Monique held her nieces and nephew for longer than the average hug usually lasted.

"Oh my God, I can't believe it," she said as tears rolled down her face. "There wasn't a day that went by that I didn't wonder about y'all." She paused for a moment. "Wait," she said, then grabbed London and Justine's hands, leading them into the house. "Michael! Michael!" she frantically called. "Look, Michael! Look!"

Michael came running out of one of the rooms and almost fainted when he saw them. "No..." His eyes filled with tears. "Is that..."

Happy, London replied, "Yes," and Monique confirmed it.

"Oh God!" He ran to embrace them.

Crying and holding each other, London, Justin, and Justine finally got a chance to meet their family. After rejoicing, Monique led them out to the yard where they were having a barbeque with the rest of the family. Monique and Michael were both married with small children. London and her siblings beamed with joy. Still, there were so many questions running through their minds, like why hadn't they reached out to them.

Ironically, Derrick and Halle were attending Monique's family event. With Halle getting there first, Monique introduced London to her cousin.

"Halle, come here. I want you to meet your cousins," Monique said, leading her to the yard. "Halle, this is London, Justin, and Justine...your cousins. These are my oldest sister Morgan's kids."

These are Morgan's children? Halle's eyes widened before she responded, "Hi. It's so good to finally meet you. Grandpa and Grandma talked about you all the time." She then greeted them with a hug and kiss.

"Is there something wrong?" Monique asked, noticing Halle's expression.

"No. It's just all surprising," Halle said, flashing a fake smile.

"Tell me about it. I wondered about you for years. I even wrote your grandfather, begging him to let me see you. I know my sister would've wanted that," Monique told them.

"Where's Anthony?" Michael asked.

London and Justine looked at each other and rolled their eyes.

"He's in New York," London replied.

There was so much stuff they had to catch up on. Therefore, Monique and Michael brushed off that comment.

"I still can't believe it. I know Mommy, Morgan, and Aunt Denise are smiling down on this moment," Monique said.

"Aunt Denise?" Justine asked.

"Yes. My mother and Denise were sisters. Come let me show you some pictures." Monique led them into the house and pulled out a family album. "You see, that's my mother, Aunt Denise, Anita, and De'shell," she stated, then flipped the page. "That's Aunt Denise, my mother, and Morgan at Morgan's sweet sixteen party."

Smiling at the pictures, Justine asked, "We were told my mother was married to our father. Is that true?"

Michael took a deep breath. "Yes, they were. We didn't find out until after Morgan got pregnant with twins. Tony and Aunt Denise were best friends. My sister had gotten pregnant by some guy. Tony stepped in to help. I guess one thing led to another, and they fell in love."

Knowing the truth, Halle remained quiet.

"So Anthony isn't my father's son?" Justin asked.

Monique and Michael looked at each other before Michael replied, "No, Anthony isn't Tony's son."

London and her siblings' mouths fell wide open.

"What! I thought they said we are all Tony's children," London blurted out.

"No, my sister had Anthony by that time." Michael explained

"Anthony and I are only a year apart. So what about my father?" London asked.

"We don't know," Monique told her. "Morgan was a very private person."

"Why didn't we live with our grandma?" Justine asked.

Michael walked over closer to them. "That's funny you should mention that. My mother died of cancer. If she was alive, there is no way you guys would've not been raised by her. The only reason Morgan lived with Denise is because she went to Dalton, and the school was in the city. My mother didn't want Morgan riding the trains by herself."

"Oh, so Denise raised Morgan?" London said.

Michael and Monique looked at each other again.

"No," Michael responded. "Our mother raised Morgan."

"What about our grandfather? He wasn't around?" Justine asked.

"Who? Felix? No, I don't even remember him being in Morgan's life. That's why we were pissed off when he took y'all," Monique told them.

While Monique and Michael answered questions, Halle looked through the family photo album. "Who is this?" she asked.

"Oh, that's our cousins Gabrielle and her husband Greg with their twins Greg jr. and Gracie"

Halle had seen pictures of them with her parents in Mr. Rubin's home.

"Monique, we're a bit puzzled. According to media, our father was married to Christina Carrington, and they were killed together in his house. But, there's no record of them being married.

However, no one knew about my mother and Tony being married until months before she died. Yet, they were married after Morgan's eighteenth birthday," Justin stated.

Michael and Monique stood with a confused look on their faces.

"Morgan didn't marry Tony until she was at least twenty-one," Monique replied.

"No, they married the day of her eighteenth birthday," London said, showing them a copy of their marriage license.

Now Michael and Monique were baffled.

"We didn't know. Are you sure this is real?" Michael asked, looking at it.

"Yes," London answered.

Michael and Monique were speechless. They always found it strange that Morgan had married Tony, but they were too young to question it.

*****

Since Gracie had been avoiding Anthony, went back to seeing this old side chick Clarice. They were meeting at Bowery Ballroom on Delancy Street. Anthony pulled up to the place in a Lamborghini, one of the most expensive cars in the world. After tossing the keys to the parking attendant, he waved to the ladies that were standing on line and then went inside.

The place was packed, and everyone greeted him as if he were Tony Flowers. The men shook his hand, while the women tried to stick their numbers in his pocket. Anthony brushed off advances as he made his way to meet Clarice.

"Hey, handsome," she said before tonguing him down in front of everyone.

One of the main reasons why Anthony liked Clarice although it's been over five years since they have been fucking around he didn't have to buy her nothing, and yet she stroked his ego.

"Wow," he said, kissing her on the cheek.

"And there's more where that came from," she told him, then licked her lips seductively.

"I can't wait," he replied, palming her ass.

A few drinks later, Anthony and Clarice were all over each other. They had great chemistry.

"Let's get out of here," she whispered while licking on his neck.

On their way out the door, Anthony spotted Gracie talking to some men. He asked Clarice to go get the car while he ran over to say hello.

Anthony walked up behind Gracie and pressed his penis against her butt. "Why haven't you returned my calls?"

Gracie turned around and damn near passed out. Ever since she found out what his father did to his mother, she'd been shunning him off.

"Excuse me," she told the gentlemen.

Anthony laughed. "Is any of them gonna get lucky tonight? If so, they should know you like big dicks," he spitefully commented.

Gracie laughed at his jealous childish comment. "How do you know they didn't get lucky already, Mr. Flowers?" she responded in a low tone.

"Knowing you, I wouldn't be surprised."

Gracie leaned closer and whispered in his ear, "The next time you decide to bring a date, let me know. I'll make sure you get the best table in the house, considering I own the place." She winked.

Her comment sent chills through Anthony's body. She snatched him by the arm, dragged him to a private area. Anthony pushed her up against the wall, and forcefully kissed her. At first, Gracie tried to fight him off, but the feel of his hard penis caused her to become aroused.

Anthony grinded against her while reaching underneath Gracie's skirt to start playing with her clitoris, making her moan. Caught up in the heat of passion, Gracie pushed Anthony off of her, dropped to her knees, and unbuckled his pants. She couldn't wait to have him in her mouth.

Experiencing a heavenly sensation, Anthony massaged the back of her head. As Gracie continued with her five-star oral sex performance, she quickly forgot who Anthony's father was. She loved sucking dick; it was her way of overpowering men.

Not wanting to bust, Anthony lifted Gracie up and stared into her eyes before leaning over to passionately kiss her. He then lifted her body up against the wall, pulled her thong to the side, and slid inside her. Gracie moaned in ecstasy at how Anthony's big cock fit her vagina like a glove. Thankfully, the music was blasting, because the way they were carrying on, their parents could have heard them from the grave.

"This dick is good, huh?" he panted.

"Yes...oh, yes," Gracie moaned in response.

He stroke in and out of her, making her body move up and down against the wall. Then Anthony stopped, kissed her again, took her legs from around his waist, and placed them on top of his shoulders. Now all of Anthony's ten inches were in her stomach, and this caused Gracie to gasp from the pain. Slowly yet forcibly, Anthony rammed in and outside of Gracie, while she closed her eyes and thought, *I guess this is what they mean about pain and pleasure being rolled up into one.*

Before Gracie knew it, her body started to tremble and she couldn't speak. "Anthony!" she managed to get out before exploding.

As for Anthony, he didn't climax. He had mentally prepared himself not to do so beforehand. A weak but satisfied Gracie held Anthony tightly, but he wasn't done yet. Anthony let her down and in a subdued way, he forced her head down to his penis, making her finish him off with a blowjob until he released in her mouth. What felt like an eternity actually took less than ten minutes.

He licked some of his cum from the corner of Gracie's mouth. "You may own this club, but that pussy..." he said, touching her between her legs, "...belongs to me." He then planted a wet kiss on her neck and walked away.

 115

*****

Finally, we're making some progress, London thought. From that day on, London and her siblings spoke to their aunt and uncle every day. In fact, they had planned a family gathering that would take place in a couple of weeks. Hopefully, Anthony and Derrick would join them.

Still in New York it had been weeks since Felix spoke to his grandchildren. Therefore, he invited them to the house for dinner to see how things were going with them. However, London and the others were supposed to have dinner with Halle, so they invited her since she was apart of the family now.

"Grandpa!" London smiled, kissing him on the cheek.

"Londie," he said. "You look more and more like your mother every day."

London blushed, while inside, she couldn't wait to tell her grandfather the wonderful news.

"Where's Justin and Justine?" he asked.

"They should be here shortly. How are you doing?" she asked, hugging him as they walked to the study.

"Well, I'm getting old, and gaining weight," he wittily replied, making London laugh. "But, I'm great. How's my great son-in-law?"

"Nyennoh is good. He keeps asking when I'm coming back."

"Well, when are you?"

London was about to answer the question, when Mrs. Marciano entered.

"Here's my beautiful granddaughter," she cheered with her hands out.

"Hi, Grandma."

"Why haven't we seen you?"

London sighed and was about to tell them the truth, when her siblings arrived.

"Can we get a home cooked meal?" Justin jokily asked.

Felix laughed. "Of course. Anytime," he replied as he stood to hug and kiss them. Seeing his grandchildren always put a smile on

Felix's face. They were the most important things in life to him. What he didn't do with Morgan, Felix made up for it with his grandchildren.

As they were about to sit down to eat, the doorbell rang. It was Halle.

"Oh, Grandpa, I forgot to tell you that we found my mother's sister and brother, Monique and Michael, who introduced us to our cousin Halle. She's Aunt Denise's daughter. We invited her to dinner. I hope you don't mind," London said.

Felix looked at Mrs. Marciano, who had a momentous expression on her face.

"Oh, not at all," she said, flashing a fake smile while looking at Felix.

While Justin and London paid no attention to Mrs. Marciano and Felix's expressions, Justine did. Smirking inside, she knew her uppity grandma was pissed.

"Hello," Halle said, greeting everyone.

"Halle, I'm so glad you could make it," London said, kissing her on the cheek. "Grandpa, Grandma, this is Halle, Aunt Denise's daughter," she introduced.

Aware of who she was, Felix smiled and responded, "Hello."

Mrs. Marciano glared at Halle for a brief second before forcing a smile. "Greetings"

A brief silence filled the room, so Justine decided to spark things up. "Grandpa, did you know my father married my mother a day after her eighteenth birthday?"

Choking on his lobster, Felix sipped some water before asking, "What do you mean?"

London rolled her eyes at Justine and jumped in to explain. "We've been doing our own little investigation, and we have a lot of questions about some things. Like why didn't we keep in contact with either side of our parents' family? Or why was there no mention of our father being married to someone?"

"Or Anthony not being Tony's real father?" Justine blurted out, glaring at her grandmother.

"Who said Anthony isn't?" Mrs. Marciano said, looking directly at Justine.

"People, but of course, you probably knew that, you probably even paid them off" Justine snapped while staring Mrs. Marciano down.

Justin looked back and forth between the two of them. He was very familiar with the blow-ups that Justine and Mrs. Marciano would have, so he jumped in. "According to our aunt and uncle, our mother had given birth to Anthony before she got involved with Tony."

Halle looked back and forth between them, while thinking, *Shit's about to hit the fan.*

"Unfortunately, we didn't know what was going on with Morgan. Those people raised her. We didn't have a say," Mrs. Marciano shot back.

"Those people?" Halle looked as if her statement insulted her.

"Halle, I don't know if you know about your family," Mrs. Marciano told her.

"What family? My family?" Halle asked.

"Halle, you must excuse my grandmother. She believes black people are only good for cleaning toilets. Isn't that right, Grandma?"

"Justine!" Justin yelled.

"It's true. Isn't that why you sent Justin and me off, because we weren't as light as London and Anthony? If we looked anything like our father's side of the family, we wouldn't be raised with this family."

"Justine..."London said

"What! Everyone knows it. Right, Grandma? Just like Anthony is your favorite great grandchild. What, does he remind you of an old boyfriend? You will cover up anything for him."

Mrs. Marciano stood up. "How dare you put your feet up under my table and disrespect me. Get the hell out of my house!"

"Grandma!" London and Justin shouted in unison.

"I stopped putting my feet under your table years ago. Remember?" Justine said, tossing her napkin on the table. "You are nothing but a miserable old bitch, and I can't wait for your day to come" the exit.

"Well you better wait in line" Mrs. Marciano retorted "And if any of you feel the same way, you can join her. Because I don't have to explain nothing, especially after all we've done!" Mrs. Marciano yelled, exiting the room right behind Justine.

Shocked, Halle just sat there watching like it was a soap opera.

While Justin ran after Justine, Felix ran after his mother. "Mother, how dare you?" he said, chasing behind her.

"If that little black bitch thinks she's gonna disrespect me, she will join her mother. And that goes for those sorry-ass grandkids of mine. After all we did, they think they can come in here and question me? They too will quickly learn," she warned, pointing in his face.

"Her mother" Felix repeated making sure he heard her correctly "If you even think about harming them, I promise you, YOU will join their mother before them."

"Watch, Felix. Remember who taught you."

"Exactly! Now don't you forget," he said, then walked away.

Listening behind the door was London. All these years, people had been saying her great-grandmother was a racist. Now London had heard it with her own ears.

She waited until Felix left to confront her Mrs. Marciano. "So now we're black little bitches...sorry-ass grandkids?"

Annoyed, Mrs. Marciano sighed. "London, you need to know one thing. All good fortunes have secrets."

"So I've heard. Justine was right. You are something else. Everyone was right about you..."

"London..."

London charged her. "Don't London me! All these years! You haven't changed," she stated through clenched teeth. "If you even think about doing anything to my siblings,"

Mrs. Marciano giggled, "now…now Londie." Referring to her by her childhood name "You and I both know you don't have the backbone"

London approached her great-grandmother "no but I have the money. And I will spend every dime sending you a first class ticket to hell, try me"

Mrs. Marciano smiled; her sweet, innocent great-granddaughter had finally grown some balls. She was about to say something, when the phone rang.

"Grandma, it's Anthony. I've been arrested."

"For what?" she asked in a high-pitch voice.

"Rape."

Before Mrs. Marciano could get any details, the phone went dead. Feeling nauseous, she took a seat.

"What happened?" London asked, forgetting what had just taken place between them.

"Anthony…" she mumbled in disbelief.

The sound of Mrs. Marciano's voice caused Felix, Justin, Justine, and Halle to come see what was going on.

"What happened?" Justin asked.

"Anthony…he's been arrested…for rape," she muttered.

Halle shook her head. *Guess the apple doesn't fall far from the tree.*

Chapter ELEVEN

The time had come for people to pay for tormenting Derrick and Halle while they were growing up, and first on the list was Ronisha, Diamond's mother. Playing the notes over in his head, Derrick knew planning was everything. Nothing should be left to chance.

Ronisha had just been released from prison and was living in Boston. Like Derrick, Ronisha turned herself over to God. He'd studied her routine for weeks. So, he knew she was on her way to church for confessions. Dressed as a priest, Derrick waited in the confession both.

Ronisha made a sign of a cross over her chest. "Forgive me, father, for I have sinned. It has been five days since my last confession. I accuse myself of the following sins..."

Once she finished, Derrick pulled the gun from his waist and while watching his hand tremble fired one shot through the window.

"Your sins have been forgiven," Derrick mumbled, then tucked the gun back in his waist and left.

Derrick hopped in the car and sped off. While killing a person was easy, the after effects weren't. He was shaking, and his stomach was churning so bad that he pulled over to throw up.

"Oh God," he cried, pacing back and forth on the side of the road while rubbing his head. "I just took a life," he slowly whispered. Taking a long, deep breath, he told himself, "Come on, Derrick. Get it together."

After a few more deep breaths, Derrick jumped back into his car and drove to his house.

Once in the house, he broke down in tears and almost broke everything in the house. Derrick dropped to his knees.

"Why me, Ma? Why me?" he cried, thinking about all he had lost because of that one prank pulled by his cousins. "Father, please forgive me," he begged, searching for his bible. "Please Father," he cried until he fell asleep.

Halle was also going through a dilemma. She knew the truth about Tony and Morgan, but debated about telling her cousin. Remembering the amount of pain she felt upon learning the truth about her mother, she knew there was no way she could do that to them. Then again, she was happy to finally know the truth about her parents.

However, after what happened with Anthony, Halle decided she would take that secret to the grave. One person Halle wished her mother had sent to hell was Mrs. Marciano. Another person Halle worried about was Derrick. She felt something was up with him. She'd left several messages for him, and he hadn't called her back. But, she couldn't think about that right now either because she was meeting with Mr. Klein to discuss her designs.

Since Greg was meeting with some investors in the big conference room, Mr. Klein decided they would conduct their meeting in Greg's office. Upon entering, Halle immediately noticed a huge wedding picture of two people. Mr. Klein noticed her focusing on the photo.

"That's Greg's parents," he informed her while laying out the designs.

Halle closed her eyes. *This can't be happening again.* Unable to focus, Halle pretended like she had a headache.

"Mr. Klein, I don't want to waste your time, but is it possible for us to reschedule? I don't feel too good."

He nodded. "Of course. How about I make some copies for you? That way, you can take them home, review them, and then call me to schedule."

Halle smiled. "Yes, please. Thank you!"

Once Mr. Klein left the room, Halle walked back over to the picture and gazed at it.

"Those are my parents," a man's voice said from behind her.

Halle turned around. "Oh, I'm sorry," she said,

Becoming leery, Greg asked, "Is something wrong?"

Before Halle could respond, Mr. Klein returned. "Here's the copy."

That's when it hit Greg.

"Klein, give us a second," Greg told him.

Bewildered, Mr. Klein replied, "Certainly. I'll just leave this here." He placed the copies on the desk before exiting the office.

There was a brief moment of silence, both not knowing what to say.

"You are Denise's daughter?" Greg finally asked.

"Yes."

Greg nodded. "How did you know?"

"Your parents wedding photo...my mother has one. What about you? How did you know I was her daughter?"

"Your name. My mother's best friend told me that Denise had a daughter named Halle. And the only Halle I know is Halle Berry."

His comment caused Halle to giggle.

Again, there was a brief moment of silence, and then Halle said, "You have a twin sister named Gracie?"

"Yes, and you have a big brother named Derrick."

"Yes."

Without saying another word, Greg embraced his long lost cousin and then took a seat.

"Wow, I can't believe it," he said.

"Yeah, me either. It's like faith brought us together."

Greg narrowed his eyes. "They told you what happened to our parents..." his voice trailed off.

Halle nodded. "Yes. Mr. Rubin, my mother's attorney, told me. He said your father and my mother were killed together, and that they were best friends."

"Yes. My godmother told me the same thing. All these years…"

"Tell me about it. My grandparents raised me. They told me very little about my parents. Growing up, my family told me that my mother was a drug dealer and a murderer."

"At least you were told something. I was just told my parents had passed," Greg said.

"Why? Why would they lie to us about our parents?" Halle asked, not expecting him to have an answer. "Why would they keep us from each other?"

Greg leaned back in the chair. "That's a good question."

Wow, this is such a small world, Halle thought. In a couple of month, she had managed to find out about her parents, aunts, and cousins. *What else is gonna surface?*

*****

On her way home, Halle pulled out her phone to call Derrick. Maybe the good news of her having found their long lost cousins would help him forgive his mother. It rang twice before he picked up.

"Well, hello to you, too, bro."

"Hey, sis," he replied in a groggy, disdainful voice. "How are you?"

"I would be good if my big brother returned my calls."

"Oh yeah. I've kinda been busy. You know, taking care of a few things."

"That's fine." Halle hated when she and Derrick fought. "Well, I'll go first. I'm sorry for questioning you about staying at the house. It was wrong."

Derrick closed his eyes. He wanted to tell his sister what he'd done, but if something went wrong, he wanted to keep her out of it.

"It's fine. I'm sorry for what I said about you using drugs. Now that was wrong. Halle, I've been going through so much. Over the past couple of months, my life has been turned upside down. Just when I think I'm on the right track, bam! Something else happens."

"I know, Dee. I feel the same way. But, we can't run from it. I know you're upset about what we found out concerning our parents, but that's life. I'm not making excuses for what Mommy has done, but if we can't forgive our own mother, then what does that say about us?"

Derrick nodded, although she couldn't see him. "You're right, sis, and I'm working on that. But, what about the money?"

"What about it? It's not where it came from; it's what you do with it. God doesn't make mistakes. Remember that."

Derrick laughed. "No, he doesn't. Well, I was thinking about donating most of mine."

"If that's what you wanna do, then that's your right."

"Halle..." Derrick sighed. "Have you ever wondered if Mommy passed on that evil trait to us?"

Puzzled, Halle asked, "What trait?"

"Well, she killed our father and other people. Maybe she was sick like Dr. Jekyll and Mr. Hyde, and it was passed down us."

Halle never thought of that, but now she started to think someone has to be mentally disturbed to kill their own husband.

"I don't know, Derrick. Anything is possible. I mean, we both have very bad tempers. But, hey, who's really normal nowadays, right?" She laughed, trying to lighten things up.

Not wanting to alarm Halle, Derrick laughed along with her. "Maybe you're right. But, I hear what you're saying about forgiving. I guess that's why I was staying up there at the house, trying to understand everything, you know?"

"I know, Derrick, and I'm here if you ever need me."

"I know, sis. I'm just working on some things right now. We will get together soon."

"Promise?"

Derrick laughed. "Promise, sis. But there's one thing I need you to know. No matter what happens, I want you to know I love you."

Halle smiled. "I love you, too. It's you and me against the world. Remember that."

"I will."

After ending the call, Derrick dropped his head. He hated lying to his sister, but there was no way she would understand. In Derrick's eyes, his mother left them that house for a reason. Hopefully, one day he could tell her. After that mild breakdown, Derrick felt good, as if that cry had cleansed his soul.

Therefore, he went back to planning his next kill, which was De'shell. Derrick found out she had moved into their grandparents' house along with Shameka and Anita. *Typical of them,* he thought while shaking his head, *but this makes it easier.*

$$*****$$

Thank you, Jesus! Derrick is finally coming around. Mr. Rubin was right. All he needed was some time. Hopefully, the time he spends in that house will help him have a better understanding about our parents. I have to admit that tape of our mother was scary. Shit, who does Derrick think he's kidding? There's no way he would pass up his share of an empire. He's holy, but not crazy, Halle thought.

Halle was happy to have met her other cousin, Greg. Surprisingly, she felt a connection to him, which was something she didn't feel with her other cousins. It was like God was giving her a fresh start on life. Boy oh boy, could she relate to Anthony's case being broadcasted all over the news and Internet. Some days she wanted to show up at the courthouse, but then she feared someone would recognize her and bring up that tape. Till this day, she worried about the video of her and her brother having sex resurfacing.

Her heart also ached for London and the others. She could only imagine what they were going through. Exhausted, all Halle wanted to do was go home, take a long hot bath, and curl up with her Harry Potter book.

Her cell phone rang with a number she did not recognize. Halle started not to answer it, but her gut told her to.

"Hello."

"Hi, Halle. This is Justine."

"Hi, Justine."

"I just wanted to apologize for my grandma's behavior."

"Awww, it's fine. How are you doing? How's your brother?"

"He's fine, but that's not why I called you. We wanted to know if you wanted to hang out."

"Sure. When?"

"Now. I know it's last minute, but we're bored to death. And with everything that has been going on, we just wanna have a good time."

Halle laughed. She could certainly relate. "Sounds like a plan. Where are we meeting?"

"Provocateur. Have you heard of it?"

"Yes. It's on 18th and Ninth Avenues."

"Yep, that's the place," Justine responded.

"Okay, see y'all there shortly," she said, then hung up.

"Yes!" Halle screamed.

It had been a long time since she had some fun. She pulled out her cell phone and called Greg, who picked up on the first ring.

"Greg," Halle said in an unsure tone.

"Yes."

"This is Halle."

"Halle, what's up? I was just thinking about you."

"Really? Wow. Listen, our other cousins, London and Justine, invited me out. I was wondering if you wanted to come."

"Sure. When?"

"Tonight."

"Tonight?" he repeated, sounding surprised.

"Yes. I know it's last minute, but they have been going through a lot and need to get out."

"Damn, tonight?" He frowned. Greg had already made plans. "I'm meeting one of my clients, but I will stop by afterwards, if that's alright."

"Sure. We're going to Provocateur. Do you know the place?"

"Of course. Grace owns it. I'll stop by after my meeting."

"Great! See you then."

Click!

*****

Instead of driving to the city, Halle called a car service. Although she had no intentions on drinking, she didn't feel like dealing with the hassle of looking for parking. Normally, there was a line of people outside waiting to get in. However, there was no one when Halle pulled up. She started to think she had the wrong address.

"Are you sure this is Provocateur?" she asked the driver.

He chuckled. "Yes. Only people with money come here."

Halle smirked at his comment. "Yes, only people with cash," she repeated while handing him a hundred dollar bill. "Keep the change," she said before hopping out the car like a star.

The bouncer ushered her in as if he knew who she was. "Right this way," he said, opening the door for her.

The place was glamorous with its black chandeliers and lavender sofas, giving it an exotic yet classy look.

"Halle!" Justine waved to get her attention.

"Hey, cousin," Justin said, dancing to Lil Wayne. "Glad you could come out."

Halle laughed. "Glad you invited me. Where's London?"

"Her boo called, so she went outside to talk to him."

The music was pumping.

"Halle, what you drinking?" Justin asked, prepared to get her the poison of her choice. "Nothing. Water will be fine," she told him.

Justin shot her a crazy look. "Water?" he repeated.

"Yes. I'm in recovery." Halle laughed at his shocked expression while she bobbed her head to the beat.

Justine overheard. "You, too?" She chuckled. "So am I. I'm in AA."

Halle's eyes widened. "What?! I'm in NA. This is crazy. Now I know we're related."

Both women gave each other high-five.

Justin smiled. "That's what's up," he said and then walked off to get the drinks.

A couple of minutes later, London joined them. She was so beautiful that every man's head in the place turned in her direction.

"Halle!" she cheered. "I'm so happy you came."

"Girl, you are stunning. You look just like your mother."

London blushed. "Thank you. You're beautiful, too."

Justine pulled out her camera to take a couple of photos of them. Justin returned with a glass of wine for him and London and bottle of water for Justine and Halle.

"To family," he said, raising his glass.

"To family," they repeated, toasting.

"What's up, everyone?" Anthony screamed as he approached them while doing his two-step.

They were surprised to see him. While Justin and London embraced him, Justine's mood instantly changed. Although she was cordial, Halle could tell something was up between them. However, it was a night of family and fun, so Justine put aside her feelings.

"Anthony, this is our cousin Halle," Justine said, introducing them.

"Our cousin?"

"Yes. She's our cousin on our mother's side. While you were out there spending money, we were locating our family," Justine sarcastically stated.

Shocked, Anthony smiled. "It's a pleasure to meet you, Halle," he said as he shook her hand.

★ ★ ★ ★ 129

"You, too. I heard so much about you. It's good to finally meet you."

Shit, he's fine as hell. Too fucking fine to be raping someone, Halle thought while trying not to stare at him. *The newspaper pictures don't do him any justice.*

They were about to hit the dance floor, when Greg joined them. London and Justine almost tripped over each other from staring at him. Greg was nothing but sexy in his black blazer, white t-shirt, and jeans. Like his father, Greg's presence spoke volumes. He had swag for days.

When Halle noticed Justine and London staring, she chuckled. "Chill out. That's your cousin Greg."

"Shit, he's fine. Are you sure?" Justine teased.

"Hello," Greg greeted with a smile.

Still gazing at him, London and Justine were speechless. Halle threw her head back in laughter.

"Greg, this is London and Justine," she finally managed to say.

Anthony and Justin, who were flirting with some girls, didn't see Greg.

"Anthony...Justin!" Halle called out, getting their attention. "Come. I want to introduce you to someone."

Both excused themselves and walked over to where the others were standing.

"This is our cousin Greg," she told them.

"What's up, man?" Justin said, giving him a pound.

"What's up?" Greg responded, returning the pound.

"Wow! Isn't this crazy?" London stated.

"Yes." Greg laughed.

"Greg, you want a drink?"

Feeling good, Greg replied, "Sure."

Happy to be around family, Anthony pulled out his iPhone. "I wanna get a picture of all of us."

Everyone laughed, but pulled out their cameras, also.

"Greg, where's your sister?" Halle asked.

Bopping his head to the beat, he responded, "I don't know. She's probably working. I called her and left several messages, but she hasn't returned my calls."

Anthony and Justin went back over to entertain the ladies, while Greg chatted with his cousin.

"Greg's sister owns this establishment," Halle told them.

Amazed, Justine and London looked at each other.

"Wow, that's great. I can't wait to meet her," London said.

They chatted it up for another hour before London and Greg called it a night. Meanwhile, Anthony and Justin disappeared into the crowd.

"Looks like it's only us two, Halle," Justine teased.

"Yep, it looks like that." Halle chuckled while looking around.

"I had a wonderful time tonight," Justine stated, grinning.

"Me, too."

Bursting into laughter, Justine added, "Now I'm starving."

"So am I. Let's get out of here and get something to eat," Halle suggested.

"Okay. Let me go close out the tab."

"Well, while you're doing that, I'm gonna run to the ladies' room," Halle told her.

While on her way to the ladies' room, Halle saw Anthony slobbing someone down in one of the back rooms. Just as she was about to enter the bathroom, she heard one of the employees say, "Look at Ms. Gracie getting her freak on." This caused Halle to stop in her tracks.

"Excuse me. You said that's Ms. Gracie, as in the owner Ms. Gracie?"

Realizing he had spoken his thoughts out loud, the employee stuttered for a second.

"No," he said before bolting out of there.

But, it was too late. Halle knew it was true. *Damn, Anthony's fucking his own cousin.*

Chapter Twelve

In her cabin house in Peekskill, New York, Gracie sat there thinking about the fact that Anthony was her cousin, but she continued to see him. Even worse, he was also a rapist just like his father. *If this ever gets out, I could lose everything,* she thought. But, she couldn't help it. Gracie was sprung. She didn't know why, but she had a weakness for cocky men with huge dicks.

Certainly, Greg would disown her. He couldn't stand men like Anthony.

But, with a man like Anthony in my life, together we could rule the world. Gracie sighed as thoughts of Anthony danced in her head.

She was in deep thought when she heard a knock at the door. At first, she thought the wind had tossed something against the door because no one knew about this place. It's where she would come to clear her head. As her father, Gracie was a loner.

When the person knocked again, Gracie hesitated for a second. *Maybe it's the park ranger checking on me.* She doubted it was her neighbors since the nearest house was ten miles down the road.

Gracie almost passed out when she opened the door and saw Anthony standing there.

"What are you doing here? How did you find me?"

Not saying a word, Anthony snatched her into his arms and tongued her down. Missing and wanting him, Gracie submitted, leading him into the house. As they groped and kissed each other,

Anthony picked Gracie up and carried her into the kitchen, sitting her on the counter.

Anthony then unbuckled his jeans, pulled out his fully erect penis, ripped Gracie's thong off, and forcefully thrust himself inside of her, causing her to gasp from the pain. Wanting her to take all of him, Anthony placed her legs on his shoulder and made her lean back to a ninety-degree angle. Grabbing a hand full of her hair, he made her look directly into his eyes while he slowly but forcefully stroked her. Gracie was in awe as pussy juice seeped out and down to her asshole. Anthony made love to her for the rest of the day.

While laying there in each other's arms by the fireplace, Gracie looked up at Anthony, who was sleeping. She knew what they were doing was wrong, but it felt so good. And sadly, Gracie wasn't about to give that up, telling herself no one was perfect. Besides, with the money and power they had, they could start a family and buy new friends. Smiling, Gracie leaned over and kissed Anthony on his lips, waking him.

"Hey!" He smiled, snuggling her into his arms.

"Hi." She returned the smile.

"You wore me out?" he jokingly told her.

Gracie laughed and then started to think about how he made her feel safe. Anthony noticed her silence.

"What are you thinking about?" he asked

"Us. How did you find me?"

"I put a device in you," he responded with a chuckle.

Gracie busted out laughing. "I bet you did." Then in a serious tone, she asked, "How are you holding up?"

Anthony faced her and leaned on his arm. "I would be lying if I said some days weren't harder than others, but I know in due time I will be cleared of all charges. I guess that's the price you pay when you have money."

Gracie nodded. "What do you mean?"

"Clarice and I have been seeing each other for year. When she realized it wasn't going anywhere, she claimed I raped her. As for the other women, they are looking for a pay off."

"Oh! How is your family holding up?"

Anthony took a deep breath. "Great. In fact, that night I saw you at the club, I met my cousins Halle and Greg. Can you believe it? After all of these years, I'm finally meeting my family."

Oh shit, Gracie thought, wondering if Greg told him about her. "How were they?" she asked, seeking more information.

"Actually, it felt good because I was surrounded by my brother and sisters, too. Everyone was very supportive. Look, I even have a picture of us" reaching for his Iphone

Gracie trying to hide her emotions replied, praying Anthony doesn't put two and two together. "That's great. In a time like this, you need family around you."

"Yes. What about you? Do you have any family or you were born an adult?" he teased.

Gracie playfully hit him. "No, silly. My parents live in Florida. I'm the only child," she lied.

"You're lucky. Both of my parents were killed. You don't know what I would do to have both of my parents."

"Both killed?" she repeated.

"Yes. I thought you knew what happened to my father."

With a straight face, Gracie replied, "I've heard stories, but I didn't know the truth."

"Yeah, I was about two years old when they were killed."

Gracie stared at Anthony. Judging by the tone of his voice, she could tell he was hurting. In her eyes, he was a kind, gentle, and loving person, whom she was falling in love with. *Damn, why does he have to be my cousin*, she thought.

Talking to him made her realize that although they were from two different worlds, Gracie and Anthony had a lot of things in common. It also made her realize Anthony was the man for her. She didn't care about his parents' past or what Anthony was accused of. She was determined to be with him. Therefore, she decided to take that secret to the grave with her.

*****

Whereas Gracie was planning a fairytale life with Anthony, Greg was getting reacquainted with his godmother and cousins. Right now, it was all about family, especially after his son Greg Jordan Brightman III was born.

Gracie was different. Lately, she had been very occupied and secretive. She also went out of her way to avoid Stevie. Stevie mentioned to Greg that every time she called Gracie, she was either busy, very curt on the phone, or didn't answer. Therefore, she stopped calling. Gracie was so tangled up in Anthony's web that she even missed Tracey's baby shower.

But, who was Gracie trying to fool? Greg knew she was up to something. He just didn't know what. Nonetheless, Greg couldn't focus on that anymore. He had a family to look after now. Tonight would be the first time Sadie, Stevie, and Halle would be under the same roof; they were all coming over for dinner. He invited Morgan's kids, too, but they had made other plans.

Sadie arrived first. "Where's my great-grandson?" she asked, smiling.

"He's upstairs sleeping."

Sadie laughed. "Well, that's what newborns do. Be grateful because that will change."

Sadie stared at her grandson. She was so proud of him. Not only was he a successful businessman, but Greg was a loving family man, also. When Sadie went upstairs to talk to Tracey, Halle and Stevie arrived a short while later. Immediately, Stevie knew Halle was Denise's daughter.

"Halle?" Stevie said as they waited for Greg to come downstairs.

"Yes," Halle answered in an apprehensive tone. "Are you a long lost cousin?"

Stevie giggled. "No, but I knew your mother Denise."

"Oh," Halle said with a sigh of relief. "Sorry. These past few months have been crazy."

Stevie nodded. "I know. Tell me about it."

By then, Greg and Sadie had returned to the room.

"Grandma, this is Stevie, our godmother," Greg informed her.

"Oh yes, I remember you," Sadie said, flashing a fake smile.

Stevie knew the smile wasn't genuine, so she gave her one back with a raised eyebrow.

"And this is Denise's daughter, Halle."

With her hand, Sadie covered her mouth that had dropped open. "Oh my God, little Halle!"

Halle blushed. "Hello."

Sadie reached out and hugged her. "I haven't seen you in years. How's everyone?"

Halle lowered her head, fighting back tears. "My grandparents passed about a year ago."

"Oh, I'm sorry to hear that," Sadie said in a sorrow-filled tone.

"What about your brother?" Stevie asked.

Halle stared at her for a second before responding, "He's fine."

Over dinner, they laughed and reminisced about the good ole days. Stevie and Sadie had them in tears with their stories. For Greg and Halle, it felt good hearing positive stuff about their parents.

The night was finally coming to an end, when Gracie walked in unannounced. "I guess my invitation got lost in the mail," she spitefully stated, glaring at everyone.

"Well, hello to you, sis. Maybe if you returned my calls, you would've known about the dinner," Greg shot back.

One thing about Greg, he was a nice guy until you pissed him off, and if Gracie didn't get her act together, she was about to find out what happened when you did.

Ignoring Greg's comment, Gracie sat down. "Tracey, you look stunning. How's my nephew doing?"

"He's fine," Tracey answered, while silently praying Greg would calm down.

"You don't see anyone else?" Greg asked in a stern tone.

"Oh, Stevie, how are you?" Gracie asked, then turned towards Halle. "Hello, I'm Gracie."

Halle looked around before responding, "Halle."

Sadie shook her head. Gracie was nothing but an ungrateful, spoiled little bitch. Sadie knew Gracie was trying to get underneath her skin, something she did when she was younger. But, that was not going to happen today.

Sadie smirked. "I'm gonna go check on my great-grandson," she stated.

Pissed, Greg glared at Gracie. "Next time you come in my house, you speak to everyone."

Gracie poured herself a glass of wine. "And if I don't?" she asked, taking a sip from her glass.

Greg smirked. "Watch it, sis. I'm not one of your little boys." The tone of Greg's voice told Gracie to calm down.

Stevie looked at Gracie and thought, *If Gabrielle were alive, she would've knocked the shit out of her.*

Avoiding the stares, Gracie asked Tracey to take her upstairs to see her nephew. After the ladies disappeared, a brief silence filled the room.

"I'm sorry about that," Greg finally said. "Halle, that's your cousin Gracie," he informed her while laughing.

"That's Gabrielle's daughter," Stevie mumbled.

"So did you tell Stevie that we met our other cousins?" Halle said, switching gears.

"Morgan's kids?" Stevie asked.

"Yeah. It was great," Greg stated.

"You heard about Anthony?" Halle asked Greg, changing the subject.

"Yeah. It's all over the papers. He appeared to be in good spirits the other night," Greg told them.

Stevie shook her head in disgust. "Boy, he's just like his fucking father."

Halle was baffled at her comment. "You knew Tony?"

Stevie and Greg looked at each other.

"Yeah. I used to date him back in the days," Stevie replied in a sickened tone.

By the tone of Stevie's voice, Halle knew it wasn't good. "Oh. Do you think it's true what they say about Anthony?"

"It won't surprise me. I mean, Tony Flowers is his father," Stevie sarcastically stated. "Guess Anthony got that honestly."

Greg and Halle confirmed her statement with a nod.

"So is it true about what Tony did to Morgan?" Halle asked.

"Yes. I was there when she told your mother. Denise was devastated. She considered Tony her brother," Stevie said. "It's funny because out of all the people in the world, Denise and Greg were the last people Tony should've crossed."

Greg looked at Halle. Both were thinking the same thing.

"What do you mean?" Greg asked.

"Everyone knew, especially Tony, that crossing Greg or Denise was like signing your own death certificate."

Meanwhile, Gracie bumped into Sadie upstairs.

"You know I won't apologize for the decision I made," Sadie told her.

"That makes two of us. Greg may have believed your lies, but I, on the other hand, know you're full of shit," Gracie snarled while walking away.

Gracie went downstairs, only to overhear Greg, Stevie, and Halle talking. So, she stood to the side listening. *Did my father and Aunt Denise have something to do with Tony's death? Did they kill Tony?* she wondered. Also, Stevie was starting to piss her off bringing up old shit about her man's father. She was going to ruin everything running her mouth, and Gracie wasn't going to let that happen.

Gracie waited until Greg walked Halle out, leaving her alone with Stevie.

"You're quiet," Stevie commented, trying to make conversation.

"Oh, I was just thinking about if you have a hidden agenda."

"I'm sorry. What do you mean?" Stevie asked.

With a glass of wine in her hand, Gracie strutted over to Stevie. "It's funny how you know all the secrets, but what secrets do you have hidden? Or maybe you're pissed that Tony married someone else, and from where I'm standing, I can see why he married someone as beautiful as Morgan. You don't look like his type," she snidely remarked. "Or maybe you're mad because you wanted to be like my mother or aunt, and didn't have the balls." Gracie looked her up and down.

Stevie laughed at Gracie's comment. Similar to Gabrielle, Stevie wasn't anything to fuck with, and Gracie needed to know it.

"Is that what you think? That I'm some jilted girlfriend who still lusted after Tony?" Stevie laughed. "You've lost your mind, but then again, a good dick can do that to you," she stated, making Gracie's eyes widen. "Oh yeah, I know about you and Anthony," she said, putting her hand over her mouth in mock surprise. "I wonder what your brother and everyone would think if they found out you're fucking your cousin. Now that's a secret."

"You don't—"

Stevie cut her off and leaned closer to her. "Tell me, did he inherit his father's bedroom skills? I mean, Tony did have a big dick and a long tongue. It's good, especially when you're not use to getting any. Is that what it is? With a good looking man like Anthony, I can see why you would go to great lengths to keep it a secret."

Gracie's silence confirmed Stevie's accusations.

Stevie laughed. "Yeah, it's that. Trust me, if you're not careful, little girl, big dicks can be deadly. Some can even cost you your life."

"You don't know what you're talking about. I would—"

Stevie laughed again. Gracie had so much to learn.

"Gracie, before you throw stones at someone's glass house,

make sure your house is clean. Nothing is a secret...nothing," she whispered. "Then you should know how crazy a woman can get when someone is coming between her and her big dick." "Gracie, do you know why I'm here and your mother isn't? Because I know when to leave shit alone. You're right. I do know all the secrets, so I think you should watch before you get spanked, " Stevie said, getting in her face. "You need to learn how to play if you're gonna play with me. You can talk to your grandma and brother like that, but not me. Because I eat little bitches like you I eat for dinner," she whispered. "Tell Greg I'll call him later." Stevie started to walk away, but then turned around to add, "One thing's for sure, you're nothing like your mother. Gabrielle was a woman with morals and class. You..." She paused to look her up and down with disgust. "...are nothing but a slut. You don't deserve to be called a Brightman."

Chapter Thirteen

Somehow Felix knew this day would come. In addition to his mental disorder, Anthony was also diagnosed with the same disorder O.J. Simpson had called *Intermittent Rage Disorder*. Felix was in the study when his mother entered with the Assistant District Attorney, who was heading up the case.

"Felix, I've asked ADA Aviles to come over so we can discuss Anthony's case."

Felix stood up and extended his hand. "Mr. Aviles, thank you for coming."

"Mr. Marciano," Mr. Aviles responded.

"Please have a seat," Mrs. Marciano told him.

"So tell me, what kind of time is my grandson facing, and is there a deal on the table?" Felix asked.

Time? Mrs. Marciano thought while shooting Felix a nasty look. "What my son means is how much will it cost us for you to toss this case?"

Feeling a little uncomfortable, Mr. Aviles became fidgety. "I'm sorry. I don't understand."

"Mr. Aviles," Mrs. Marciano said in a calm yet serious tone, "my grandson will never see the inside of a cell."

Just as Mr. Aviles was about to respond, Anthony walked in.

"Mr. Aviles, this is my grandson Anthony."

Mr. Aviles smiled. "Mrs. Marciano..."

"Just name your price, Mr. Aviles."

He cleared his throat, looking at all of them before answering. Anthony stood there with a smug look on his face, while Felix had an embarrassed expression on his.

"Mrs. Marciano, do you realize what you're asking me to do? I can lose my license or even go to prison."

Shrugging her shoulders, Mrs. Marciano answered, "Then don't tell anyone. Everyone has a price. Name yours."

Aware of the seriousness of this case, Mr. Aviles nodded. "I will not toss the case, but I can present a weak case. Although, I don't control the jury's decision."

Mrs. Marciano smiled. "You let me worry about that."

Mr. Aviles nodded and then smiled. That was his cue to leave. Mrs. Marciano signaled Anthony to walk Mr. Aviles out so she could talk to Felix.

"What was that all about?" she huffed.

Pissed with the whole situation, Felix stood up and snapped, "What was what all about, Mother?"

"You wanted to make a deal. The Marcianos don't make deals. I'm starting to wonder about you," she said, getting up to leave.

"That makes two of us. My daughter was raped and yet—"

"Don't chastise me about Morgan being raped, when I wanted to remove her from that house. I told you when she came here that something was wrong with her. But, you sent her back to those mullies," she scolded, pointing in his face.

Felix shook his head. For years, his mother had blamed him for Morgan's death among other things. However, this was different; she was condoning the very thing that had happened to Morgan. She knew Anthony had been sexually assaulting women. They had been paying them off.

Felix walked up to his mother. "One day, you're gonna learn money can't buy you everything."

"No, son. You're gonna learn everything has a price," she shot back before exiting the room.

Felix sat back down, folded his hands as if he was praying, and rested his face on them.

Meanwhile, Anthony, who had overheard the tail of the conversation, was fuming. "Grandma, is everything okay?"

"Of course, but I want to talk to you," she said, leading him to a private area.

Mrs. Marciano took a seat. "Anthony, I wanna tell you something. Felix was furious when he found out Morgan was pregnant by your father. He ordered her to have an abortion."

"Why?"

Mrs. Marciano took a deep breath, pretending like it was painful for her to discuss. "Because he was black."

"I don't understand."

Mrs. Marciano grabbed Anthony's hand, forcing him to sit down. "Felix was engaged to marry Jasmine, Morgan's mother, but found out she was cheating with another man who was black."

Anthony lowered his head. All these years, he had looked up to his grandfather as a father figure; and now to find out he was a racist bastard was quite disappointing. Mrs. Marciano smirked inside. She could tell Anthony was pissed, which was perfect for what she was about to plan.

"And now he wants to be King of your father's empire," she added.

"Well, he's not."

"No, Anthony. The only way to remove a King is...." She paused choosing a different approached "Even still, that can take years."

Anthony stared at his grandmother with a bewildered look. "So what are you suggesting?"

Mrs. Marciano sat back in her chair and said, "What do you think?"

With that, it was on.

*****

Though Anthony was hurt by what his grandmother revealed, there was no way he wanted his grandfather dead. There had to be another way. That's why he asked his siblings to meet him...so he could tell them about their grandfather. Ironically, this would be the first time Anthony went to the house in Alpine, New Jersey. For months, he had avoided this place. Anthony didn't want to remember his father like this.

He pulled up to the huge mansion and took a deep breath before getting out. Upon ringing the bell, he was greeted by Justine.

"Sis," Anthony sarcastically said.

Justine looked him up and down before walking away. He was dead to her years ago. Oblivious, Anthony shrugged Justine's attitude off and followed her. *She'll get over it,* he thought.

"Anthony," Justin said, coming out of a room. "How are you holding up?" he inquired, hugging his big brother.

"I'm good. Are you gonna be there in court?" Anthony asked.

"Of course, with bells on."

Anthony smiled while following his brother into the room to meet with the others.

"Anthony!" London chimed, running over to hug him. Ever since he had been charged with rape, London had been worried about him. "How are you?" she asked in a concerned tone.

"Good, sis. Knowing I got my family behind me, I'll be fine."

"You do. Trust, we will get through this," Justin chimed in, patting his brother on the back. "But, wasn't it great to finally meet our cousins?"

"Yes. I can't believe all these years we never met them," Anthony proclaimed.

Justine stood there with her hands folded; glaring at them, but everyone ignored her. Right now wasn't the time for Justine's childish behavior. Anthony was going through something serious. Even so, Justine didn't feel sorry for him.

"So what brings you here?" London asked. "Are you hungry? I was about to make us something to eat."

Anthony playfully roughed up his sister. "You know I love your cooking."

All pitched in to prepare a meal, and it actually felt good, even to Justine, who had put aside her feelings and joined them. It had been a long time since they laughed and snapped on each other.

Anthony looked around. "So this is where it happened?" he inquired in a melancholy tone.

A brief silence filled the room before everyone looked at each other and responded, "Yes."

"How can you guys stay here?" he asked.

"It's home, Anthony," London replied.

"What are we gonna do about the other properties?" Justin asked.

"I say keep them, especially this one. It's an historical place," Justine said.

"Yeah, like Gracie Mansion and Neverland Ranch," Justin joked, causing everyone to laugh.

Anthony took a deep breath. "Has anyone given any thought to running the business?"

When everyone sighed in unison, Anthony held up his hands. "Wait. Before you guys curse me out, I was wrong. I should've talked to you guys. But, in my defense, you always shoot me down. Don't you find it strange that Grandpa hasn't even considered turning it over to us? It's like he's hiding something," Anthony stated, setting the next plot up.

Judging by the looks on their faces, they were thinking about what Anthony had said. It also didn't help that they found out stuff about their parents that their grandfather didn't share with them. Maybe Anthony was on to something. Why was Felix hesitant to turn over control? It's not like they weren't educated to take over their father's business. Then again, was Anthony up to something? While London and Justin were somewhat in agreement, Justine thought, *Anthony is full of shit.*

"Wow, Anthony. We never looked at it like that," Justin said.

"Exactly. Now don't get me wrong, I'm grateful to Grandpa, even though I found out he didn't like our father because he was black. It's still our company and—"

"Whoa! Whoa! What do you mean he didn't like our father because he was black?" Justin asked with his face frowned up.

"I found out that our grandpa wanted Mommy to abort me because our father was black."

London and Justin looked at each other in total shock and then back at Anthony.

"If this is true, he isn't the only one," London commented.

"What do you mean?" Anthony asked.

London took a deep breath. "The night you were arrested, Halle came over for dinner, and Grandma referred to her as *'those'* people."

Anthony brushed it off. "She's old, London."

"No, Anthony. I confronted her, and she didn't deny it."

"Well, she told me that it's Grandpa who's the racist. He didn't want Mommy to have me because our father is black," he stressed.

Seeing through his bullshit, Justine blurted out, "Or maybe he didn't think Tony was your father."

London and Justin shot Justine an evil eye, but Anthony was getting tired of Justine's slick comments.

"Funny, I heard the same thing about you," he shot back.

London tightened her lips, scowling at Justine. "Okay, guys, let's not lose focus. Anthony, I think we need to have a seat down with Grandpa and Grandma. If both of them feel like that about our father, then I agree they shouldn't be involved in our father's company."

Fuming, Justine jumped up and shouted, "He's lying! Grandpa would never say that. He and Grandma are trying to get us to turn on Grandpa. Can't you see? Well, I'm not gonna allow you to do that. I will give it all away before I watch you destroy it," she warned and then stormed out, leaving them speechless.

******

Against his lawyer's advice, Anthony continued to stay in the public's eye, attending different kind of events. The only thing he hadn't done was be seen with a lady. That was only because he was dating Gracie. Over the past couple of months, they had become serious. Once the trial was over, Anthony decided he would go public with her. Certainly this would help with his image.

Anthony didn't want to admit it, but this trial was taking a toll on him. It didn't help that his grandmother kept pressuring him about killing Felix. Stressed out, he started using drugs frequently. When he wasn't sniffing, Anthony was drinking heavily.

Anthony had just received word that the jury was back with a decision, and he was scared like shit. Although his grandmother assured him everything would be fine, he still had an eerie feeling like something bad was about to happen. Faced with something like this, most people wanted to be around their loved ones. Anthony, on the other hand, preferred to be alone. Since his inheritance, Anthony never had the chance to soak it all in. So, he was sitting in his luxury penthouse alone with his thoughts. Suddenly, there was a knock at the door. Anthony sighed. *This apartment costs too much to have shitty-ass doorman service.*

Anthony ignored it, but the person knocked again, this time harder. He exhaled, figuring it was his grandmother or someone she sent to check up on him.

"Can I help you?" he asked upon opening the door.

"Anthony?" she said, recognizing him.

"Yes. Sorry, do I know you?" he asked, wondering how she knew his name.

"I'm Monique, and this is Michael. We're your aunt and uncle...your mother's siblings," she told him, getting his attention.

Anthony's eyes widened. "Oh, come in...please," he said, opening the door wider and waving for them to enter.

Unlike the reunion with the others, everyone felt awkward. "We won't keep you," Monique said, while Michael couldn't believe how much Anthony looked just like Morgan.

"Don't be silly. London and them told me that they found you."

"Yes," Monique said, then looked around with a saddened look.

Anthony noticed. "Is there something wrong?"

"The last time we were in this apartment was when Morgan died," Michael answered.

Anthony lowered his head. "I didn't know. Come in. Can I offer you something to drink?" he asked, changing the subject as he led them into the other room.

"No…no," Monique said. "We won't be long."

"No, please," Anthony insisted. "This is the first time I'm meeting someone from my mother's side," he answered, excited.

One thing for sure, Anthony had tons of pictures around the house of his family, causing Monique and Michael to smile.

"You have a Basquiat painting," Michael commented, noticing the framed artwork.

"Oh, yes."

"Your mother loved his work. In fact, your grandmother loved his work, too. She has a degree in Art History."

Anthony blushed in amazement. "Wow! I can't believe this."

"Me either. But, how are you doing?" Monique asked with a voice of concern.

Anthony shrugged his shoulder and lowered his head. "I'm holding up. It's in God's hands now."

"Yep. Don't worry. You will be fine. If you need anything," Michael said, "don't hesitate to— "

"I won't," Anthony said, interrupting him.

Again, there was an awkward moment of silence.

"Well, we won't keep you," Monique said, getting up to leave.

"Wait. You won't be in the courtroom tomorrow? I would love to have you there."

Michael and Monique looked at each other. "We tried but were told we couldn't. That's why we came to see you."

Puzzled, Anthony asked, "Who told you that? You're family."

"It's okay, Anthony," Michael said in a comforting tone. We know things are crazy right now, and with the media making up stories, we just wanted you to know we are here for you."

Anthony nodded. "Alright, but why don't you stop by here after court, please?"

"Okay, we will do that," Monique told him.

They hugged each other before exiting. Astonishingly Anthony felt good after seeing them. Maybe what he was going through was a blessing in disguise.

While getting ready for the next day, he heard his cell phone ring. It was his grandmother. He felt like sending it to voicemail, but knowing her, she would just call back.

"Hello, Grandma," Anthony answered in a dry tone.

"Why you sound like that? Is everything okay?"

"Yes, everything is wonderful. In fact, my mother's sister and brother just left here."

"Who, Monique and Michael?"

"Yes," Anthony responded.

"What made them stop by?" Mrs. Marciano asked.

"To see how I was holding up. They tried to come to the courthouse, but were turned away."

"Oh, that's sad, but be careful, Anthony," she told him.

"Why?"

"You have money, and money brings out the worst in people. A lot of family members are gonna contact you now. Remember, everyone has a hidden agenda."

Anthony rolled his eyes. "I don't think that was the case with them."

"Oh? Well, why didn't they reach out to you when you were a child? Where were they before the money?" Mrs. Marciano pointed out. "My number or address hasn't changed."

Anthony nodded. His grandmother was right. Where were they when he needed them? But then he remembered London saying they had found Monique and Michael.

"Anthony!" Mrs. Marciano called out, making sure he was on the line.

"I'm here."

"You know I love you, and I'm always here for you. Why don't you do a background on them first?"

While Anthony thought that was a little extreme, he agreed. "Okay."

"Great. I will get a friend of mine on it. Now get some rest. Tomorrow you will walk out that courtroom a free man."

"Are you sure about that?"

"As sure as the day my mother gave birth to me. Anthony," she said in a calm voice, "one thing you can always count on is Grandma. You will walk out that courtroom with me. Understand?"

"Yes, ma'am."

*****

"The courtroom is filled to capacity during the trial of the infamous Anthony Omari Flowers, Jr., who is accused of first-degree rape, sexual assault, and kidnapping. His father, rap legend Tony Flowers, was killed by his ex-girlfriend Christina Carrington in a murder-suicide. His siblings, London Justin and Justine, joined Mr. Flowers in court. Also in the courtroom are his grandfather Felix Marciano and his great-grandmother," the newscaster reported.

"It's hard to believe someone with great looks and with more money than some countries could do this," another reporter stated.

"Well, they say money doesn't fix everything."

"So true," the reporter agreed. "Now we take you inside the courtroom, where the key witness will be taking the stand momentarily."

"All rise!" the bailiff announced.

"You may be seated," the judge instructed as he took his seat and adjusted his robe.

"Clarice Brown, raise your right hand," the bailiff said as he prepared to swear her in. "Do you promise to tell the truth, the whole truth, and nothing but the truth, so help you God?"

"I do," she replied.

"You may be seated," the bailiff told her.

"Ms. Brown, how long have you known the defendant, Mr. Flowers?" the prosecutor questioned.

"For about a six years," Clarice responded.

"Intimately?" he asked.

"About five years."

"Can you tell us what happened on...?" The prosecutor paused to walk back to the table and pick up a piece of paper. "...October 21st?"

Clarice looked over at the jury. "I bumped into Anthony at a party at Trump Towers."

"And?" the prosecutor asked, prompting her to continue.

"We had a couple of drinks, and he invited me back to his place. I really liked Anthony, so I said okay."

"What happened when you got there?"

Clarice looked over at the jury again. "He started acting strange. He snorted some coke and ordered me to take off my clothes so he could snort some off my stomach."

"Did you do it?" the prosecutor inquired.

"Yes. I mean, I thought it was cool..." she said, her voice trailing off.

"What happened next?"

"He snorted a couple of lines off my stomach. Then he put some on his penis and asked to have sex with me."

"Coke?" he asked, wanting to be clear with her statement.

"Yes, and again, I said okay."

"Then what happened?"

"I started to feel numb down there and asked him to stop."

"Did he?"

"No. He flew into a rage and started choking me."

"Out of the blue, he just started choking you?"

Clarice began to cry. "Yes. I tried to remove his hands, but he overpowered me. He grabbed me by my neck and tossed me across the room."

Gasps echoed throughout the room, and some of the jury members looked over at Tony.

"Then what happened?" the prosecutor asked.

"He raped me," she said, breaking down on the stand.

"No further questions. Your witness," he told the defense attorney.

Bill Fish, Anthony's high-profile attorney, stood up, buttoned his suit jacket, and walked over to the witness. "Ms. Brown, you stated that out of the blue, my client started choking you and then raped you, correct?"

"Yes."

"So why did it take you three weeks to report the rape?"

"I was confused and scared," she responded. "Anthony is very powerful."

"Or is it because my client refused to give you any money?" Bill asked spitefully.

"That's not true! He raped me!" Clarice shouted.

"Your Honor, I would like to enter Exhibit L. This tape will show Ms. Brown plotting to extort my client. At first, she told him that she was pregnant. When that didn't work, she accused him of giving her an STD, and now rape."

As the tape started to play, mumbles filled the room. This time, everyone glared at Clarice. Women twisted their faces up, while men shook their heads.

"He did rape me!" Clarice cried. "Anthony is a monster!"

"Sure, he did," Bill responded sarcastically. "I have no further questions, Your Honor."

Anthony sat with a smug look on his face, staring at Clarice as she stepped down from the stand.

*****

It was the day when a jury consisting of twelve men and women would decide Anthony Omari Flowers' fate. He entered the courtroom accompanied by his family, friends, and legal team. Most people would've been nervous, but not Anthony. At his mother's request, Felix had everything covered. Five members on the jury had been paid off. Even the prosecutor had been paid off to present a weak case. So, either way, Anthony would walk away scot-free

"All rise!" the bailiff said.

"Has the jury reached a verdict?" the judge asked.

"Yes, Your Honor," the foreman replied.

"Will the defendant stand and face the jury," the judge instructed Anthony.

The courtroom was so silent you could hear a pin drop. Like the O.J. Simpson trial, this case had divided a country. Some believed greedy women were setting up Anthony, while others believed he was a serial rapist, with money, power, and political connections, who would get off.

Anthony looked back at his family. His great-grandmother nodded, letting him know everything was going to be fine.

"How do you find the defendant?" the judge asked.

The foreman stared into the defendant's eyes and then at the paper. She knew the world was watching and waiting. As she looked around at the victims in the courtroom, her eyes started to tear up.

"How do you find the defendant?" the judge repeated.

Before she gave the verdict, she said a silent prayer. *God, please forgive us.* Then she replied, "We, the jury, find the defendant not guilty."

The courtroom filled with mixed emotions. Some were crying, while others cheered.

"Order! Order!" the judge yelled, banging his gavel. "Mr. Flowers, the jury has found you not guilty. You are free to go."

Anthony hugged his attorney and then reached over to hug his great-grandmother.

"I told you only in America can you buy this kind of justice," she whispered in Anthony's ear.

Mobbed by the media, with his family and legal team proudly standing behind him, Anthony spoke with reporters.

"Anthony, how do you feel about the verdict?" one female reporter asked.

"I'm happy, of course. I'm happy to be able to put this behind me."

Bill interceded. "There will be a full press conference tomorrow. Thank you."

Family and friends went back to Anthony's penthouse to celebrate. There, Felix pulled Anthony aside.

"Got a second?"

"Sure, Grandpa," he said, walking with him to the other room.

"I think you should lay low for a while. Let things cool down," Felix suggested.

Anthony nodded before smiling.

"I'm serious, Anthony. Next time, you might not be so lucky," he angrily whispered while staring directly into his face.

"As long as I got money, I will always be lucky," Anthony replied arrogantly.

Felix laughed. "Your father would've said the same thing."

"Well, my father was a wise man."

Felix glared at Anthony. The only reason he didn't put a bullet in his grandson's head was because it would've broken his mother's heart. Anthony was everything Felix despised in a man.

"A.J.," he said, using his nickname, "you're my grandson, so I will always be there for you. But, if you rape any more women, I will not help you."

Anthony, being the self-righteous bastard he was, stepped up to Felix. "Help? My father left me a shitload of money. What makes you think I need your help?"

Felix released a devilish chuckle. "You are your father's child...a punk who raped women."

"My father never had to rape women, just like I don't. They just need help saying yes."

It infuriated Felix to hear Anthony praise his father. Maybe if he knew the truth, he might think differently.

"Your father always felt he had to have the best. That's why he's not here today, because the best cost him his life. Now you listen to me, you punk motherfucker. It's only because my blood runs through you that I tolerate your ass. Because if I had it my way, your sorry ass would be spending the rest of your life in prison where you belong with the rest of the niggers."

Anthony smiled. "Now I know how you've really felt about me all of these years. It killed you that my mother married a black man. I knew you were a racist bitch. You never liked my father because he was black."

"No, I never liked your father because of what he did to my daughter," Felix quickly interrupted.

"Bullshit! My father treated my mother like a queen. You didn't like him because he was black. But, that didn't stop you from taking over his estate."

"Is that what you think?" Felix started to tell him the truth, but changed his mind.

"Well, my mother loved my father, and it's because of her that I don't take you out of your misery," Anthony shot back.

"Watch it, boy. Before I forget—"

Anthony jumped in his grandfather's face. "I already did. Now get the fuck out of my house before we do something we both regret."

Felix smirked. Anthony didn't know who he was dealing with.

"There's my favorite great-grandson," Felix's mother cheered, entering the room.

"Hi, Grandma," Anthony said, kissing her on the cheek.

"Be a dear and get your grandma something to drink."

"Sure," he told her, then glared at Felix before exiting.

Once Anthony was out of sight, Felix's mother turned towards him. "What was that all about?"

"That young punk has the nerve to challenge me, when it's because of his fucking father that my daughter is dead."

"Felix, he's your grandson."

"Don't remind me."

Still steaming, Anthony went into the other room to cool off and take a hit.

"Anthony?" London said, knocking on the door before opening it.

With white powder on his nose, he replied, "Yeah."

"You never did stop," London snapped.

"What is it, London?" Anthony said, tired of everyone judging him. "What the fuck you want now?"

"You're a son of a bitch, you know that?" London yelled.

By that time, his brother and sister had joined them.

"What the fuck?" Justin said.

"Alright, so I'm caught. Considering the amount of stress I've been under, I deserve a little recreational play."

Everyone looked at him in disgust, while thinking the same thing. *What's the point? Anthony is going to be the cause of his own downfall.*

"Fuck you," Anthony screamed under the stares of the judgmental eyes. "Fuck all of you! This is my father's empire, and he left it to me! I am the king of this empire!"

Standing afar and listening, Felix thought, *And sometimes kings needs to be overthrown.* He'd had enough of Anthony's shit. This case just made Anthony believe he was untouchable. He knew Anthony wasn't going to stop hurting women, and Felix wasn't about to let that happen. It was time to tell the kids the truth, and hopefully, they would help their brother.

Chapter Fourteen

Halle shook her head. Her aunt De'shelle waited almost two weeks to tell her about Ronisha, and the only reason why De'shelle called was because they were going to put a lien on the house if they didn't pay the taxes the next day. It really sickened Halle the way they just moved in right after her grandparents. Although Halle felt like they deserved to be on the street, there was no way she would allow her grandparents' house to be auctioned off. Until she and Derrick could figure out what to do with the house, Halle would pay the taxes. They were lucky Halle was in a giving mood, or else they would've been fresh out of luck.

She reached out to Derrick, letting him know what happened and about the house. Indeed, he was sad, but he didn't offer to help. One thing for sure, Halle wasn't putting any money in their hand. She was going to fly down there tonight, check on the house, handle her business, and catch the next flight back to New York.

Halle exhaled and glanced at her watch. *How the hell am I gonna pull this off?* It was going on three o'clock, and she still hadn't left the house. One her peers were celebrating a year clean, and Halle had promised to stop by. She needed to drop off the contract at Greg's office and submit her clients' weekly progress notes to her supervisor.

Halle's phone rang, and she growled. "Who is this now?" she grumbled, searching for her keys. It was Justine. With her being so busy, Halle hadn't spoken to her cousin in a while.

"Hi, Justine," she answered.

"Hi, Halle. How are you?"

"I'm great! I read Anthony was acquitted. I know you're happy."

"Yeah, I guess, but that's not why I called you," Justine told her. "I was wondering if you and I can go to eat or take in a movie?"

Halle looked at phone and thought, *Now?* She really had to go home and pack, but the tone of Justine's voice really sounded like she needed someone to talk to.

"Okay, but I can't stay long. I have to catch a flight to Atlanta tonight. They're gonna put a lien on my grandparents' house if someone doesn't pay the taxes."

"Dag, okay. Next time?"

"Sure," Halle responded.

"Well, call me if you need anything."

Click!

***** *

Meanwhile, Derrick was in Atlanta. He'd been there for the past couple of days. He waited until it was dark outside before entering the house. Dressed like the Omen, Derrick surprised everyone.

"Derrick!" His aunt Anita smiled, showing her missing tooth. "What brings you down here?"

With a somber look on his face, Derrick just nodded while assessing the area. "Just checking up on my loving family."

Anita led him into the other room, where De'Shell and Shameka were sitting.

Damn, they tore this house up. It looks fucking disgusting, he thought.

Just as he was about to grab Anita and choke the life out of her, De'shell popped up out of her seat. "Derrick! Damn, you just missed Kasheem and Diamond. They went to Diamond's old man's house," she said.

Lucky them. Derrick flashed a wicked grin and kissed her on the cheek. Unfortunately, it would be the last kiss. He looked at his mother's two sisters. Only if they knew if it weren't for his grandparents, they would've been gone a long time ago. Sadly, there was no one to save them tonight. Derrick was determined to carry out his mother's wishes.

Look at them, Derrick thought to himself. *They grew up to be pieces of shit. I'll be doing them a favor by putting them out of their misery. Shit, they look dead already. Anita looks like she has the monster (HIV), and De'shell looks like a pimp beat the life out of her.*

Shameka, who was talking on her phone, looked like a dope fiend. "Is that my mother's fucking cousin?" she asked." I heard you a preacher now."

"Yes, I am a man of God with sinister talent." He smirked, confusing them.

"Ooookay," Shameka said, then returned to her phone conversation.

"Alright, I'm gonna go upstairs to take a long, hot bath," Anita informed
Derrick."Are you staying the night?"

Looking around he knew there was no way in hell he was staying in that rat hole.

"Uh, no," he answered.

Once Anita left, Derrick talked to De'shell for a couple of seconds before making an excuse to go upstairs. Knowing his room would look like shit, Derrick went anyway. It was worse than he thought; clothes, food and beer bottles were everywhere. *Damn, they destroy everything they touch.* Remembering his mother's words of advice, he checked every room in the house. The last thing he needed was any surprises. Derrick pulled out the cross from under his shirt, held it tight, and silently prayed for the sin he was about to commit. Then he walked into the master bedroom; Anita was in the master bathroom's Jacuzzi.

Another rule his mother stated was to always use gloves so you don't leave any fingerprints. Pulling out a pair of gloves from his pocket, Derrick put them on. Anita, unaware of her destiny with faith, had her iPod on full blast and her eyes closed. Derrick, who was now standing over her, dropped to his knees and forced her head under the water while reciting a scripture from the book of Revelations. She struggled for a few seconds before her body just floated.

"Your sins have been forgiven," he mumbled, sweaty and wet.

He went out to his car, opened the truck, and got two gallons of gasoline. Then he went back inside. Clueless as to what happened upstairs, De'shell took her sleeping medication dosed off into sleep in the family room, while Shameka was still on the phone in the other room. De'shell didn't smell or feel Derrick pouring gasoline around the couch and on her. As he reached into his pocket to get a match, Shameka entered.

"What are you doing?" she asked, smelling gasoline.

"I was…" He tried to think of a response, but Shameka saw the two containers of gasoline by his foot.

"Oh my God!" She tried to make a dash for it, but Derrick snatched her by her weave.

"Where are you going?" he said, putting her in a full nelson.

Cutting off her air supply with his bicep, he snapped Shameka's neck like a chicken. She wiggled for a second before her spirit left her body.

"Your sins have been forgiven." Derrick dropped her lifeless body to the floor.

Then a voice screamed, "Derrick! What have you done?"

He turned to look. It was Halle standing there with her hand covering her mouth.

In a psychotic state of mind, a sweaty Derrick turned around while breathing heavily.

"Halle…" he gasped.

"Derrick! What…" Completely paralyzed, a teary-eyed Halle couldn't speak.

 162

Perturbed, Derrick slowly walked towards De'shell, reached into his pocket, and pulled out some matches. "Halle, they ruined our lives. Mommy would've wanted this."

Distraught, Halle shook her head and cried, "No, Derrick!"

Angry and deranged, Derrick yelled, "Yes! She told me." He looked like Jack Nicholson in *The Shining*. "Now, either you're with me or against me. Either way, I'm gonna send them all to hell. The question is, Halle, are you going with them?" he asked, tossing a lit match onto De'shell.

The intense pain of her burning flesh caused De'shell to wake up screaming in pain and rolling about.

"Derrick...we have to go," she said as the fire ignited. "Derrick!" she screamed, afraid the police were going to come in a couple of seconds.

Finally coming to his senses, Derrick nodded. "Let's go."

Halle looked over at Derrick, who had completely lost his mind. There was no way in hell she was letting him drive.

"I'm driving," Halle said in a stern voice.

Derrick looked into Halle's eyes. She, too, had a temper. He looked back at the house. It would only be a matter of time before the fire engulfed the house. He tossed her the keys and then jumped into the passenger's seat. They hauled ass out of there.

Scared to death, Halle drove fifteen hours back to New York. If she didn't have to stop for gas, she would've been there sooner. There was no way she was taking Derrick's ass to her house. So, she drove straight to the house outside of New York. As for Derrick, he slept like a baby on the ride home.

While pulling up to the house, she said a silent prayer. Then she looked over at Derrick who was still sleeping. *He has completely lost his mind.*

She nudged him awake. "We're here."

Oblivious to where he was, Derrick looked around. "Where are we?" he asked in a groggy voice.

"Where you think?" she retorted, getting out of the car.

Once inside, Halle lit into Derrick ass. "What the hell is wrong with you? Have you lost your fucking mind?"

Standing there like a child being scolded, Derrick twiddled his thumbs as he stared down at the floor.

"What is wrong with you, Derrick? Do you understand if they find out what you did, you're going away for life? Haven't you learned anything from that last incident?"

"They deserved it, Halle!" he exclaimed. "They deserved it!"

"Who said, you? Now your God?" Halle griped.

"Mommy. You saw her on tape," he pointed in the direction of the television. "She said if it wasn't for Grandma and Grandpa, she would've killed them a long time ago. I just finished what she started."

Halle nodded. Now it was all starting to make sense. "So is this why you went to Mr. Rubin, to get the tapes? To finish what Mommy started? Is that what you call forgiving her, carrying out her wrath?"

Derrick removed his shirt. "I don't have time for this now, Halle," he said, tossing his shirt on the chair. "I'm doing what my mother would've wanted. You don't think she left us this house for a reason? She knew people like Kasheem, Diamond, and Tony exists in this world!" he yelled, picking up the tapes and tossing them across the coffee table. "And it's people like us who they are always hurting. Our fucking cousins!" he shouted, pounding on his chest as if he was an ape in the jungle. "They made us have sex with each other. Tony raped our cousin, and for what?" he said, spit flying from his mouth. "Because they can. Well, not me, sis. I'm done being their fuckin' sucker. So, yes, I'm gonna continue my mother's wrath," he warned, staring intensely into Halle's eyes. "I'm gonna send them all to hell. Hopefully, when they get there, Mommy can finish them off."

Halle nodded. It was pointless arguing with him. She slowly walked up to him. "You do that, Derrick. I don't want any part of it. But, if you ever," she warned, grinding her teeth, "ever threaten me again, I guarantee not even praying will not save you." Rolling her eyes, she then exited the house.

Pissed, Derrick punched the wall, while outside; Halle hopped in her car and sped off. She had to get out of there before she did something she would regret. Further down the road, she pulled over and broke down in tears. Just when life seemed like it was going good, this shit happened. Right now, Halle could use a hit and a stiff drink. But, no, she'd come too far to let anyone jeopardize her sobriety. Times like this she needed to talk to someone when she started thinking about picking up. But who could she talk to? This wasn't easy. It's not every day you find out your brother just committed murder. Then she thought about Mr. Rubin, who had been there from day one. Halle drove out to see him, praying he could make sense of all this.

Mr. Rubin was in the garden when Halle arrived.

"Hi, Mr. Rubin," she said, getting his attention.

"Oh, Halle, I didn't even hear you come in. How are you?" he greeted, struggling to get up.

Halle ran over to help. "I'm good. Mr. Rubin, I need to talk to you."

Mr. Rubin knew something was wrong by the sound of her voice. Not to mention she looked like hell, just as Denise did when she was in trouble.

"Halle, is something wrong?"

Trying to keep it together, Halle said, "Mr. Rubin, its Derrick. He's done something terrible"

Mr. Rubin led her over to the table. "What is it?"

Halle exhaled. "Derrick killed my aunts and cousin. He feels like that house she left us was her way of saying we should continue her wrath. Mr. Rubin, was she a murderer?"

Mr. Rubin rubbed his face. He was afraid this would happen. It's not every day he had to tell someone's child that their parent was considered one of the most dangerous people in the world.

Before he started, Halle made a statement. "Mr. Rubin, no matter how hard it is, I need to know the truth."

Mr. Rubin nodded. "Fair enough. Denise was something else."

"Mr. Rubin!" Halle said, getting frustrated.

"Yes, she killed, but she wasn't like these other killers out here. You had to cross her. Denise had to feel as if her life was threatened."

Halle got up and started pacing. "And that's supposed to make me feel better. Look at Derrick. There's only two ways he's gonna end up, dead or in prison. Is that what our mother wanted for us? I thought you said she loved us, that we were the best part of her. Why would she do this?"

"I don't know. I do know people like Denise and Greg in this world. Halle, I've been a lawyer for over thirty years, and I've watched innocent people get hurt. Take the case with you and Derrick. Because your cousins were jealous they set out to ruin you. What if I didn't have the money to pay them off? You guys would've still been in jail. And for what, because you defended yourself?" He stood up and walked over to a shaken up Halle. "In the world we live in, sometimes justice isn't always served."

"Yes, but that's not up to us to decide. God will handle them."

"Sometimes God takes too long."

Halle left Mr. Rubin's house more confused than ever. While she did agree with him, there was no way she believed there was anything right about what Derrick was doing. He was taking people's lives. No matter what anyone said, Derrick was heading down the same road as her mother, and Halle couldn't allow that to happen.

Exhausted from not having slept in twenty-four hours, Halle went straight home. Derrick's bullshit would have to wait until the morning. After arriving at home, she immediately took a shower. However, afterwards, she tossed and turned in the bed. Not even a nice hot shower could put her to sleep. She couldn't get those images out of her head.

Worried about Derrick, Halle got dressed and drove back up there. As she pulled up, she noticed a car parked in front of the house. It hadn't been there when she left. Then again, Halle got out of there so fast that she wouldn't have recognized it. Then she heard cries coming from the house. It sounded like Derrick.

Is he praying again? After what he did, he should be, she thought.

But, there was something strange about his cries. Halle listened closely and heard what sounded like something cracking.

"I told you, nigga, I was gonna get your ass back."

"Fuck him up," a lady's voice cheered on.

Immediately recognizing the voice, Halle gasped. It was Kasheem and Diamond. "Oh my God," she muttered as Derrick's cries grew louder. "They are torturing him," she cried.

She had to do something, but what?

"Ahhh!" he screamed as Kasheem smashed his skull with a crowbar.

Halle frantically looked around for something she could use as a weapon. "Shit!" she yelled, hitting the steering wheel. Then she tried to calm down. "Halle, think. Think, Halle," she said, talking to herself. Then it dawned on her that this was Derrick's car. She looked in the back, but there wasn't anything there. *Maybe it's in the trunk.*

Again, Halle heard Derrick's cries. She was running out of time. Derrick would be dead soon if she didn't take action. She popped open the trunk and got out of the car, praying they didn't see her.

"Yes, here's a gun." Halle looked into the sky. "Thank you."

She picked it up gun and having watched enough movies, she knew to check the safety latch. *My only chance is the element of surprise,* she thought before going in.

Untrained and outnumbered, Halle realized this wasn't any movie. Running up in there could get them both killed. So, Halle crept around to the back door.

"Please let this door be open," she mumbled. "Yes," she said as the knob turned.

While tip-toeing inside, Halle could see Derrick. He was shirtless and tied to a chair. They were taking turns hitting him. Blood was everywhere. Halle pointed the gun at them.

When Kasheem spotted her, he yelled, "Bitch," and charged at her, but the bullet that entered his stomach caused him to drop to his knees.

By then, Diamond saw her. Halle fired another shot, hitting her in the throat. Her hand was trembling so bad that she didn't even think she would hit them.

Once she saw they were down, Halle went to check on Derrick. His skull was crushed, his eyes were closed, and he had numerous stab wounds in his torso.

Crying, Halle kneeled down. "Derrick…"

"Sis…" he whispered in pain.

"I'm gonna call the ambulance," she said, trying to untie him.

Derrick murmured, "No, let me go. I won't make it."

"No, Derrick," Halle said as tears rolled down her cheeks.

Derrick nodded and swallowed hard. "Please, Halle, I wanna go home. I wanna go be with Mom and Dad."

"No, Derrick!" Halle pleaded, falling in his lap.

"Sis, please. You were right. It has to stop."

Halle looked in Derrick's face as she gently massaged his wounds. He was the only family she had left.

"Halle, please," he struggled to say, while coughing as blood and fluid filled his lungs. "It has to stop…"

Numb, Halle nodded and wept. Then she grabbed the gun and stood up, facing him. A single tear dropped from Halle's eye.

"Have…my…sins…been…forgiven?" he gasped, coughing up more blood.

Nodding and crying, Halle replied, "Yes, Derrick." Then she raised the gun to his head. "Your sins have been forgiven."

She fired a shot into his chest, silencing him.

She looked over at Diamond, who was groaning in pain. Halle walked over and stood over her.

"Halle…" Diamond cried as if begging for her help.

Halle fired two shots into her head and then Kasheem's. She then went back over to her brother, untied him, and held him in her arms.

Chapter Fifteen

So you eat bitches like me for lunch, huh, Stevie? Well, swallow this, Gracie thought. In her line of business, Gracie came across some hungry, crazy people who were willing to anything for a dollar. Unlike her parents, Gracie didn't believe in getting her hands dirty. She had too much money for that. Therefore, she hired a couple of goons from Miami to take care of Stevie and Sadie.

Gracie wanted it to be quick and painless. However, before they left this earth, Gracie wanted Stevie and Sadie to know it was her who was sending them to hell.

Gracie received word saying Stevie was at her condo in Miami. Ironically, Gracie and Anthony were five buildings down from her condo. Once Gracie gave the order to go ahead with the hit, the men wasted no time busting in the apartment. Luckily, Stevie was in there by herself.

They carried Stevie out to the balcony. One of the hit men pulled out his cell phone and called Gracie. "You ready?" he asked her.

"Yes," Gracie replied. She grabbed her binoculars off the table and walked on to the balcony. "Put that bitch on."

"Hello," a shaken Stevie said.

"Tell my parents I said hello." Gracie smiled.

"You bitch!" she shouted.

"Mrs. Bitch to you."

Click!

From afar, Gracie watched as two huge men dragged Stevie back into the room. Although she wanted them to toss her off the balcony, the men opted not to. They weren't sure if someone was watching. So, they took Stevie back inside and executed her.

"What are you looking at?" Anthony asked, hugging and kissing her from behind.

Gracie laughed. "Oh, nothing."

*****

Greg was devastated to learn about the death of Stevie. He knew something was wrong when she didn't return his call. According to her husband, not only did they kill her, they beat her up so bad that there had to be a closed casket.

Greg, Tracey, Gracie, and Sadie attended the service. It was beautiful. They finally got a chance to meet her two beautiful children that got up and spoke about their mother. Greg hurt for Stevie's husband, who didn't even cry. Greg figured he was still in shock.

While Greg and the others went back to the house, Gracie hopped on a private jet to Fuji, where she was meeting Anthony. They were staying at his private island. Greg felt she was being very insensitive, but Gracie couldn't care less. Stevie wasn't anything important to her.

The death of Stevie made Greg value life even more. Yes, he was a millionaire, but in his eyes, friends and family made him rich. That's why he made sure he was home every night with Tracey and his son.

Greg was getting ready to leave the office, when Klein came in.

"Greg, have you heard from Halle? I've been calling her for two days. Her phone is going straight to voicemail."

"No, I haven't."

Klein did a motion with his hands, turning them up with his palms open. "Well, if you do, please let her know the contracts are ready for her to pick up."

"Alright."

That's strange, Greg thought while on his way to the elevator. Just as he was about to get on the elevator, he turned and went back into the office.

"Klein, you have an address for Halle?"

Klein searched for her file on his cluttered desk. "Yeah, here," he said. "Is everything okay?"

"I'm sure it is. I'm just gonna check on her," Greg responded, not wanting to alarm Klein.

When Greg pulled up to Halle's house, all the lights were off, but her car was in the driveway. He looked down at the paper to make sure he had the right address. *Yep, this is the place.* He got out and rang the bell, but no one answered.

"Guess she isn't home," he muttered and started back toward his car.

As he was walking, another car pulled up. It was Justine.

"Greg!" she called to him as she jumped out of her car. "Have you seen, Halle? We were supposed to meet for dinner, but she never showed."

"No, and her phone is going straight to voicemail."

"Maybe she's still in Atlanta," Justine said.

As they turned to walk to their cars, they heard what sounded like glass breaking. They looked at each other from a brief moment and then quickly ran to the house.

"Halle!" Greg shouted while banging on the door.

"Halle, are you okay?" Justine yelled.

Suddenly, they heard the locks being unlatched. Then the door opened and Halle emerged wearing bloody clothes. Justine and Greg looked at each other in shock.

"He's gone. My brother is gone," she cried, falling into Greg's arms.

Greg and Justine looked around to make sure no one was outside, and then took Halle back into her house. She had been sitting in the living room since the incident. In order to find out what happened, they needed to clean Halle up. Justine took her

up to the bathroom and bathed her, while Greg looked around the house for clues.

Finally, Justine and Halle come down to the living room.

"Halle what happened," Greg asked. "What are you talking about?"

Still in distress, Halle mumbled, "Derrick…he's dead."

Greg and Justine looked at each other again.

"Dead?" Greg repeated. "What do you mean he's dead?"

Halle sniffled and threw her head back. If she didn't tell someone, she was going to go crazy. She took a deep breath, but as she was about to say something, there was a knock at the door, causing all of them to jump. Greg got up and walked over to look out the peephole. It was an old white man with a cane standing outside.

"It's a white man," he turned and said before opening the door.

"I'm looking for—"

"Mr. Rubin!" Halle jumped up and ran over to hug him. "Mr. Rubin," she cried.

"What's wrong?" he asked, leading her back into the house.

Greg and Justine just looked at them, but didn't comment.

"Sorry, guys. This is Mr. Rubin. He knew our parents," Halle explained. "Mr. Rubin, this is…"

Mr. Rubin looked at Greg. "My God, you look just like him," he said, cutting Halle off while extending his hand. "You are Greg's son."

Greg smiled. "Yes."

"And this is Tony's daughter, Justine."

"How are you? I knew your father," he said.

"Mr. Rubin, please take a seat," Halle told him, noticing him struggling to stand.

"Now, Halle, what's going on? I heard there was a fire at your grandparents' house that killed your aunts and cousin."

Halle looked them in the face; she knew they were waiting for an answer. But, where would she begin without revealing

Morgan's secret. Again, she heavily exhaled before starting to explain. By the time she finished, they all had an expression as if they had seen a ghost.

"The bodies are still at the house?" Mr. Rubin asked.

With tears rolling down her face and while nodding, she answered, "Yes."

Mr. Rubin lowered his head. "I was afraid this was gonna happen. I told Greg to make Denise get rid of that house years ago."

"Wait. You said you told my father?" Greg asked.

Now it was Mr. Rubin's turn to explain. "Like I told Halle, there was so much more to y'all parents than people knew." He raised his hand. "That doesn't mean they didn't do a lot of shit. Excuse my French. But, if you measure up the two," he said, demonstrating, "the pros outweigh the cons. Your father was many things, but as I said to Halle, Greg and Denise were different. Back when your father was growing up, things were different. A lot of people sold drugs; it wasn't just a Black or Hispanic thing."

"Let America tell it," Justine grumbled.

"Who, the government? Shit, they were the users," Mr. Rubin humored, making them giggle. "But, aside from that, your father was a honorable man. He believed in people. If it weren't for him, there would be no Tony Flowers."

"My father?" Justine said.

Mr. Rubin leaned forward. "Yes. That was Greg's company; he was the one who saw the talent in Tony. He was the one who encouraged him to get out of the street life. He did the same thing for Denise. Your father," Mr. Rubin preached, "was a father to a lot of people. Yeah, he made everyone in his circle get their high school diploma. Denise even went on to get her Master's." Mr. Rubin leaned toward Greg. "What man you know would accept a life sentence knowing he didn't committee the crime? Greg could've brought a lot of people down, but he didn't," he said, raising an eyebrow.

Greg listened and stared intensely into Mr. Rubin's eyes. "I didn't know that," Greg said.

Mr. Rubin slapped his knee. "Of course, you didn't, because they won't tell that. But, I was there. I remember going to see your father when he was in Riker Island. I told him to talk, but he looked me straight in the face and said he would rather do his time as a man than live out there free as a coward. You see, most people didn't understand there's only two outcomes in that lifestyle: death or prison. Greg and Denise did."

"I was telling Greg it was you who told us about our inheritance," Halle said.

Mr. Rubin giggled. "Denise was something else. She was smart, loving, and loyal, but don't fuck with her. I've watched her blossom into a strong black woman. Before her death, she liquidated her assets and put them in a trust fund for the kids. She made sure I was the executor of her estate."

"Why?" Greg asked.

"Because she knew what you do in the past can sometimes affect your future. She knew I would make damn sure her children got what they deserved, and money can bring out the worst in people, especially family members," Mr. Rubin stated, raising an eyebrow.

They nodded in agreement. Mr. Rubin had clarified so much stuff for them.

"What about my mother Gabrielle?" Greg inquired.

Mr. Rubin chuckled. "Now Gabrielle…she wasn't your average wife. She loved your father; she kept him grounded. Most girls all they care about are clothes and money. But, not Gabrielle. She went to school, became a lawyer, and made her own. In fact, she was the one who brought your father home. She believed in family. She loved your father so much that she stopped speaking to hers."

"Yes, so I heard. I didn't know she was the one who brought him home," Greg said.

"Yes, and she had very high standards that she would never lower for anything." Mr. Rubin stared directly into Greg's eyes. "Let me tell you something, son," he said, sensing something was wrong with Greg. "Your parents were the kindest people you would want to know. But, if you ever crossed them, you would regret it." He turned to Halle. "Well, I think I said enough. Don't worry about anything. I'll handle it."

"Mr. Rubin..."Halle said.

He winked. "I owe this to your mother..." he told her before leaving.

Astonished, they all sat there quietly while absorbing everything that had just been told to them.

"So now what?" Greg asked.

"I don't know. I tell you one thing, our life will never be the same after tonight." Justine sighed, still stunned.

"Guys, I know I have no right to ask you to keep a secret like this. So, if you feel like going to the police, it's fine."

Greg and Justine looked at each other. They couldn't lie. This wasn't a little secret. People had lost their lives. However, after hearing her story, they didn't blame her. Especially Greg, he didn't know what he would do if his own family hurt him.

Greg moaned and then said, "It's cool, Halle. Your secret is safe with me."

"Me too," Justine agreed.

Halle got up and embraced them. "Thank you," she cried.

"Are you sure you're gonna be okay?" Greg asked, preparing to head home.

"Yes," Halle told him.

"Call us if you need anything," Justine said.

Halle nodded and then hugged them again. Since they agreed to keep her secret, it was only right she told Justine about hers. Before she walked them out, Halle went over to her bag that was on the table and pulled out a couple of tapes and a dairy.

"Here," she said, handing them to Justine. "You should see this. It will explain everything."

Baffled, Justine nodded and took the tapes. "Okay."

*****

On his way home, Greg played everything back. Although the past couple of months had been interesting, he wouldn't have it any other way. For years, he wondered about his parents. Now to hear how his mother fought for his father to come home and how his father had inspired so many lives made Greg smile. He even chuckled at Mr. Rubin; his father had a white man praising him.

And Halle had been through hell, having lost her entire family in less than three years. While she didn't know it, Halle was strong as a motherfucker. Guess that's why Greg felt a special connection to her as he did Stevie.

Greg also wondered if Mr. Rubin knew about Tony raping Morgan. Greg was sure he knew. He was just happy Mr. Rubin didn't reveal it. Greg couldn't handle any more drama.

Tracey had just put their son down for bed, when Greg entered the house.

"Shhh, he's sleeping," she said.

Realizing how truly blessed he was, Greg ran over to kiss his wife and son.

*****

Meanwhile, Gracie and Anthony had fallen deeply in love. She'd never felt this way about any man. With Anthony, Gracie let her guard down. She wasn't the exclusive cocky bitch people perceived her to be. She put away the iPad, five-inch pumps, and diamond earrings. Around him, she wore flip-flops, cut-off jean shorts, and tank tops. She felt free and relaxed.

Surprisingly, Anthony was the same. He, too, put away the designer suits and arrogant attitude. When they weren't relaxing on the beach, they laid up watching movies.

Gracie was in the bedroom when she received a call on her phone.

"Gracie speaking?"

"It's a go! Make the call," the male caller told her.

She almost forgot about the hit on Sadie. Things had been going so great in her life that she wanted to call it off. But, nah, keeping her alive might ruin everything. *Who knows what else she is hiding,* Gracie thought. Once Sadie was gone, there would be no one left who could ruin her relationship with Anthony.

"Alright, conference me into her iPad," Gracie said.

Sadie was so predictable. Every Tuesday, she went over to her friend's house to play gin. However, what Gracie didn't know is Sadie wasn't driving; Tracey was. Sadie was in the back seat with Greg III. They were going to Tracey's sister's house.

Ring!

Sadie looked down. Normally, she didn't answer calls from unknown numbers, but she thought it was one of her daughters checking on her.

"Hello," Sadie answered.

"Grandma, I want to tell you this is the price you pay when you lie."

"What? Gracie, what are you talking about?"

"You'll find out. Goodbye, Grandma."

Click!

"I swear that child—" Before Sadie could get the words out her mouth, the car exploded.

*****

Greg was meeting with a client when he got the news. He was so devastated that he couldn't even identify the body, let alone make funeral arrangements. Thank God for his aunts, Justine and Halle, or Greg wouldn't have made it.

In a blink of an eye, his entire family was gone. They tried to reach Gracie several times, but she was out of the country and had turned off all communication devices. What Gracie didn't anticipate was her sister-in-law and nephew being killed. She had just gotten off her private jet, when she received several text messages from everyone.

Gracie sighed, put on her game face, and called Greg.

Halle answered. "Hello."

"Hello," Gracie said, not knowing who was answering Greg's phone. "This is Gracie. Tracey?" she asked.

"No, this is Halle."

"Halle?" Gracie looked at the phone to make sure she had dialed the correct number. "I'm looking for my brother Greg."

"Oh yes, he's here."

"Well, can I talk to him?" she asked with an attitude.

"Gracie, I think you should come over here. He's too upset to talk."

Gracie frowned. "Alright."

Sadly, she was about to experience the surprise of her life.

When Gracie arrived at Greg's house, her Aunts Gail and Grace greeted her. "We've been trying to reach you."

"What? What happened?" she asked, feeling the somber mood.

Grace lowered her head, making Gracie ask again, "What happened?"

"There was an accident. Mommy's car…" Gail cried. "Mommy's car blew up."

"Oh my God!" Gracie covered her mouth.

Gail then dropped another bomb. "Tracey and Greg Jr. were in the car."

"What!" Gracie asked, her eyes widening.

"They were in the car."

Gracie's heart rate accelerated, and she started feeling chest pains. "They were in the car?" She gasped, trying to catch her breath. "No, please," she wept. "Please…"

She fell to the floor. *What have I done!*

★ ★ ★ ★ 178

Chapter Sixteen

Damn! What the hell is going on? Justine thought. *First Halle and now Greg.* This was getting scary. Even with all the bullshit she went through with her family, she didn't know what she would do if something ever happened to them. Even with Anthony's raping ass, Justine would be hurt. Someone was definitely looking over them.

Since the trial was over and everything appeared to be returning to normal, London flew back to Africa. Justin was vacationing with some girl in Dubai, and Anthony had been keeping a low profile. Felix and his evil mother flew back to Italy. Finally, everyone went back to living their lives.

Meanwhile, Justine and Halle grew closer, both taking turns checking on Greg. With both being recovering addicts, they understood each other. Halle even persuaded Justine to spend some of her money. So, Justine purchased a beautiful home in Saddle River, New Jersey.

After months of begging Justine and Halle finally convince Greg to leave the house. Today, they were coming over for lunch and to help Justine unpack. They arrived ready to help.

"Welcome to my humble abode," Justine joked.

"Yeah, you better feed the workers, or we gonna call the Department of Labor on your ass," Greg replied, making them laugh.

For the rest of the day, Justine, Halle, and Greg unpacked boxes and hung up pictures. They were in the living room eating pizza when Greg noticed Justine's family photo.

"Justine, your brother Anthony doesn't look anything like your father. He looks just like your mother."

Justine laughed. "Yes, he does, but that's because he isn't my father's son."

"Huh?" Halle said. "He isn't?"

Justine exhaled. She didn't want to say anything, but hey, they were family. "No. My mother had Anthony already when she married my father. I guess that's why I never felt a connection to him."

"So Anthony isn't your brother?" Greg repeated.

Justine shook her head. "No. My mother got pregnant by some guy, and my dad accepted Anthony as his own."

Halle looked away. She knew Justine hadn't read the diary or looked at the tape she had given her a couple months ago.

"Justine, do you still have the book and tape I gave you?" she asked her.

"Yes. It's in the other room in a miscellaneous box. You want it?"

"Yes," Halle replied with a blank expression while trying to avoid eye contact with Greg.

Greg and Halle both knew the truth. Shit was about to hit the fan again.

"Here," Justine said, handing the items to Halle, who exhaled.

"Justine, that's not true. Anthony is Tony's son."

"Impossible. My father was with Christina Carrington when Anthony was born."

Halle swallowed hard. "No...no." She paused before handing the book back to her. "Read it."

After reading, Justine looked up. "What's this?"

Halle looked at Greg and then back at Justine. "It was your mother's diary."

"Diary?"

"Yes." Halle took a seat next to her.

"How did you get it?"

Lowering her head, Halle responded, "It was in my mother's things. My mother must've found it when your mother passed."

Bewildered, Justine looked back and forth between Halle and Greg. "I don't understand," she stated in a scared tone.

"Justine, your mother was repeatedly raped by your father," Greg said, sitting across from them.

"What?"

"Yes. He started raping her when she was fourteen years old. When she turned eighteen, he forced her into marriage."

Justine's heart sank. She threw her head back, allowing the tears to roll down her temples. "What about Christina?"

"Christina was just a cover up," Greg told her.

Justine didn't know if she was too shocked to cry or pissed off. But, it all made sense. She got up and started pacing.

Halle and Greg looked at each other again and then up at Justine who was rambling about something.

"Anthony...he raped those women," Justine cried.

Although devastated, it was such a relief for Justine to know the truth about her parents. After shedding many tears, all she could do was laugh. How could her mother marry her rapist and have his children? After learning this, Justine instantly lost all respect for her mother. As for her father's money, they could take Justine's half and shove it in their asses.

She had a strange feeling this was the information her grandfather had been hiding. Well, all was about to be revealed. Justine reached out to Justin and London, deciding to leave Anthony out of it for now. So as not to alarm them, Justine asked them to meet her at their parents' house in New Jersey, claiming she had some great news to share with them. They needed to know the truth.

Justine arrived first. Knowing emotions and tempers were going to flare up, she put a box of tissues on the table. Justine also asked Greg and Halle to join them.

Oddly, Justin and London pulled up to the house at the same time.

"Hello!" London yelled, entering the house. "Justine!"

"In here," Justine answered from where she was in the room watching the tape of her parents.

"What are you watching?" London asked.

"Is that a sex tape?" Justin questioned.

Justine shut it off. "Yes."

Justin and London looked around, noticing papers and pictures everywhere.

"Justine, what's going on?" London asked.

Justine giggled. "I'm glad you asked. Have a seat," she said, standing up. "Remember when Addy told us that Mommy and Daddy married a day after Mommy's eighteenth birthday? How there was evidence of them dating?"

"Yes," they both replied, wondering where she was going with this.

"Well, it turns out that Mommy was seeing Daddy. In fact, she started seeing him when she was fourteen." Justine's voice cracked and her eyes got teary. Still, she remained calm.

Justin and London sat there looking confused, wondering if Justine had started drinking again.

Growing impatient, London asked, "Where are you going with this?"

Justine smiled and tossed Morgan's diary to them. "Maybe this will help you understand."

By then, Halle and Greg arrived.

"Justine!" Halle called out.

"We're in here!" she responded.

"What's this?" London asked, opening it.

"Read," Justine told her, unable to hold back the tears.

London and Justin looked at Justine, then at each other, and then up at Greg and Halle who had just joined them.

"What's going on?" Justin asked in a leery tone.

"Oh my," London muttered as she read the contents of the diary.

★ ★ ★ ★ 182

Justin snatched it from her. "What?" he asked and then started to read. "What is this? Is this someone's diary? Whose fucking diary is this?" he asked, afraid of knowing the answer.

"It's Mommy's," Justine huffed. "She was being raped by our father."

This news sent shockwaves through the room.

"No, it's not true," London wept. "You're lying."

"No, Londie," Justine said. "I wish I was. Here, look at this." She turned on the tape.

After they killed Tony, Denise and Greg came upon two tapes hidden in the house. On the tapes were Tony beating and raping Morgan repeatedly.

"Turn it off!" Justin screamed. "Turn that shit off," he scolded, slamming his hand against the table.

Looking at them hurting made Greg and Halle cry, especially after all the shit they had been through.

"Why?" London cried. "Why?"

Hugging her, Justin answered, "I don't know, sis. I don't know."

"How did you get the tapes?" Justin asked.

Halle exhaled. "From me. It was in my mother's belonging. She found out that Tony was raping Morgan. I'm sorry."

Disgusted by the whole thing, London brushed Justin off of her. "Don't be. We needed to know the truth about our parents. It was better we learned it from you than the media. It was bound to come out."

"So Anthony is Tony's son?" Justin asked.

Greg nodded. "Yes."

"How did you know, Greg?" London asked, reaching for a tissue to wipe away her tears.

"My godmother Stevie used to date Tony. He did the same thing to her. She was there when my mother made Morgan tell Denise."

"Do you think Grandpa knew about all of this?" Justin asked.

"No. Didn't Addy say Grandpa wasn't around when Mommy was growing up. He had no way of knowing," London explained.

However, Justine knew better. She had done some digging. "He knew," she said, handing them some papers. "He's known. That's why he's been paying off women." Making them all confused, Justine continued. "Anthony has been raping women for year, and Grandpa and Grandma knew it. They paid off many women."

"What?" the room echoed.

Justine walked over to her bag, handing them more documents. "Here are receipts of the payoffs."

The room was quiet. Everyone was in complete shock.

Then Halle blurted out, "So what now? Where do we go from here?"

Still shaken up by all this, Justine blurted out, "I don't know. But, one thing I know for sure is I don't want any part of Daddy's money. I don't want to be associated with him."

"Justine!" London said.

"No, London! He's a rapist, and because of him, our brother raped women." she huffed deciding to tell them the truth about Sofia "Sofia killed herself because Anthony raped her. One night, I came home drunk. I heard noises coming from the guesthouse. I thought it was Anthony with another one of his girls, but the person was crying and begging him to stop. I went to see what was going on. It was Sofia. Anthony was on top of her, raping her while Grandma held her down. Sofia looked over at me, wondering why I was allowing it to happen. Grandma saw me and took me back to my room to lay me down. The next morning, she told me that I had been dreaming. It wasn't until I saw the scratches on Anthony's back that I knew it wasn't a dream."

Justin got up and started pacing. *This can't be real.* For years, he blamed himself for Sofia's death. Now to learn she killed herself because his brother had raped her was just too much. Justin wanted to kill him.

"So he got off. He really did rape those women," he mumbled.

"Justin!"London called out. "We don't know—"

"He's just like our father," Justin confessed, cutting her off. "Anthony is a rapist," he added, staring them in the face.

Damn, Halle and Greg thought.

"He's sick," Justine stated, getting everyone's attention. "Anthony suffers from a mental illness that most people would consider normal or just mildly eccentric. Most serial rapists and sexual abusers are diagnosed with this illness. Daddy suffered from this, and more than likely it was passed on to Anthony."

"Does Anthony know any of this?" Greg asked.

Disoriented, Justin grabbed the diary and yanked the tapes out.

"Justin...Justin," London called for him, and he slowly turned around. "Where are you going?" she asked.

"To have a chat with my big brother," he said.

*****

Anthony had just came back, only to find Justin in the dark watching the tape in their father's old office.

"What the hell are you watching?" Anthony asked in a surprised, yet angry tone.

"This is my father's house, too, or did you forget? I'm watching Daddy," Justin replied, putting his feet on the table.

Anthony was about to turn around, but the cries from the young girl on the tape caught his attention. "Is that..." he mumbled, walking closer to get a better look.

"In the flesh," Justin said. "That's Daddy, and you see that little girl right there?" He pointed. "That little girl who's bleeding from her mouth is our mother. She was fourteen when he started beating and raping her."

Like the others, Anthony was in complete shock. "Turn it off!" he screamed.

Justin chuckled and then turned the tape off. "Why? You hate watching yourself on TV."

"What the fuck are you talking about?" Anthony shouted.

Justine got up and clapped his hands. "Rape. We all know you raped those women?"

Appalled, Anthony shouted, "I don't have to rape any fucking body! I get pussy thrown at me."

"You are just like him! You are just like that motherfucker!" Justin screamed, leaping over the desk and punching Anthony in the face. "You bastard! You killed her!" Justin cried while throwing jab after jab.

Anthony blocked and swung back. Getting his brother in a bear hug, he body slammed him on the desk. "You wanna fight me, motherfucker?!"

Feeling his ribs being crushed, Justin pounded on Anthony's back, which wasn't doing anything. So, he reached for the stapler on the desk and started smashing it against Anthony's face.

"Take that, you fucking rapist!"

Anthony loosened up just enough for Justin to squirm his way out. Justin then started tossing everything at Anthony—books and pictures.

"You are just like Daddy!" Justin whined.

Justin was about to charge him again, but remembered he had the diaries. So, instead of leaping at Anthony again, he ran, picked up the book, and tossed it at him.

"What's this?" Anthony asked, catching it in his hands.

"Read it!"

Anthony glared at Justin for a split second before opening the book and starting to read.

"Whose is this?" he asked.

"It's Mommy's. She kept a diary on how Daddy repeatedly raped her."

Anthony's eyes widened. "You're lying!"

"He'd been raping her since she was fourteen!" Justin shouted with tears in his eyes. "The same way you raped Sofia and those other women."

Anthony dropped the book. "Rape? That can't be true," he mumbled, taking a seat.

Although Justin wanted to kill him, he felt sorry for his big brother. Both bleeding from their injuries, Justin took a seat next to Anthony.

"I know you don't wanna believe it. None of us do."

"How did you find out?" Anthony mumbled.

"Halle gave Justine Mommy's diary and tape."

Anthony lowered his head. "So you're telling me those fucking family tapes were a lie? None of it was real?"

"I don't know, bro."

"Do you realize we are a product of rape, Justine? Rape," he emphasized. Anthony stood up and started pacing "Why? Why?" he repeated. "Why did this have to happen to me...to us?"

Justin stared at his brother who had a sad puppy look. "I don't know, Ant. We may never know."

"All those women..." He sighed and hit himself in the head with the book. "And Justine...she knew that's why she hated me all these years!" he stated in sorrow.

Justin nodded. "Yes. She saw you rape Sofia. Grandma covered it up."

Anthony tightened his lips, closed his eyes, and threw his head back. "Sofia ..." he whined.

"Why?" Justin asked.

"I don't know. I don't even remember that night. All I remember is waking up with a hangover."

Now Justin lowered his head. *Damn.*

"Justine said you suffer from some kinda mental disorder that a lot of serial rapists and sexual abusers have. According to Justine, Daddy suffered from this, and it was passed on to you. Did you know this?"

With tears in his eyes, Anthony shook his head. "No. All they gave me were some pills, claiming it would help with my panic attacks and headaches. But, the side effects were killing me."

"The pills were supposed to help you with this illness."

Anthony sighed. He felt like a ton of bricks had fallen on top of his head. The last thing he wanted to do was hurt women, but most of all his family.

"So our father is a rapist?" he muttered, sucking his teeth.

"Yes. The infamous Tony Flowers..." Justin highlighted.

So many things were running through Anthony's mind that he thought it was going to explode.

"Why, Justin? All these years we wondered about our father..." he said, breaking down. "...wondered what he was like. You know how good it felt to know our father was Tony Flowers. It wasn't about the money, Justin. I was proud to know people respected him. Every son wants that."

Tears rolled down Justin's face as he nodded. "I know. Even after watching that video and looking at pictures, I was happy to learn they were married."

"Is that a lie, too?" Anthony said, sucking his teeth.

"I don't know. Mommy supposedly married Daddy a day after her eighteenth birthday."

Pissed, Anthony cut his eyes. "Why? Why did she marry someone who raped her? Where was Grandpa? Why did he allow this to happen," he rambled, thinking out loud.

Unable to answer, Justin asked, "Are you gonna be okay?"

Anthony flashed a half smile. "I have no choice. How about London and Justine? How are they doing?"

Justin placed his hand on Anthony's shoulder and took a deep breath. "It's a shock to all of us, but together we can get through this. I mean, it's not every day you find out your father is a rapist, you know?"

"So we are a product of rape. Is that what you're telling me?"

"It looks like that." Justin sighed.

Anthony pushed Justin's hand away in disgust, realizing his life had been just one big fucking lie. He felt like killing someone, mainly his father for ruining his life. Shaking his head, he tried to fight back tears. Anthony thought, *Why do I have to be the one with the illness*? When he thought about all the women he had hurt, Anthony felt like shit.

"You know how many women I've hurt?" he exclaimed, looking at Justin. "Why didn't any of them press charges against me?"

"They were paid off."

"Paid off? What do you mean?" Anthony asked.

Justin shot Anthony a look that said it all.

"But, of course, our grandma wouldn't want this to get out."

"Grandma..." Justin mumbled in disbelief.

"Yes. She was the one who paid off the ADA and jury," hesitated, surprising the hell out of Justin.

Now that Anthony thought about it, it was Mrs. Marciano who told him to stop taking the medicine. "Grandpa wanted me to get help, but it was Grandma who told me to stop taking the pills. She knew what I was doing to those women."

Anthony released a fake laugh. Now that he looked back, it was Mrs. Marciano who had planted terrible things in his head about Felix and his siblings.

He was about to stay something, when Justin's phone rang.

"Hold on a second," Justin said, pulling his phone out of his pocket. "It's London. What's up, sis?" he answered. "Are y'all alright?"

"Yes. Did you see Anthony?"

"Yes. He's standing right here next to me."

"Did you tell him?" she asked.

"Yes."

"How is he taking it? What did he have to say?"

"You don't wanna know."

"We are on our way," London informed him.

"Alright. See ya when you get here." After disconnecting the call, he turned to Anthony. "London and Justine are on their way."

"Good. It's time we get to the bottom of the bloody lies," Anthony responded.

Chapter Seventeen

Halle was already emotionally drained and now this. Even though Mr. Rubin took care of everything, including having Derrick's body cremated, Halle was still on pins and needles. In a matter of months, she became a millionaire, found out her mother was murdered and had murdered her father. Her brother went crazy, killing her family. She found her other cousins, who were a product of rape. All of this was enough to drive a person insane.

All of these secrets and lies started to make her wonder if this was the reason why her mother was killed. According to everyone on the streets, Denise wasn't anything to play with. So, how did someone manage to get that close to her? Truthfully, Halle didn't even want to know, fearing it was probably someone she knew.

With everything that had been going on, Halle made sure to check on her cousins, because right now, all they had were each other. The last time she spoke to Justine, they decided to confront their grandparents. In addition, they all agreed to donate half of their father's money to domestic violence victims. But, Halle swayed them into opening the center so they could stay involved.

Justine told her that Anthony was in rehab and back on his medication. She also told Halle that they all were going to therapy to help them deal with this issue. Halle did the same, because many nights she woke up in a cold sweat after dreaming about her brother.

Greg was still copping with the death of his family. It didn't help that the police didn't have any leads.

Halle was on her way to a Narcotics Anonymous meeting; it had been a long time since she attended one. Afterwards, she was going to run to Barneys. Tonight was Mr. Rubin's birthday, and his wife was giving him a dinner. She and Greg were attending the event.

To her surprise, Halle bumped into Gracie in the dressing room area of Barneys.

"Halle, right?" Gracie said in an unsure tone.

"Yes, Gracie…"

Both ladies giggled with a sigh of relief.

"I'm sorry to hear about your brother. I wish I would've met him," Gracie said.

"Thank you. Oh, I'm sorry to hear about your godmother."

"Oh yeah," Gracie answered in a nonchalant tone. "Well, if you ask me, she ran her mouth too much," she replied while modeling a dress in front of the mirror.

A little taken aback at the comment, Halle simply replied, "Okay."

"It's not like I knew her. She popped into our lives telling stories about people. Maybe she told the story about the wrong person."

"Wow! Isn't that a bit harsh?"

"Well, you wouldn't be saying that if she told the world about you and your brother's little sex tape," Gracie malicious stated, giving her a look as if to say, *Oh yeah, bitch, I do my homework.* "Now that would be a bit harsh, don't ya think?"

If this were years ago, two things would've happened. Either Halle would've burst into tears and ran out of there, or she would've tore Gracie's head off. However, since she was in therapy and already scared of the police finding out about Derrick and the others, she laughed. *Bitches like Gracie, their bark is worse than their bite.* Gracie reminded Halle of her cousin Diamond, who was always talking shit but couldn't back it up.

"Yeah, that would be harsh, but you know what would really be fucked up?" Halle said with a smug look as she walked over to Gracie. "If the world knew about you and Anthony."

Gracie's eyes damn near popped out of her head. Although she tried to hide it, it was too late.

"Yeah, I know about you and Anthony. I saw how you guys were all over each other. Shhh!" Halle chuckled, putting her finger over her mouth like a kid. "You see, the difference between my secret and your secret," she said, touching Gracie's chest, "is everyone knows mine." She leaned closer, as if she was going to kiss Gracie on the neck. "But they don't know yours, "she whispered.

Gracie backed up. "Watch it, cuz. I would hate for something to happen to you."

Halle laughed "you think so"

Gracie smirked, "unlike your drug dealing mother, my mother left made Queen of her empire. So if I was you-"

"You don't have—"

"Don't need the heart when I have the money," Gracie stated, interrupting her. "A couple of dollars get bitches like you taken care of, especially when they cross me."

"You think so?" Halle smiled. "Send them, but before you do..." She paused for a moment. "...I'm gonna advise you to go back and do *your* homework. Find out what happens to Queens in this family especially when they cross this Queen." She winked and then walked out.

$$*****$$

Halle arrived at Mr. Rubin's dinner looking stunning. Greg was already there. Halle shook her head, wondering if Greg and Gracie came from the same mother. She had to laugh when she thought about the confrontation at the store. *The nerve of the bitch. Cuz or no cuz, let her try it, and I will gladly out a bullet in that stuck up bitch ass. Greg better watch Gracie might have that shit*

Derrick had…crazy, Halle thought as she made her way to Greg and Mr. Rubin.

"Alright, cuz, you look stunning," Greg complimented.

"You don't look so bad yourself."

Mr. Rubin stood there like a proud grandfather. *After all these two have been through, they still remain strong.* It warmed his heart to see how they turned out.

"Only if your parents could see you now. They would be so proud of you, just like I am," he stated.

"Awww, thank you," Halle said.

Halle and Greg didn't know it, but although Mr. Rubin was over seventy years old with two hip and knee replacements, he loved to dance. For the rest of the evening, Greg, Halle, and Mr. Rubin hit the dance floor, dancing the entire night away.

As the evening came to an end, an exhausted Mr. Rubin sat down to admire everyone.

"Are you okay?" Halle asked, taking a seat next to him.

With a blissful expression, Mr. Rubin replied, "Yes. I had a wonderful time."

"I'm glad. I did too, Mr. Rubin," Halle said, taking a deep breath and grabbing his hand. "I just wanna say thank you. Thank you for everything. I don't think I could've made it without you." Halle's eyes filled with tears.

Mr. Rubin patted her hand. "You're welcome. Your mother was like a daughter to me, which means you are my granddaughter."

Halle blushed. "I just wish I knew who killed her."

"What's going on over here?" Greg asked, joining them.

"Nothing. I was just telling Mr. Rubin that with everything that has been going on, I wish we knew who killed our parents."

Greg nodded. "I don't think they even care. Remember our parents were considered murderers. Right, Mr. Rubin?"

"Right. The police really didn't investigate."

"If my mother hadn't killed Tony, I would've thought he had someone kill her."

Greg's eyes widened. "Your mother killed Tony Flowers?" he said, looking back and forth between Halle and Mr. Rubin.

"Yeah. Once Denise found out about Morgan, she just snapped. She wiped out Tony's entire family," Mr. Rubin explained further.

"Exactly. He was the only person that had a reason to kill our parents."

"It doesn't make sense," Greg chimed in. "Then who killed our parents?"

"Well, all I can say is it was hit that was carefully planned out. Within minutes, your mother, father, and Denise were killed execution style. If I know Greg and Denise, they were caught off guard. The only people who carry out hits like that are the mob," he affirmed, giving them a mysterious look.

* * * * *

The next couple of days, Halle pondered over Mr. Rubin's words. Halle started thinking her mother left them the house and tape for a reason. She liquidated all her assets, putting it into a trust fund. Only someone who knows they are not going to be around does that.

Needing more information, Halle thought about her mother's house. There was no way she was going back there. But, the DVD was in the house, and then she remembered Mr. Rubin had sent some of Derrick's things over from the house. Halle went into the other room, and there it was right on top of the box.

Halle had watched the DVD a million times trying to make sense of this whole thing. This time, she looked for clues. On the tape, not only did Denise confess to killing their father, but Tony, too. Then Halle noticed something.

Denise said, "Morgan..." Her voice trailed on in sorrow. "Why? How can you love a man who brutally raped you? How can you bear his children? She didn't understand I needed to make it right. Tony was one of my best friends, so not only did Tony violate her, but he violated me, too. And where I'm from that's punishable by death." Denise lowered her head. "She chose him over me. What was I supposed to do? I had my two kids to think about, and not even Morgan came before them." Denise smiled. "She made her choice, and I made mine. Tony didn't deserve that kind of loyalty. I just hope someone is taking care of her children. Would you believe before she took her last breath, Morgan asked me to take care of Tony and the kids?"

Halle froze. Her mother had killed Morgan.

Then she thought about what Mr. Rubin said. *Only the mob could've carried out a hit like that.* Halle shut off the tape. It was clear.

"The Marcianos killed my mother."

Halle jumped in her car and headed over to Justine's place. Justine and London were there.

"How are you holding up? How are the others doing?" Halle asked, pretending to check on them.

"We're good? London is upstairs talking to her fiancé. We've called our grandparents and asked them to come out here so we can confront them," Justine informed her.

Halle nodded. "They know y'all know?"

"Of course not. Anthony called my grandma begging her to come. You know he's in rehab, right? London asked my grandpa. I can't wait to see the looks on their faces when we confront them. They can't lie their asses out of this one. Come, you want something to eat or drink? I was fixing London and me some leftovers," Justine said, heading to the kitchen.

Looking around, Halle noticed Justine had removed all the family photos from off the wall and replaced them with paintings. "No, thanks. I see you removed some pictures."

"Yes. Why have the phony pics up?" she said, placing food on the plate. "How are you holding up?'

"Great. The other shoe dropped today."

Justine slammed the spoon on the table. "What now? Don't tell me that we have another cousin or some shit. I can't take anymore?" Her comment made them chuckle.

"Hi, Halle," London said, entering the room and kissing her on the cheek. "What brings you here?"

"What happened now?" Justine asked, staring at Halle.

"Hi, London." Halle smiled, ignoring Justine's question.

"No. What happened?" Justine asked again in a more serious tone.

"Your grandma killed my mother," Halle affirmed.

London looked over at Justine and then at Halle, who was waiting for one of them to respond.

"It wouldn't surprise me," Justine finally said.

"It doesn't surprise you that she killed my mother?" Halle asked. Getting upset, she started to gasp for air.

"Halle!" London and Justine yelled, trying to calm her down.

"Take a deep breath, Halle." London rubbed her back while Justine went to get her some water. "Halle, you have to calm down."

Still gasping, Halle's tears rolled down her face. "That bitch killed my mother."

"Here, drink this," Justine said, handing her a glass of water.

"Why would my grandma kill your mother? She didn't hurt my mother," London asked.

Oh shit, Halle thought. *Mrs. Marciano must've known my mother killed Morgan.*

"Because the bitch is evil. She probably didn't like Denise because she was black."

But, London wasn't buying that excuse. Mrs. Marciano was vindictive, but only when you fucked with her family.

"No," London said, moving away from Halle. "It was something else." She gave Halle a side eye look.

"Now you're siding with her?" Justine yelled.

"No, but, Halle, I want you there when we confront our grandparents. It's time we get to the bottom of this once and for all."

Halle nodded. She couldn't wait.

Chapter Eighteen

With so many things going on and secrets floating around, Greg hired a private investigator to investigate his family's murder, and the investigator believed he had found out who was behind it. Greg was meeting him at his office.

"Before Sadie died, she received a phone call."

"Okay. So?"

The investigator continued. "The person used FaceTime."

Anxious, Greg replied, "Okay. So how does this help?"

"Well, FaceTime records all calls and the callers' faces."

Greg paused. "What?"

"Yes. Even though the car blew up, the call was saved in the cloud."

"Was it able to save my grandma's call?"

"It did something better. The FaceTime cloud saved not only the call, but it saved the face."

The investigator reached into his pocket and handed Greg a flash drive.

Judging by the look on the investigator's face, Greg wasn't going to like it. So, Greg paid him and thanked him for his services before departing.

Once home, Greg went into his private office to see what was on the flash drive. Afraid of what he was about to see, he took a deep breath.

"Here goes nothing."

Greg was completely traumatized at what he saw. It was Gracie threatening their grandma; she was behind this. Gracie had killed his family!

Like his father, when provoked, Greg could be dangerous, and his sister just did that. Greg grabbed his keys and the flash drive,

then headed out to confront his dearest sister. When the door opened, Greg damn near passed out. It was Stevie.

"Stevie, I thought you were dead."

"We need to talk," she said, pushing Greg back outside.

"Stevie, I don't have time," he scolded, trying to brush past her.

"Before you go and do something stupid, you need to hear this." Stevie guided him inside.

Greg heavily exhaled. "Make it quick," he said while walking into the family room.

"Okay. A couple of months ago, I found out Gracie put a hit out on me."

"Gracie?" Greg said in disbelief.

"Yes."

"But why?" he asked.

"Because I found out she was sleeping with Anthony, Tony's son."

Greg paused for a second. He raised his hand to stop Stevie from continuing. "Wait. You said she was sleeping with Tony's son, as in Anthony our fucking cousin?"

Stevie closed her eyes. "Yes. They've been seeing each other for months now. Anthony doesn't know Gracie is his cousin. But Gracie knows."

Greg closed his eyes and started rubbing his baldhead. He was so upset that all he could was laugh. "Un-fucking-believable. Whoa!" he said, letting out a loud breath of air. "You're telling me that my fucking sister killed my grandma, wife, and son to keep her fucking secret," he recanted in anger. "That's what you're telling me?"

"I don't know why she killed your grandmother, but she ordered a hit on me because I knew she was messing with Tony."

With a frightened expression, Greg started rubbing his chin, reminding Stevie of his father.

"Well, let's go find out," he told her.

*****

Gracie had flown out to China to meet with some investors about opening up a few hotels out there. This would be a great opportunity for her and Greg. This could take them to another level. That's why Gracie was baffled when he declined the offer, but she just brushed it off as him still grieving.

Gracie spent the next few days mingling with the rich and powerful. One thing for certain, she had the gift of gab. By the time she left China, Gracie had signed a two hundred million dollar deal to build hotels in China. *Who said I'm not the queen of my fucking empire.*

She had just landed when Anthony called her. He had been in a rehab program. Gracie wasn't aware he had a drug problem, but learning this made her love him even more.

It was his first weekend out, and he wanted to see her. They were meeting at her house upstate. Gracie couldn't wait to see him; she missed him so much. She was back to being in his life. Their chemistry was off the chain.

As they snuggled in their love nest, Anthony told her, "Hey, I want you to meet my brother and sisters."

"Okay," Gracie answered, wondering why.

For months, Anthony had been begging Gracie to meet his family. She would either cancel at the last minute or change the subject. Her avoidance made Anthony start to think she wasn't serious about him.

"For months you've been telling me okay. When are you gonna meet them?" he asked in a stern tone.

"I don't know. Why is it such a big deal?"

Gracie wasn't aware, but Anthony had turned over a new leaf. After learning what his father did to his mother, Anthony vowed to never hurt another female again. When he looked back at all the women he had hurt in his life, Gracie was the only one he hadn't hurt.

Anthony pulled her close to him. "Gracie, a couple of weeks ago, I found out that my father raped my mother when she was fourteen."

"What?" Gracie pretended like she was hearing this for the first time. "Are you serious?"

"Yes. He had some sort of mental illness."

"Anthony, I'm sorry. I didn't know," she said, caressing his head.

"As a result, while growing up, I hurt women, too. That's why I checked myself into rehab. So I can get better," he said, facing her. "Gracie, I looked up to this man. I was proud that he was my father, and to learn he raped my mother…to find out I was doing the same…" His voice cracked as it trailed off.

Gracie lowered her head. She couldn't believe what Anthony had just said. Now would be the perfect time to declare her secrets, but somehow she couldn't. Anthony had already endured enough pain. There was no need to add to it.

"Anthony, I'm sorry for everything you've been through. I'm here if you need me."

Anthony looked into her eyes. They seemed sincere. In fact, he had fallen in love with her. Gracie was everything he wanted in a woman. Right now would the perfect time for him to propose, but he chose not to. He planned to propose to her after she met his siblings.

"I love you," he told her.

Gracie's heart melted. "I love you, too," she exclaimed, leading them to make love.

After making love for most of the day, Gracie stood in the kitchen preparing something to eat while Anthony took a shower. Dancing and singing like a teenager in love, Gracie was happy.

Then there was a knock at the door. She wiped her hands with the towel and tossed it on the counter.

"Babe, are you expecting anyone?" she shouted while going to open the door.

"What?" Anthony shouted back.

"I said are you—" Her sentence was cut short by the sudden state of shock. "GREG!"

"Sis."

Anthony came out of the shower with a towel wrapped around the lower half of his body.

"What did you say?" Anthony asked, wondering what the hell was going on.

Gracie stood frozen with a scared yet troubled look on her face. "Greg…"

By then, Greg had brushed past her. "So it's true," he said, entering the house.

"Greg…" Gracie repeated, unable to say anything else.

Anthony was puzzled. At first, he didn't recognize Greg. Then he looked closer, and it was him.

"Greg my ass! How could you, Gracie?"

"What is going on?" Anthony asked.

"He doesn't know?" Greg glared at Gracie. "You killed my family."

Growing nervous, Anthony replied, "I don't know what you're talking about. Gracie, what's going on here?"

With an impish grin, Greg responded, "Tell him, Gracie."

Gracie brushed her hair back, praying this was some kind of sick joke. She was unable to say anything.

"Tell me what, Gracie?" Anthony shouted, fearing the worst.

Both men glared at her, waiting for an answer.

Then it hit Anthony. Gracie was Greg's sister.

He smirked. "You're Greg Brightman's daughter…my cousin, right?"

Gracie's eyes became watery as she swallowed hard. "Anthony…"

"How long have you known, huh? Did you know before or after you started fucking me? I guess that's why you didn't want to meet my family, because they would've known."

"I didn't know. It was after I feel in love in love with you."

"In love?" Anthony chuckled. "Bullshit! The only thing you love is this big dick," he said, grabbing himself. "You knew who I was from the start," he grumbled, shaking his head.

Gracie ran over to him, trying to touch him.

✦ ✦ ✦ ✦ 203

"Anthony...please," she begged. "I swear..."

But, Anthony wasn't trying to hear it. He pushed her away. "Get off of me. You disgust me," he said, tossing her to the side and then went to gather his clothes. "I never wanna see you again."

Hysterical, Gracie got up and reached for his arm. Enraged, Anthony smacked the shit out of her. He smacked her so hard that Gracie flew across the room.

"Don't you ever touch me. You hear me? You hear me! Don't you ever!" he shouted before departing.

Greg shook his head. "Was it all worth it? Huh? Was killing my family worth it?"

Gracie's eyes opened wide to the size of quarters. "I don't—"

"Don't you dare fucking lie to me? You killed my family, Gracie!" he said as tears rolled down his face. "You killed them!"

Gracie ran over and tried to stop him from leaving. "Greg...please. I'm so sorry. I didn't know they were gonna be in the car. I swear, Greg," she wept. "I would never do anything to hurt you. Please, you gotta believe me."

Greg grabbed her by the arm. "I believe you're an evil bitch who will do anything to succeed. You are dead to me." He tossed her to the side and attempted to walk out, but Gracie made a dash for him again.

"Greg, please," she pleaded, pulling his arm. "Please, I'm sorry, Greg. Please don't do this. You're all I have left."

Greg turned around and grabbed her by the throat. "It's only because we came out the same pussy that I won't kill you. But, if I were you," he said, squeezing tighter, "I would stay the fuck away from me." Her flung her to the floor and then walked out.

Gracie curled up in a fetal position and sobbed. Sadly, her troubles were about to get even worst. The door opened again.

"Greg...Anthony!" Gracie called out, but it wasn't either of them.

"My...my...what do we have here?" It was Stevie, with three men following her.

"What?!You're dead!" she gasped.

Stevie smiled. "That's the problem," she said, playing in her hair. "That's the fucking difference between new money and old money. They don't know how to spend it."

"Fuck you" Gracie said, getting up off the floor.

"Didn't I tell you if you weren't careful big dicks can be deadly?" Stevie said, while strutting away. "Make it look like an accident! You hear me?" she ordered, then took one last look at Gracie before walking out.

"FUCK YOU!" Gracie screamed. "FUCK YOU, BITCH!"

Chapter Nineteen

Just when Anthony turned over a new leaf, this shit happened. He was so hurt that Anthony felt like having a drink. He drove back to his penthouse, only to be greeted by his little brother Justin. Judging from his disheveled look and glossy eyes, Justin knew something was wrong.

"Ant, what's wrong?"

Anthony took a long, deep breath. "I found out this girl I was seeing..." He paused.

"Yeah?" Justin said, holding his breath.

"She's our cousin. She's Greg's twin sister."

Justin started rubbing his head while looking around. For a second, he thought he was being punk'd. "You slept with her?" Justin asked.

Anthony confirmed with a nod, then walked over to the bar and poured himself a drink. "I didn't know she was our cousin. We were at her place when Greg came in." Anthony exhaled. He was about to put the glass to his lips, but looked at it and threw it against the wall. "Justin, it wasn't about the sex. I fell in love with her. Why did this have to happen to me...to us?"

Justin stared at his brother, who had the most saddened look on his face. "I don't know, Ant. We may never know."

"All those women..." He sighed, hitting his fist against the wall. "I guess that's what I get, huh? The first real woman I fall in love with turns out to be my fucking cousin. What else is gonna happen?"

Justin nodded. "I don't know, but you'll be alright. London called. It's time. They're on their way over to Grandpa and Grandma's," he stated

*****

Felix was in the den looking at some old photos of Morgan and the grandchildren. *Damn, I miss my daughter.* He knew Morgan was looking down at him disappointed. Not because he bribed the ADA and jury, but because he didn't get Anthony the professional help he needed. It was only a matter of time before Anthony ended up like his father. Maybe it wasn't a good idea for Felix to get custody of the kids. For the first time, he regretted killing Denise. Felix knew she loved Morgan to death and would've raised her kids.

That's why Felix decided to turn over his share to the kids and go back to Italy. Hopefully, he taught them enough where they could run their father's empire. If they allowed Anthony to mess it up, that would be their problem.

One thing for sure, he wouldn't let his mother play on his emotions again. She was the one who claimed to have proof that Denise killed Morgan. She also blackballed Justine from the family. Mrs. Marciano convinced Felix to send Justin and Justine to New York. Now that Felix thought about it, Justine was right; Mrs. Marciano treated them different because they didn't look Italian.

He was in deep thought when a familiar voice said, "It's funny how time flies." Recognizing that voice, Felix smiled and then looked over. It was Justine and London.

"Justine...Londie." Relieved, he smiled and embraced them. "How are you?

They smiled and hugged him back.

"Great, Grandpa, and you?" Justine asked.

"Better now," Felix said, leading her over to the sofa.

"Where's Grandma?" London asked.

"She's probably in the living room."

Justine looked over at the photos. "May I?" she asked, picking them up.

"Of course," he said, happy she was there.

"Wow, London. You do look like Mommy."

"You have some features of your mother, too," Felix said.

"Boy, pictures do say a lot." London smirked.

Bewildered at her comment, Felix replied, "I guess. How's Halle?" he asked changing the subject.

"Halle's great! In fact, she will be here shortly. Come on, Grandpa. Let's go say hi to Grandma," Justine said, flashing a deceitful grin.

Mrs. Marciano was finishing up a call when they entered. "Well, look at my granddaughter. Londie!" She smiled with her arms outstretched.

London looked at Justine before obliging her with a hug. "Hi, Gram. How are you?"

"Wonderful. Hello, Justine," Mrs. Marciano snidely said.

"Mrs. Marciano," Justine responded dryly.

"So," Mrs. Marciano said, turning her attention back to London, "how's my great son-in-law?"

Felix looked over at Justine. *Mother can be such a bitch,* he thought. "So, Justine, how's school?" he asked.

"Hello!" It was Justin and Anthony.

"Oh my God!" Mrs. Marciano beamed. "What's going on here? All my grandchildren came to see me. Felix did you have something to do with this?" she blissfully asked.

"No. We actually came up with a decision about our father's estate," Anthony said.

"Oh, you did?" Mrs. Marciano's voice now had a sad tone. "What did you decide?"

"To give it up," Anthony informed her.

"Huh?"

As rehearsed, they looked at Justine, giving her the signal to start.

Justine walked over to the fireplace. "It's funny. Even though we've been fighting over the past few months, we managed to set aside our differences and have become really close. We even hung out with our mother's siblings and cousins. You know, the ones you deliberately kept us from," she sarcastically stated.

"That's good. I'm pretty sure your mother would've wanted that," Felix said, ignoring her slick comment.

"Really? So why did you keep us from them?" London asked.

"What are you talking about? I didn't," he responded, but was caught off by London.

"They never reached out to us. In fact, Grandma lied about Aunt Monique and Uncle Michael not wanting them around us," Justin informed. "They've been trying to reach us for years. Isn't that right, Anthony?" he said, giving him his cue.

Anthony smirked and pulled out a book. "Maybe you were afraid we would find out this." He tossed it to Felix. "Remember we couldn't figure out why Mommy married Daddy after her eighteenth birthday? How there was no evidence of them dating?"

"Why don't you tell us why, Grandpa?" Justin asked.

Speechless, Felix lowered his head.

Justin yelled, "Answer me goddamnit!"

"I tried to protect you," Felix said, getting choked up. "I wanted to protect you…"

"Tell us the truth about our mother and father," Justine cried. "We deserve to know."

Felix sighed. "I didn't know. I wasn't exactly in your mother's life when she was growing up."

Shaking, London asked in a stern tone, "Why was Mommy seeing Daddy since she was fourteen? Was it because she was being raped by him?"

The looks on Felix and Mrs. Marciano's faces said it all.

"How could you?" London screamed. "She was your daughter!"

"I didn't know she was being raped. I was deported when your mother was five years old. I wanted her to come with me, but her mother said no. I swear I didn't know!" he shouted in a weak voice. "I found out after Anthony was born. Denise came to see me in prison and told me everything. We didn't even know Tony was Anthony's father. I cried!" He ground his teeth. "Morgan was my only daughter; she meant the world to me. That's why I wanted the son of a bitch dead when I found out. But, she had fallen in love with him, London," he said, walking over to her. "By then, you and your brother had already been born, and Morgan was pregnant with Justin and Justine. What could I do? She loved him."

"I don't believe you!" London cried.

Halle entered. "He's telling the truth!" she said, pulling out Morgan's final diary and reading a passage. "She wrote, 'Good can come from evil. Tony has given me the greatest gift in life, my children'."

London sobbed uncontrollably, taking this news hard.

Also crying, Justin went over to console her. "It's okay, London."

"Londie," Mrs. Marciano called out, afraid to go over to her. "I swear we didn't know."

"But you did know about Sofia," Anthony said, getting Mrs. Marciano's attention.

"You knew I raped her. You know I raped all of those women."

"What are you talking about?" Mrs. Marciano asked in a high-pitched tone.

"Sofia killed herself after I raped her."

"No! I don't know anything about the rape," Mrs. Marciano said in a defensive tone.

"Yes, you do. You held her down while I brutally raped her, didn't you?" Anthony shouted. "Just like you know I suffer from a mental illness. You knew!"

"You knew he was a danger to women. You knew!" London screamed. "You know Anthony raped those women."

"How many were there?" Anthony asked, slowly moving towards Mrs. Marciano.

"How many were there?"

"Many," Felix answered. "For years, we've been paying women off."

"Did you pay off the ADA?" Justine asked.

Felix looked over at his mother. "I can't believe I allowed you to ruin their lives!"

Annoyed by his tone, Mrs. Marciano responded, "I beg your pardon? Don't give me that bullshit. You know Anthony raped Sofia."

"I knew after the fact," he said.

"Oh please! Sofia wanted Anthony to fuck her! You know how those people are. They want to be us. They want our pretty eyes, olive skin, and beautiful skin. Justin couldn't grant her that."

"Those people?" Anthony asked. "You mean Black and Latino like us?"

Mrs. Marciano became speechless.

"Come on now, Grandma! Don't stop on our account. What people?" Anthony repeated.

Mrs. Marciano held her ground and poked her chest out. "Yes. So I said it. I wouldn't be in this predicament if these men like your grandpa and great-grandpa would've kept it in their pants," she snapped, pointing a finger.

"So you're upset that they cheated?" London asked, confused.

Mrs. Marciano released a forced laugh. "Ha! It wasn't the sleeping around that bothered me. It was who he slept with. I guess those nappy-headed bitches were good in bed after all."

Anthony was in total shock. His grandmother was a bigot. "And Sofia?"

"What about her? She was from Africa. They get raped all the time. Shit, we did her a favor, just like we did you."

"You bitch!" Justine went to charge her, only to be grabbed by Justin.

"She isn't worth it," he told his sister.

✶ ✶ ✶ ✶ 212

Anthony lowered his head, trying to remain calm. "What favor?"

Mrs. Marciano frowned up her face. "Well, look at you. Do you think you would have turned out like that if your mother weren't Italian? Have you seen your father's family? Trust me, if you did you, wouldn't be questioning me. Why you think your mother's mother had a baby by my son? She wasn't stupid. Everyone wants beautiful kids."

"You are so fucked up it's sad, and to think I looked up to you," Anthony grumbled. "It's because of you that I raped my brother's girlfriend. It's because of you that I hurt women," he said while slowly walking towards her.

"It's because of me that your ass is free!" Mrs. Marciano retorted. "If you wanna blame anyone, blame your grandfather for allowing your mother to be raised by those animals."

Felix shook his head. "This is how you felt about my daughter?"

"Oh please! How did you expect Morgan to turn out? Her mother had three different babies' fathers. Then you!" Mrs. Marciano shouted. "You had the nerve to allow your only child to be raised by a drug dealer. No wonder her kids are screwed up. Look at their parents. And Morgan, please" she rolled her eyes "we all have to make sacrifices...in her case it was her virginity"

"You knew Tony was raping my daughter..."

"Of course I did...unlike you I know everything. And I wouldn't call if rape, if you've seen the tapes." Mrs. Marciano snide raising her eyebrow

"I should've killed you..." Felix grumbled " Denise loved Morgan more than you would ever know. She treated my daughter as if she was her own," Felix stated.

Mrs. Marciano laughed again. "If she did, why did she kill her? Tell your grandkids who killed their mother."

"Is it true, Grandpa? Denise killed our mother?" Justine asked.

"Yes and that's why they killed mother. You killed my mother," Halle said, holding her mother's .45 in her hand.

"Halle…" Justine was about to walk over to her, but Halle raised her hand, stopping her.

"No, Justine! I wanna know. Did she kill my mother?" Halle asked in a stern tone.

"No, I did." Felix stepped forward. "She promised to take care of my princess. She told me if anything should happen, she would lie down."

With tension in the air and everyone watching each other's moves, Justine whispered, "Halle…"

If Halle thought Mrs. Marciano was scared, she had another thing coming. As she had stated plenty of times, she didn't reach eighty years of age by being scared.

"Don't try to stop her. Yes, I ordered the hit on that bitch."

"Mother!" Felix yelled.

Mrs. Marciano shot Felix a nasty look. "What!" she answered in her Italian accent. "It's time they know the true," she said, strolling from around the desk. "What you kids don't know is that all good fortunes have secrets." She smiled and then continued. "For years, I watched your father mess around with the black bitches while I sat there like a pretty little wife. I had to deal with the snickering behind my back, so I decided to give your father a taste of his own medicine."

Mrs. Marciano reminisced, closing her eyes and thinking about her true love. "You see, with your father, it was just about sex. But, for me, it was about love. Not only was it a passionate love affair, but he also treated me like a queen. When I think back…" She paused and sighed. "He was my true love. I was ready to give it all up for him."

"What happened?" Felix asked.

"She took him away," Mrs. Marciano stated.

"Who?" Anthony asked.

"Denise," Mrs. Marciano responded.

Bewildered, Felix repeated, "Denise?"

"Yes. That bitch took the one thing that meant something to me."

"Denise? What does she have to do with anything?" Justin asked, puzzled like everyone else.

Thinking she may have said too much, Mrs. Marciano waved her hand. "It's nothing. Let's forget it."

But, Felix wasn't ready to drop it. "What does Denise have to do with this?" he asked again in a stern tone. Then it dawned on Felix what his mother was talking about. His silence made her a little nervous.

Mrs. Marciano threw her hands up in the air. "Grant...she killed him," she said with a sigh of relief.

"This was never about Morgan, was it?" Felix asked.

"Morgan? Oh please! So what she was beaten and raped a few times, that's the price you pay to become a Queen. If she played her cards right and kept her mouth close, she would still be here."

"How could you say that about your granddaughter in front of your great grandkids" Felix asked in disbelief.

Mrs. Marciano sucked her teeth, "These are not my grandchildren. I just took their asses in because you were my son. They are nothing but fucking animals. I tolerate Anthony and London because they look Italian, but at far as I'm concerned, they're just as fucked up as their parents, and that includes your daughter. She fell in love with her rapist. How fucked up was she? Leaving them here for us to take care of. That just goes to show you they are just like their parents."

"You're right about that," Halle said, itching to pull the trigger.

However, Mrs. Marciano wasn't the least bit worried. "Be careful, dear. You might hurt yourself."

"Halle!" London called, but Halle was like a lion locked on its target.

"You killed my mother."

"Yes, I did...after I helped her kill everyone else," she said, causing everyone's eyes to widen. "Let me give you a little history." She smirked. "I knew Grant had a problem. I knew about the children and women he pimped."

"He was a pimp, and you love this man," Felix said in disgust.

Mrs. Marciano shot Felix a nasty look. "Oh, like your father was any better? He did the same thing. He just put a suit on doing it. I didn't care what Grant did, as long as he didn't do it to me. The night he was murdered, I saw Denise and Greg coming from his apartment."

"So this was about Grant! All these years you had me believing it was about Morgan...family...when it was about some dick you lost?" Felix shouted.

"So now you know," she snidely responded. "Even though I would've been ruined if it got out that I was sleeping with Grant that still didn't give Denise the right to take him away from me," she angrily stated. Then in a calm voice, she said, "That's why when I found out what Tony did to Morgan, I knew Denise would kill him. So, I indirectly helped her by keeping the police off her ass. The Marciano name runs deep in this city. "

"You are sick," Halle said.

Mrs. Marciano laughed. "Dear, not as sick as you. I'm not the one who fucked my brother. Oh yeah, I heard about that. Just like I know you killed him and your cousin. You see dear we all have secrets some worse than others. "

Halle was so upset that her body was on fire. Justine, London, Justin, and Anthony, who were on pins and needles, slowly surrounded her.

"Halle!" they called again. "Put the gun down."

In a daze, Halle thought about everything that happened over the past couple of months. So many people she loved were now gone. Killing Mrs. Marciano wasn't going to solve anything. The killing had to stop. Therefore, Halle took a deep breath and dropped the gun. With nothing more to say, they just left, leaving Felix and Mrs. Marciano standing there confused.

*****

As planned, they headed over to a small diner on the Westside where they were meeting Greg, Mr. Rubin, and Stevie to discuss the next steps.

"How did it go?" Mr. Rubin asked, but judging by their faces, he knew it wasn't good. "That bad, huh?"

"I can't believe she killed my mother," Halle said in shock.

Anthony, London, Justin, and Justine, still stunned by what happened, remained quiet.

"Listen, guys, I know for the past couple of months your life has been turned upside down. But, you have to know everything happened for a reason. And I don't care what anyone says, your parents were close."

"Yes," Stevie chimed in. "Yes, they were like a family. I have no doubt in my mind that Denise didn't want to hurt Morgan. She loved her. She was in a different state of mind. Someone she loved crossed her, and she had to do something. As far as Tony..." Stevie's voice lowered. "He needed help, but I know he loved y'all. You guys were the best thing that happened to him. Like Greg, you and your sister were the best thing that happened to Gabrielle."

"Stevie's right. You guys have lost so much. It's time for you guys to put the past behind you and start living," Mr. Rubin advised.

"What about the money? It's blood money," Justine said.

"All money is blood money. It's not where you got it. It's what you do with it," Stevie said.

Halle sighed. "With everything we have learned, we can either call it a truce or..."

"I say truce," Justine said, looking at her siblings. "Haven't we lost enough?"

All nodded in agreement.

"We just gonna let them get away with it? We lost our parents for God sake," Anthony grumbled.

"Who said they were?" Greg smiled, looking at Steve and Mr. Rubin.

"Come," Mr. Rubin said. "It's time to take a trip down memory lane."

Waiting for them outside of the restaurant were two black SUVs.

*****

It will be a cold day in hell before I speak to those little bastards. Ungrateful mullies, Mrs. Marciano thought. After what just took place, Mrs. Marciano and Felix didn't want to stay another second in the city. They were catching a red eye out of New York. Both couldn't wait to get back home. Although Felix wasn't speaking to his mother, he was happy everything was out in the open. He couldn't believe how all these years she manipulated him. But like everyone, her day is gonna come, and sooner than she think.

"You see after all we did, they turn on us like that. Niggers!"

"Can you blame them, Mother? Especially when you treat them like shit."

"Oh please! It's because of us that they turned out great."

"You really believe that bullshit?"

Mrs. Marciano stared at Felix. "It's only because you're my son that I tolerate that tone from you, but you better watch it."

Felix chuckled. "Mother, Mother…only if you knew," he said, patting her on the knee. "Knowing is half the battle."

Mrs. Marciano knew he was just blowing smoke out of his ass. However, Felix knew it was only a matter of time. What Mrs. Marciano didn't know is that Felix had met with Mr. Rubin and Stevie a couple of days before, and they told him it was Mrs. Marciano who gave Denise the access code to Tony's house. He also learned that Mrs. Marciano was planning a hit on him. Therefore, along with Mr. Rubin and Stevie, Felix decided it was time to put Mrs. Marciano out of her misery.

Exhausted from the day, Mrs. Marciano sat back and closed her eyes, while Felix's mind drifted off into space. Suddenly, the driver came to an abrupt stop, causing Mrs. Marciano's body to jerk.

"What the hell is going on here?"

"I'm sorry, ma'am," the driver said.

"Can't you people even drive?" she spitefully asked the black driver.

"Sorry. I think I hit something," he said, cutting off the car. "Let me check." He hopped out of the SUV.

"They can't even drive," she grumbled.

As it happened twenty-five years ago, the light turned green, but the car didn't move.

"What's the problem now?" she asked in an annoyed voice, wanting to get out of New York.

"Hush, Mother. Sit back and enjoy the ride. We're going home" Felix told her with a smirk.

"What? What do you mean? Is that—?"Mrs. Marciano asked while looking out of the window.

Joined by Stevie and Mr. Rubin, who were standing there with smiles on their faces and their arms folded, Greg, Halle, Anthony, London, Justin, and Justine waved.

That's when it hit her. It was a hit. Mrs. Marciano tried to open the door, while Felix released a high-pitched laugh.

Strangely, he was proud of his grandchildren. "Isn't revenge sweet?" He laughed before the car exploded.

When Halle told Greg who killed their parents, like Gracie, he felt they should pay. But, unlike his father, Greg didn't get his hands dirty. So, he reached out to Mr. Rubin and Stevie for their assistance to come up with the perfect plan.

*****

Luckily this was just a figment of Stevie's imagination which left grandparents horrified by the story. They looked at each other while trying to digest everything. They never thought about it in that way. Assuming by not telling the children they were protecting them. Sadly they forgot one thing, the secrets they buried.

"I'm sorry, I didn't get your name," Mrs. Marciano stated.

"Oh, I'm sorry. My name is Stevie. I was a friend of theirs, and I can assure you they would've wanted their kids to be raised together."

"We have no intentions—" Felix attempted to say, but was interrupted.

Stevie laughed, raising an eyebrow. "Really? Then why did you file papers for sole custody," she said, causing everyone to look at him. "He's not the only one, Mrs. Dodson. You filed to have your grandkids' last name changed, and, Mr. Taylor, I know about your meeting with Mr. Rubin."

"And your point is, dear?" Mrs. Marciano asked.

"Unlike their parents, these kids inherited money, power, and respect. But, as secrets are exposed and new business develops, they will learn an old saying, 'whatever doesn't come out in the wash will comes out in the rinse. You of all people should know that."

"I don't see how that could happen if they aren't raise together" Mrs. Dodson stated causing Stevie to smirk "Mrs. Dodson have you heard of a story called *Roman Revenge*, it's a story of a bloody lies and family ties. These kids were left empires," she said pacing back and forth "whether you like it or not these children are considered Kings and Queens of their kingdom I guarantee their empires will collide" Stevie laughed "do you know these kids come from parents that some may call demons of the underworld. If you keep them apart, it's like leaving the leaves on the family tree to fall in the devil's playground,"

Mrs. Marciano annoyed with Stevie's analogy asked "and how do you know all of these?"

"Because you and I both know the apple doesn't fall far from the tree" she said, then exited, leaving them speechless…

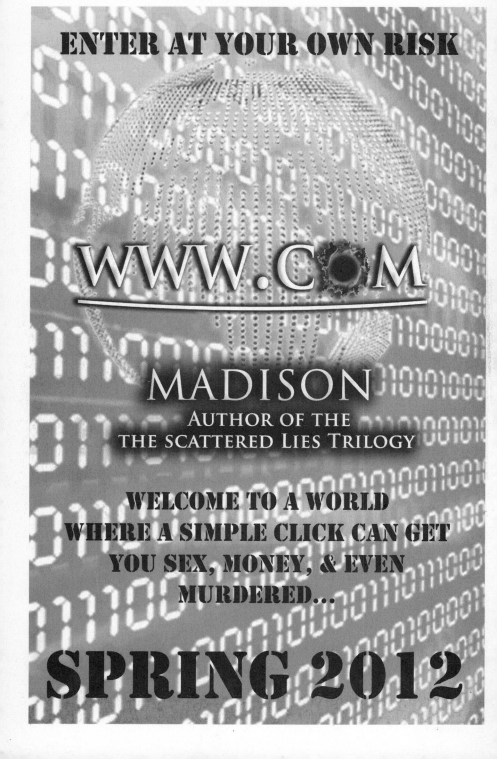

PUBLICATIONS PRESENTS

WELCOME TO THE JUNGLE

WHERE LOVE AND LOYALTY DON'T EXIST

NOW AVAILABLE

PUBLICATIONS PRESENTS

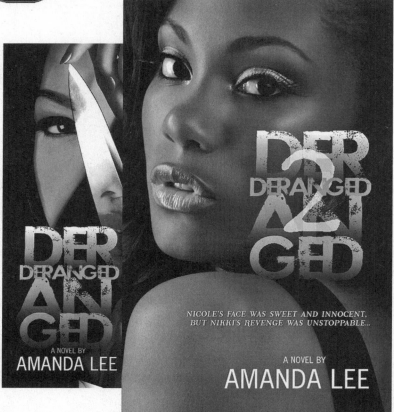

NICOLE'S FACE WAS SWEET AND INNOCENT,
BUT NIKKI'S REVENGE WAS UNSTOPPABLE...

A NOVEL BY
AMANDA LEE

In Deranged, Nikki achieved her goal of capturing
Jeremy for Nicole, but fell short as Cowboy spoiled their
plans. One year later, Nikki refuses to fail and no longer
needs Nicole or her assistance. In Deranged 2, Nicole's
face was sweet but Nikki s revenge was unstoppable as
she moved heaven & earth to be with her man and live
the dream life that they planned together. Once free,
AND she sees he's cheating and living their dream life
with someone else, Jeremy and his family have nowhere
to hide. The question is: Will she finally get what she
wants or will she die trying?